BIG FOOT Mamas

a novel

also by pamela foster

the perfect victim
my life with a wounded warrior
clueless gringos in paradise
noisy creek
soldier's heart
bigfoot blues

BIG FOOT

Mamas

a novel

pamela foster

RADIANCE

RADIANCE

An imprint of Roan & Weatherford Publishing Associates, LLC
Bentonville, Arkansas
www.roanweatherford.com

Library of Congress Cataloging-in-Publication Data
Names: Foster, Pamela, author
Title: Bigfoot Mamas/Pamela Foster | The Bigfoot Trilogy #2
Description: Third Edition. | Bentonville: Radiance, 2025.
Identifiers: 978-1-63373-206-3 (hardcover)
ISBN: 978-1-63373-207-0 (trade paperback) | ISBN: 978-1-63373-208-7 (eBook)
Subjects: | BISAC: FICTION/Romance/Romantic Comedy | FICTION/Women
Fiction/Romance/Contemporary

Radiance trade paperback edition June, 2025

Cover & Interior Design by Casey W. Cowan
Editing by Gil Miller

Shirley McDaniel
Avoca, Arkansas

This one is for my sister, Vickie.
You've held my hand in plenty of dark woods.
Thank you.

acknowledgements

SO MANY PEOPLE played a part in getting this book into your hands. Velda Brotherton and Dusty Richardson were mentors extraordinaire. Casey Cowan and Gil Miller made the magic happen. Ruth Weeks, Jan Morrill, Linda Apple, and Patty Stith wove their circle of support. Mike Miller held me to a higher standard than I knew I could attain, and he did it by simply being his own talented self.

one

THERE'S NO REASON for the little hairs on the back of my neck to bristle in warning, tickle the collar of my Carhartt.

Not this morning, on a foggy length of beach, the ocean eerily quiet on my left, the ochre bluffs invisible across a narrow stretch of muggy creek bed—no logical basis for my turning in a slow circle to squint through the velvety mist.

Dad dropped me off at Gold Bluff Campground an hour ago. By now he's sipping hot coffee at the Teepee Café in Orick. He and Ranger Donaldson swapping tales of deep-throated bellows that pierce the night and rocks tossed at campfires.

The ocean sleeps under its gray blanket, ground clouds so thick they mute the lap of the waves against the sand. Not even a halo of sun to mark the dawn. Just a paling, incremental movement in shading, from charcoal to pewter.

The tracks of my Wolverines are vanishing shadows on wet, steel-gray sand. When I turn to look back, all trace of my footprints are gone, absorbed by the sea. From the hidden ocean on my left a seal's bark, muted in the thick, vaporous air, is followed by the higher-pitched voice of her pup. These two animals have been with me since I left the trailhead.

I've had this happen before. There are those who would say the mother has been conditioned by fishermen to follow humans in the hopes of an easy meal. That could be the explanation. But, in this gray soup, with a cold breeze skimming over her exposed head, how does she track my progress? What connection keeps her there barking, what sure as hell sounds like a warning?

Picturing them, those sleek heads riding the surface of the dark water, mother and pup together, an ache, like pushing on a bruise, twists in my center. Since the birth of the twins, I have become increasingly hungry for information about my own mother. Which is to say, I have begun to wake from perfume-laced dreams, hungry for the touch, the acceptance of a woman I know only from one much-studied photo and a near-empty bottle of fragrance.

I stand looking back the way I've come, reach under my jacket, unzip the belly pack pressing against my pelvis, enjoy the cold feel of the .38 against my hand. The combination of fog, the muted whisperings of the waves, and the soft sand underfoot all conspire to give any would-be stalker an unfair advantage. Even in the midst of this ridiculous paranoia, the bite of salt laden air is a welcome gift. I draw the cold deep into my lungs, leave the belly pack unzipped for ease of access, and turn inland, away from the barking of the seals and murmurs of the ocean.

Somewhere along here Redwood Creek narrows, becomes jumpable. Most years there's a driftwood bridge to keep a hiker's feet dry, but in this morning's fog, it's unlikely I'll find it. The soft sand gives way reluctantly to patches of swaying grass. Just before the beach surrenders to a narrow strip of shoulder-high, emerald green cut-grass, thick brown stalks of shaggy cat-tails, and a slightly bitter, almost rancid stink my mind can't quite place, I turn once more and stare back into the mist.

Nothing moves. My body twangs with a near electrical warning.

I am not alone.

If someone is out here with me, they can't see or hear me any better than I can them. I turn my back on vague premonition, weave through the grass toward the meandering creek and the bluffs that guard the dirt road to Fern Canyon.

In testimony either to my sense of direction or to the truth of the adage that God watches over fools, the variegated gray of the driftwood bridge appears out of the luminous mist. It takes both hands to pull myself up onto its rough surface. The added height of the bridge is a last opportunity to turn in a slow circle, squint into the thinning fog, weigh paranoia against time-proven instinct.

The rustle of thick, skin-slicing grass in a pale sea-rich breeze.

A dancing veil of pearly fog.

Nothing else. No movement.

The mist lies heavy in thick patches at ground level along the creek. Something not quite right about those fifty or so mounds of paler, somehow wetter air. Well, whatever is causing those nearly life-like humps of denser fog, there's no way it can have anything to do with someone following me.

My booted feet shuffle carefully along the slick, uneven surface of the silvered driftwood. Directly in front of me now, the flat top of the bluff accepts the dawn's first sun, a thin line of ochre transforms to rich gold. For a moment, I am alone with the universe. In that second of connection, I relive another moment across a U-shaped meadow on Blue Mountain. An encounter that changed my life. Or, maybe allowed me to see who I had been all along. Sheltered in a cocoon of oneness, wholeness, I pull one last salt-laden breath into my core and jump flat-footed from the bridge down into the tall grass at the other side of Redwood Creek.

And reality comes crashing up out of the mist in a noise like a hundred claps of thunder.

A herd of elk stands as one entity, up from the dense ground fog, materializes as in a nightmare from both sides of the creek to tower all around me. Jesus God! I have woven my way through these sleeping giants, picked my path around their slumbering forms. So focused on an imaginary, human stalker, I've stumbled into something far more dangerous and unpredictable. A threat to which my little Colt .38 is a joke and an insult.

Warm breath clouds around the shaggy heads of the elk. This explains the thicker patches of fog at ground level. Standing now, fifty or so cows and their calves, one ragged, worn-velvet-antlered king, and a small contingent of sleek, young bulls along the periphery—every reddish-brown eye is focused on the two-legged intruder in the middle of their bedroom.

"Fuck, fuck, *fuck.*" An incantation I take back immediately. If these are my last words, I can do better than that.

"Oh,God, oh, God, oh, God." Better, but fear still welds my boots to the mucky ground.

My babies! Stubborn Victoria and sweet Dharma. Heavy blue-black hair and skin like burnished mahogany, Hawk's legacy to his daughters. Glacier blue eyes, my contribution to their DNA. My girls!

Stop!

Think, dammit. I refuse to die today and leave my babies. Without my discipline Bubba will spoil those girls to ruination.

My right boot takes one small step.

The bull doesn't move, but the two nearest cows lift their heads higher, tip big ears toward me. I bring my left foot even with my right.

There now. Still alive. Not gored. Not stomped into the rich black muck of the creek.

A headline forms in the air in front of me. *Local Bigfoot author and bar owner, Samantha Foster, smashed to bloody pulp by herd of angry elk.*

Bad thought. Bad thought. Concentrate on my babies. Bubba. Dad. Today is NOT a good day to die. No dying. Keep walking.

Another step, focus on the tops of my boots. Do not make eye contact with any of these sharp-hoofed animals. Slow, steady steps.

The nearest cow whistles for her calf. I keep moving, in a kind of trance, or possibly shock, one slow step at a time. Part of me sees I'm fifty yards from the packed sand road that fronts the bluff. In the thick of the herd now, the closer to the road I shuffle, the fewer elk there will be. Unfortunately, the animals along that edge of the group are the young bulls. Raging testosterone combined with precious little life experience—a dangerous combination in any species.

The morning sun eases its path along the Bluff. I walk steadily toward the cliff's golden face, look to neither the right nor the left.

It's an old cow elk that saves me. Touched by instinct with the knowledge that the intruder in their midst is harmless, a laughable threat, or nudged by the hand of God. Either way, she turns, one long-legged stride at a time, pushes through the tall grass, knob-knees her way slowly back toward the campground. Away from me. The remaining cows hesitate and then, one by one, show me their sides, then their wide rumps. The young bulls, confused and distracted, follow the cows. I do not pull a full breath of elk-infused air until the reigning bull exhales one last hot blast into the morning air, turns, and joins his herd.

Still no turning, no thinking, keep moving. I walk. One scuffed boot in front of the other. For an hour? A moment? No thinking, dammit, just keep walking. Eventually, the packed sand road along Gold Bluff turns sharply east and I'm in a shadow world of verdant green.

Perpetual shade reigns along the creek bed here. Steep fern-covered walls of the narrow canyon nearly join high above the clear waters. Maidenhair ferns dominate. Thousands of delicate, black-veined fingers flutter in a light breeze. Darker, hardier sword ferns are sprinkled throughout, accentuating the waving sea of pale green. Some part of my mind drinks in this peaceful green mile-and-a-half of the hike. Mostly, I just keep walking, one stride at a time. Very little thinking, movement is all I can manage.

When the trail leads out of the magic of Fern Canyon and up into the deeper, more ancient secrets of old growth redwoods, I stop, allow myself to think about my latest near-miss. With the soft bark of a tree older than the birth of Christianity at my back, adrenaline pours from my body. Great wracking sobs and full body tremors force me flat on my butt, onto the thick cushion of thousands of years of death and rebirth that is the forest floor.

Those young bulls. Muscles taut. Staring, eager for the chase. Smoldering testosterone turning away at the last possible moment from stomping my life into the ground, leaving a bleeding bloody mess. Me, so intent on a human stalker that I wandered directly into a far greater danger. When the sobs stop, hysterical laughter disrupts the deep quiet of the forest. This here, this faulty judgment as to the genesis of true danger—this is the story of my freakin' life.

two

HIS BIG HANDS cover my naked hips completely. My palms braced on the sill of the bay-facing bedroom window, the pounding rain inches from my face, I watch his reflection behind me. The refracted face of my husband shatters as the wind, like the very breath of God, roars through the heavy streaming veil, slams against the glass. A pitched cry arches up from my center, a noise louder than any mother of two napping daughters ought to make.

When my body settles, he turns me to him, walks me backward to the bed where I straddle his girth and rock gently while the wind shakes the windows and I remember how to breathe.

"You remember the first time we did this here?" His deep rumbly voice is warm oil poured over already aching need. His hands support my breasts. The world's best Living Bra.

"Ah, yeah."

"You remember what y'all said?" He shifts the rhythm, cups my ass in calloused hands.

"Ah, yeah."

Aren't men reputed to recite baseball statistics in their heads or think about mowing the lawn during these times? This man, this beautiful giant of a man, he talks.

"Tell me what you said." He pulls me against him. Harder. Faster.

"Not. Now."

Thunder rumbles along the surface of the dark bay. Below us, the unmistakable sound of a door pushed open by at least one small, demanding girl child. The low bark of a very large dog on guard duty. I shift my weight forward ever so slightly. In the split second pause between the rise and fall of his broad chest, I reach around and cup his heavy balls in my warm hand.

That ends the talking.

My breath is still ragged, my mind slipping in and out of the here and now, when four little fists pound on the locked bedroom door.

"Go away." My words are muffled against Bubba's wide chest which shakes in either laughter or, possibly, the last great shudder of his finish.

"We want in there!" Veronica demands.

He lifts me from him and his withdrawal, the movement of air over flushed skin, raises goose bumps. I flail in the twisted sheets, find the edge of the thermal blanket, and work it up and over my still trembling body. He heads for the bathroom, returns to pull on jockey shorts, soft blue jeans, and a dark green t-shirt before he sits on the bed's edge, pushes a lock of pale hair from my face.

"I'll get the girls some cocoa. Tide em over till Hawk gets here."

His mouth is hot and salty on mine. When he pulls away he keeps his face so close I can see every gold fleck, every glimmer of green in his brown eyes.

"But you gotta say it." His smile is that of a debauched archangel. "What you said that first time we was together. Over yonder, cross the street, in that itty-bitty tree house bedroom of yours."

I work my hand up under his t-shirt.

More pounding at the door. Amazing how much noise tiny fists can make.

"Mama!" Dharma this time.

"This ain't over," he whispers.

Six long strides and he's at the door, throws the latch, disappears into the hallway.

"I believe." His voice comes through the heavy wood, recedes with three sets of footsteps down the stairs. "Y'all promised me you'd take a nap before your Daddy Hawk gets here."

"Up! Up!" And I know he's got a child thrown across each shoulder. The thunder of Bubba's footfalls on the stairs, accompanied by the excited bass barking of a mastiff, mixes with little-girl giggles and fades away.

I snuggle under the cover, stare out the window, think again how clever it was of Bubba to insist on making our bedroom the entire third floor of the old Firehauser Furniture warehouse. Gives us an extra layer of privacy. Smart of me also to demand a wall of bay-facing windows. As the only three-story building in a two-block area, we have an unobstructed view of the bay and no need of window coverings.

Still in a euphoric afterglow, I watch the rain and think back to that first night Bubba and I slipped out of our jeans and t-shirts together. Accustomed to Hawk, who moved over my body like a musician playing a careless tune on his favorite instrument. My only other sexual experience one night in an elegant hotel with the man who would turn out to be my nemesis and who approached the sex act like a contestant waiting for the judges to hold up those rating numbers. I give him a six for precision of execution, a three for difficulty.

Neither of these experiences prepared me for Bubba.

Lovemaking with the big man from Georgia is like rolling around inside an electrical storm. If such a thing were possible while still knowing, with every fiber of my being, that I am safe from all harm. Sex with Bubba is sanctuary in the midst of rumbling power and exploding energy. It's as though I spent my life thinking I knew how to swim because I'd stuck a toe or two into a bathtub and then came into full-body contact with the Pacific Ocean at its rogue-wave-producing, roaring best.

I was already four months gone with the twins—Hawk and my babies—when Bubba and I crossed that line between friends and lovers. That first night, with the bluish glow from the street light behind him, my need already a hot pulse, I'd taken one look at him naked and blurted the exclamation he was never going to let me forget.

"Oh my God," I gasped. "I got nowhere that thing is gonna fit."

It was his answer that always makes me giggle.

"Now, darlin'," he'd drawled. "This here ain't the first time you been wrong."

I fling back the covers, still giggling at the memory, head for the shower.

The monthly meeting of the Tri-county Bigfooters starts in under an hour and, as unofficial spokesperson for the ragtag group, it'd be good if I didn't show up smelling like sex. I may represent, as a reporter in Dallas put it when I spoke there on my book tour last year, "flannel-shirted lunatics," but I do have some standards.

Besides, I want a few minutes with my girls before leaving them for the evening. With my inherited bar, Victor and David's, right across the street flashing that crippled neon V and then D into the fog, I rarely miss an evening of tucking the twins in at night. The lavender and vanilla scent of the shower gel Bubba bought me last week mixes with the hot steam of the shower and creates a warm oasis. In the midst of all these lovely sensations—warmth, flowery scent, glorious sexual satiation—my longing for my daughters triggers a feeling of grace.

A few hours away from Victoria and Dharma and my longing for the smell of their skin, the feel of their tiny hands on my face, the sound of their sweet, demanding voices, is an ache in my center. Yet my own mother, after running away while eight months pregnant, returned only long enough to drop me like unwanted baggage with a man who was not my blood father. A man who nevertheless raised me as his own and brought me up strong and cherished.

It is not lost on me that Bubba, who stepped up when Hawk backed away from my pregnancy five years ago, has done the same. A cycle of love and honor. My life blessed twice by the selfless love of two good men, each of whom could have walked away from duty not his own and instead strode into my life with open arms.

Out of the shower, one towel wrapped around my body, another worn turban style on my wet hair, I step from the bathroom to the bedroom and am greeted by two small girls and a very large dog. Victoria sits on the bed, pillows tucked behind her. Dharma's back is to me. She stares out the rain-streaked window, her reflection superimposed on the silvery rain and the ghostly fog outside. The dog, Rufus, is stretched the length of the forest green rug that protects my bare feet from cold wood floors each morning. He opens his bloodshot eyes and stares balefully at me.

"We picked out your clothes," Victoria announces. She rolls her hand *à la* Vanna White toward my best jeans and a pale blue V-neck sweater.

Dharma runs from the window, tiny feet slapping the floor, hits like a miniature linebacker. She wraps her arms around my bare leg. I drag her with me and collapse on the bed where Victoria pounces full-body along my length. The three of us, with Rufus drooling on the bed in seeming approval, fall into a tickling fight which only ends when Bubba's voice breaks through the squeals and giggles.

"Your Daddy Hawk done pulled up on that Indian motorcycle he rides. You girls wanna chance to crawl all over the durn bike like a couple of monkeys, you best jump to it."

three

THE BAR IS already filling with Bigfooters when we get there. David, Hawk's dad, supervises the setting up of a trio of new foot casts. Found by a half-dozen women hunters up near Bluff Creek, the footprints aren't the biggest I've ever seen, but they're pristine, as though the creature had vanished into thin air an instant before the women appeared out of the forest's dense fog.

I can't help but smile, remembering how many times in the past I rolled my eyes over this exact same type of conjecture. Of course, that was before I was carried through a moonless night, laid on a bed of soft ferns, and marked with the lifeblood of these very creatures. My snorting, eye rolling, heavy sighing days were before I was born into faith while looking across a greening meadow into red-rimmed eyes.

VD's has hosted a Tri-county Bigfooters' meeting each month since Dad and David took over the bar in 1953 when they returned from the Korean War. Until the 1967 Patterson tape, the meetings were sporadic and usually took place on quiet Sunday afternoons. Since the October 20th filming of Patty, the Bigfoot whose picture hangs over the bar in the place of honor, the meetings have been held on that date each month.

It was Dad's Great-Aunt Mandy who originally owned and operated the business. She ran a brothel in this building from 1917 to 1932. Which is why the bar is so damned chopped up. Dad built a loft bedroom for me, a sanctuary in which I grew up and still miss, while he lives in what is now one room behind the bar, but used to be six small cribs for Mandy's working girls. The room that was Hawk's bedroom until four years ago is just to the right of the front door and juts out into a gravel parking lot that separates VD's from a small medical marijuana clinic. If family legend is accurate, and that's always debatable, Hawk's old room was where Mandy hosted, and I use this term euphemistically, the likes of Tom Mix and Errol Flynn.

When Dad and David turned the bar over to Hawk and me ten years ago, I intended to replace the missing neon on the sign flashing in the window. Victor and David's sounds ever so much better than VD's. Hawk had other ideas. By the time he finally let me buy him out so he could concentrate on the job for which his PhD prepared him—teaching anthropology at Humboldt State University across the bay in Arcata—I had grown sentimentally fond of, or at least resigned to, the crippled neon.

I did however remove the hand-lettered poster that used to be directly below the flashing VD which proclaimed *Fresh Local Crabs*. I have the crustacean sign in the store room. I'm keeping a ledger. When the one hundredth customer asks me about it, I'll put the damn thing back in the window and throw a capitulation party. I thought that was a safe bet with myself. But I removed the poster four years ago and I still get old-timers asking about it. The count is currently at eighty-one.

I'm behind the bar, bent over, restocking the open trough of longnecks, my arms elbow deep in crushed ice.

"How's my favorite redneck mutha?"

"Lefty. How's it going? Beer?" In answer to this purely rhetorical question, I set a brown, dripping bottle on the bar.

He removes his ball cap, shakes his head like a scrawny crossbred Labrador, showers the polished wood of the bar top and the Bigfooters on both sides of him. I glance automatically to the front window. It wasn't raining ten minutes ago when Bubba and I walked across the street from our house. Now First Street is black and slick with rain, the streetlights wet halos in the glooming.

"What are you doing here tonight?" I ask. "Did you forget there's a meeting?"

Lefty was right there in that meadow with me five years ago, but he has always denied seeing anything, insists he was in some sort of fugue state and can't remember any part of what happened on that ill-fated trip to Bluff Creek. I don't hold it against him. Faith is a personal decision.

"You thought any more about that business proposal I mentioned?"

"Ah, yeah. That was not a business proposal. That was a harebrained, drunken idea."

I wipe scattered rain from the bar, toss a towel to Buddy and Chesty Ambrosini, the drinkers to Lefty's right and left. The brothers carry their beers to the table under the head of the cauliflower-eared whitetail. Chesty's glare in Lefty's direction is completely wasted, my childhood friend oblivious to subtlety.

"You're missing out on a golden opportunity here, Sam. Let me build you a cage in the courtyard and we could draw in the big names. The Undertaker. Might get The Edge. Hell, you never know till you ask. Maybe even convince an old timer like Jake the Snake to come up."

"Give it a rest," I say. "We're not enclosing my courtyard in the hopes of seducing the World Wrestling Federation into staging fights at VD's. I've got enough beer-fueled, fist-swinging idiots to deal with. No need to import them."

His scowl wrinkles his narrow forehead. His wet ball cap on the bar, a ragged line of white is exposed, an inch or so of freckled vulnerability from his hairline to mid-forehead.

"You been getting work roofing?" I pop two maraschino cherries in my mouth, one for each cheek.

He turns sideways on the gold Naugahyde seat of the stool, rubs his right knee with his left hand. His right hand, of course, keeps a firm grip on his quickly emptying longneck.

"When it's not raining." The mind of this wiry, hardworking, somewhat odd man is as easy to read as that flashing sign in the window. "We don't gotta start with the big names. What about this? How about if I can talk Bubba into wearing a furry caveman kind of sarong deal? He's near about as big as a Sasquatch. He can wrestle as Bigfoot."

This idea is wrong on so many levels, I'm struck temporarily dumb. It does conjure an interesting image. I admit that. My sweet, beautiful Bubba in caveman mode. You man. Me woman.

I shake my head. "Any wrestling Bubba's going to do will be with me. Now drop the subject."

"Lord, Sam, since you sold that book and gallivanted around talking to folks, you *have* gotten all uppity. No fun at all. I ain't complaining or nothing, but you're different now. And I don't necessarily mean in a good way, either."

Across the room, Dad directs Bubba in the hanging of the photo of my belly, bloody handprint from "unknown primate" like a 3D imprint disappearing around my waist. You've seen the poster. It's for sale in every head shop, Walmart, and t-shirt store in twenty-two countries. Lefty's correct, that book tour changed me. Shut me up about wanting to see more of the world than this ratty bar. Turns out, Dad was right. Humboldt County really is the most beautiful place on the face of the earth. It just took one hundred and sixty speeches and book signings in fourteen different countries for me to come to that truth.

"This about the bar tab I made you pay out of your income tax return?" I ask Lefty.

Since his bypass surgery I'm nervous about how excited Dad gets at these meetings. He and David are talking with Dr. Bernstein. Three wispy-haired old men, two in flannel and one in motorcycle leathers, their heads together, eyes dancing with joy. I've got about ten more minutes before I need to turn the bar over to Bubba and take my place up front.

"That there now," Lefty whines. "That hurt my feelings. You know I always pay my tab."

I raise my eyebrows. Keep my mouth shut.

"One way or another. I pay." The bottle goes to his mouth again, his Adam's apple works one, two, three, four times before he sets the empty bottle on the bar. "And I ain't talking about no tab. I'm talking about I saw you coming out of The Eureka Inn yesterday. You looked right through me like as if you never saw me before in your life. Me, your amigo since kindergarten at Alice Birney Elementary."

"What? I was nowhere near The Eureka Inn yesterday. I was hiking from Fern Canyon to Prairie Creek."

I pop two more cherries into my mouth, bite down on them with my back molars.

"Well now, if that weren't you then you got yourself a dopley-gangster. Anyways, it ain't none of my business. You wanna get all dolled up and hobnob with ladies what walk like they got a stick up their butts and with men in fancy suits, hey, it's no never mind to me. Figured it had something to do with your book or maybe with you being the Bigfoot Whisperer or some such a deal. It just hurt my feelings, is all, you pretending not to know me."

Again, in his own sarcastic way, Lefty's correct. Not about seeing me yesterday. I've got no earthly idea what the hell he's talking about with that. But I have taken over the leadership of the Tri-county Bigfooters. My official title is Chairperson, but Letticia, who is currently flitting across the bar coming directly toward us like a hollow boned chickadee amidst a flock of pelicans, calls me the group's Reluctant Messiah.

I lean around the five-gallon Beaver Mustard jar with its honor system stash of bills to give her a hug, but she pulls back from me, fixes me with the ol' stink eye.

"So," she says in the same tone she used when I was three and basted the lower three feet of her refrigerator with cold-pressed olive oil. "You don't speak to me now when you see me in public?"

"What?"

"Coming out of Bank of America. Some City Slick helping you into an Escalade."

"What?"

Lefty has a look of vindication on his face, though this triumph is partially impaired by the fact that he's out of beer.

A Cadillac Escalade? Bank of America?

"You going to tell me you didn't see me?"

"What?"

"I walked right up. Tried to give you a hug. This gray-suited midget pushed me out of the way like I was some crazy street person trying to assault Your Highness."

"What?'

"For a writer," she says. "You got yourself a regular way with words."

"Ah, yeah," I say. "You're right about that but, honest to God, whoever you saw, it wasn't me."

"Uh, huh." Letticia looks across the room at Dad and Bubba, cuts her eyes sideways to Lefty. "Could be I should have talked to you about this when you were alone?"

"What?"

She rolls her eyes, slips her cat's eye glasses down her nose so she can glare at me over the top. I cringe, fight the urge to confess to whatever she suggests I did. Anything. Just to stop this seventy-eight-year-old matriarch from looking at me like a bug pinned to a specimen board.

"All right," she says finally. "I don't know what your story is, but I'm willing to let it slide this time. You ever slight me like that again though, and, I may be coming up on eighty, but I'll pound you like steak picado." She leans across the bar and lays her warm hand on the back of my neck. "You got that?"

Holy Mother of God, this woman is as scary as a repressed nun with a metal-edged ruler.

"Wha... yes ma'am."

Strange things have been happening around here lately. I mean, stranger than usual. Which is saying something. It all started with my Fern Canyon walk. I spent a good part of the seven-mile hike through the mystic redwoods ducking behind tree trunks as big around as rooms, peering through sword ferns, searching for the answer to why every hair on the back of my neck insisted on rising up each time my boots carried me over an exposed patch of trail.

Then, on the ride home, with Dad snoring lustily in the passenger seat, the nose of a metallic brown Toyota Camry kept poking its way into my rearview mirror. Not that Toyotas aren't as common as fog in Humboldt County, but I've seen the same car twice more since returning home yesterday. Both times it was staked out within sight of VD's.

This morning, looking out the kitchen window while cradling a steaming cup of Humboldt Roast Sumatran, I got a look at the driver. A balding guy dressed in a black windbreaker. Maybe mid-fifties. Didn't look like anybody I knew. I grabbed my loaded belly pack and snuck out the backdoor, hoping to come around behind him, but by the time I got to the sidewalk all I saw was the brake lights of the Toyota as it made the turn out onto B Street.

I haven't mentioned this to Bubba yet. The man has a protective streak as wide as Bigfoot's ass. Whoever the watcher is, he's probably harmless and, if not, I'm a better shot than my husband anyway.

"You Samantha Foster?"

I look up from behind the bar where I'm bent over stacking a crate of longnecks. Well now. This might turn out to be an interesting night.

"You the guy that's been following me?"

He's wearing black jeans, the windbreaker open and hanging to just below his waist, a bump of menace at his right hip. I unzip my belly pack as I stand. Below the bar, inches from my left hand, is the Remington pump, but in a crowd like this, the shotgun's not much use to me as anything but an attention-getter.

His eyes drop to my cupped hand inside the belly pack. It's distressing that some fairly large part of me hopes he'll reach for that gun on his hip.

He holds both hands in front of his chest, palms toward me, asks permission.

"I'm going to reach in my jacket pocket for some papers."

"I don't believe I'd do that if I were you." I shake my head slightly.

The posse is here. Bubba, Dad, Lefty, and David all stand directly behind my stalker.

By now I'm fairly certain this guy isn't going to draw on me, probably never meant to do any such thing. But there's enough adrenaline coursing through my body to send him flying across the bar with nothing but psychic energy. I force three slow, steady breaths of stale beer, mildewed wood, and wet flannel in and out of my lungs.

"My husband is going to reach around and take that itty-bitty gun from off your hip there. You got any sort of problem with that?"

He puts his hands flat on the bar. His eyes are gray, the black pupils swollen in the dark of the bar. He hasn't looked away from me since I stood up.

"Under the circumstances? No problem whatsoever."

Bubba unfastens the snap on the hip holster, lifts a dull gray Beretta semi from the web pouch, and drops it into the pocket of his own coat.

"Happy now?" the intruder asks.

"Not quite yet. You been following me for days. Why?"

"My client wanted to know a little about you before she approached."

An eerie silence has settled over the bar. Fifty or so curious, mostly unarmed adrenaline junkies hold their breath as one unpredictable creature, watch, wait to see what is about to unfold.

"Your client?"

"She'd like to set up a meeting."

Neither of us has blinked since he walked in the bar.

Bubba slides his bulk onto the bar stool next to the guy. Lays a heavy arm, like a thick steel trap, over his shoulder.

"Y'all need to explain yourself right quick," he drawls, his voice pitched so low I expect the glasses behind the bar to shake with its growl.

"I'm Joe Stanton, a private investigator from out of The Bay Area." Most people by now would have transferred their focus to my six-foot-five, brick wall of a husband. This guy's good, though. He's correctly pinpointed the epicenter of danger.

"One more time." I lean toward him. My hand still rests on the metal security blanket in my belly pack. "Why are you following me?"

The Bigfooters are a suspended half-moon around the action. About a quarter of them, in complete disregard for the law and my explicit instructions, are carrying somewhere under all that corduroy and wet Carhartt. Time for me to kick it down a few dozen notches.

Whatever Stanton's intent, he didn't walk into this crowded bar, in the middle of a monthly meeting of armed individuals, to cause me any harm. Though PIs usually precede lawyers like wind blowing dirty scum off the whitecaps of the bay, this one isn't going to shoot me—but those papers he's got hidden in his jacket are apt to cause me nearly as much damage as a bullet.

"How about you just give me the paperwork." I lean in and lay both my hands between his on the bar.

His right hand moves slowly to his jacket pocket. He's like a buck under the gun, exposed, edging incrementally toward the safety of the forest. Nobody breathes until the folded packet of paper has been transferred to me.

"Get out," I say amiably.

He doesn't move. "You might want to look at those. I can't tell you much, but I can answer a few questions."

"I do have one question. Did you follow me to Fern Canyon and then hike just behind me along the beach and through the redwoods?"

He blinks, cocks his head slightly.

"I followed you and your dad to the turnoff to Fern Canyon. My client asked for a general idea of your lifestyle. I was gathering information on what you did on your off time. But I wasn't on the trail behind you. There wasn't any need. I called the Park Service, found out the only outlet for that hike was Prairie Creek. I picked you up again once you hit one-oh-one headed south back to Eureka."

"Go now," I say. "Go quickly."

Bubba lifts the confiscated Berretta from the pocket of his jacket, every movement slow and calm and practiced. The pistol aimed at the ceiling, he drops the magazine, pulls back the slide, and ejects the blunt-nosed bullet onto the bar. The sharp sound of well-machined, properly-oiled metal focuses the attention of every person in the bar. The weapon open, exposed, empty, Bubba pockets the mag, lays the gun on his open palm, and offers it to the PI.

Stanton's exit brings into the bar cold, wet air from the street and a group exhalation of hot beer breath. It also leaves me with more questions than answers. If this PI didn't follow me through the redwoods, who, or what, was behind me sending shivers down my back each step of that eight-mile trail?

four

THE OVERHEAD LIGHT has been turned off, but the end table lamp is switched to low and throws a soft, yellow glow over the sleek, dark heads of my daughters and their biological dad. Hawk sleeps with his mouth open. Victoria is wedged against the high back of the couch, one fuzzy, pink, footsie-pajama leg thrown over his chest. Dharma, her favorite green and red plaid nightgown tangled around her hips, snuggles along his right side. Rufus's heavy, furry girth presses along the outer edge of the sofa. The dog is the only one still awake and, it would appear, the only thing keeping Dharma from rolling off onto the storybook-strewn rug.

Two weeks ago, after returning from a day with Hawk, Victoria tapped the toe of her pink tennis shoe and informed me, "Ordinary little girls only got one Daddy. I'm special, 'cause I got Daddy Bubba and Daddy Hawk."

"Ah, yeah," I confirmed. "You and Dharma are lucky to have two daddies that love you so much."

That's what came out my mouth, but what I was thinking was, Thank you Jesus and Mary for taking a monumental screw-up on my part and turning it into a blessing.

Tonight, returning from the PI-invaded Tri-county Bigfooter's meeting, Hawk's sleeping face framed by those of our daughters, my hand firmly in Bubba's, I am swept with a feeling of grace and well-being. In the midst of this blessing, a premonition overcomes me in a rush of icy cold that catches my breath, causes me to lean into the wide body of my husband, memorize the moment. Some small voice whispers that in the weeks ahead, this instant will become a luminous pearl strung on dirty string, a thing of precious beauty to be taken out and caressed between shaking fingers.

Rufus whines a greeting like the creak of a rusty-hinged door. Hawk opens his eyes. The man blinks, tightens his grip on his daughters. The dog leaves his post and comes to me. He rubs his giant head under my hand and presses his weight lightly against my left side, anchors me between him and Bubba. The air is infused with the smells of home. Wet dog, damp wood, and strawberry no-more-tears shampoo mix with Bubba's spicy musk. Tonight there's a hint of Hawk's slight woodsy scent as well, but all traces of him will be gone five minutes from now when he shuts the front door behind him, straddles his powder blue Indian motorcycle, and roars off into the dark, wet night.

"Guess I fell asleep." Hawk yawns.

Bubba steps around the coffee table, scoops up Dharma, while Hawk struggles to sit up with Victoria cradled against his chest. The girls' bedroom is on the second floor. Actually, the girls' room is the second floor. A big kitchen and the living room with its wall of high, west-facing windows, with a small bathroom tucked under the stairs, comprise the entire first floor of the old furniture warehouse. Up the stairs is a huge bedroom and attached bath for Dharma and Victoria. The third floor is Bubba's and mine.

The dog stays with me while Bubba and Hawk carry the girls upstairs to bed. Framed in one of the high, street-facing windows, a bat feasts on soft-bodied moths, swoops in and out of the streetlight's fuzzy halo. The bay-facing windows were salvaged from a two-hundred-year-old Victorian behind what is now Target. On rare cloudless afternoons, the setting sun hits these imperfect windows and transforms the light into waves of peach-tinted magic, fills the room with what the twins call *water light*.

The private investigator's folded papers are a flame drawing my fluttery hand to my coat pocket. Dad and David, hell the entire congregation of Tri-county Bigfooters, are eager to know what those papers portend. I'm saving that news, want just Bubba and myself to see what words are written in legalese, before sharing any information with a larger audience.

"How'd the meeting go?" Hawk returns from putting Victoria to bed.

"It was quiet." I turn from the window, leave the moths to their fate, don't mention the near shootout with the private investigator, Joe Stanton. "Haven't been many sightings in the last few months."

"I thought the women hunters from out near Peckwan had some new casts," he says as Bubba joins us.

My husband slips his arm around my waist and draws me to him in a clear, if gentle demonstration of our relationship. His need for this display is an irritation to me, but I've grown to accept it as one of those guy-things over which I have zero control.

"It makes me feel like property," I told him the very first time he did the maneuver in front of Hawk, well over four years ago.

"Well, now." He kissed my forehead and the tip of my nose before I pulled away to glare up at him. "You got to get over that 'cause it truly ain't got nothing whatsoever to do with you. This here is 'tween me and Hawk."

"Yeah, I get that. And I'm the bitch you two stud dogs are posturing over."

Tonight, I lean into my husband for a moment before walking to the couch, plopping myself onto its worn cushions, and resting my booted feet on the coffee table.

"The women hunters," I tell Hawk, "are the only ones having any Bigfoot contact at all. The creature seems to have disappeared back to wherever it comes from."

"You still thinking Doctor Bernstein's string theory and the existence of other dimensions explains the sightings?" Hawk asks.

I untie my boots and slip them off. Bubba sits at the other end of the couch, lifts my stocking feet onto his lap.

"I don't know what to think," I tell Hawk, suppressing a moan of pleasure as Bubba massages the balls of my feet. "I keep picturing the whole bunch of us as blind fools running our hands over different parts of an elephant. We all end up with very different ideas of what the animal is, but that doesn't necessarily mean we're not touching the same creature."

Hawk shrugs. "I've got an early class to teach tomorrow. Cultural Anthropology. I'm taking the girls next weekend, right?"

"Ah, yeah." I swing my feet to the floor. There is no way I can concentrate with Bubba's hands on any part of my body and that evidently includes the calloused soles of my feet. "The girls have that nutrition play at school on Friday. They're playing pinto beans. Remember?"

"They mentioned that." Hawk's halfway to the door. "I'll be there if I can," he promises without asking what time the play starts.

Bubba waits until the bike's throaty roar has disappeared into the night.

"You gonna look at those papers tonight? Or you wanna just wait till they burn a hole clean through your pocket?"

five

DHARMA'S ALREADY KICKED off the quilt, twisted the bed sheet into a knot at her bare feet. Pete, her one-eared, love-mottled elephant, peeks from under a dimpled elbow. I untangle the sheet, tuck the quilt around her warm body, stretch out along the edge of the bed. She rolls into me, throws both arms around my neck, and nuzzles against my breasts. Instinct borne of hundreds of nights of nursing. Or maybe just love. Pure, simple, sweet love.

Usually, this is a moment of anticipated calm in my day, when I let myself sink into the quiet joy of motherhood. Tonight, the encounter with the PI in the bar has left me shaky, my questionable ability to guard my children's vulnerability a hot knot of fear in my throat.

When Dharma's breathing returns to its slow, deep sleep rhythm, I slide gently from her bed and walk four steps to look down on Victoria. During the day this is the daughter who never stays still, who questions and butts heads and demands answers. In the night, the girls reverse roles and, while Dharma tosses and turns and calls out from her dream world, her sister simply lies on her back, closes her eyes so that her long, dark lashes shadow her rounded cheeks, and drops into restful sleep.

Veronica's forehead is warm and dry when my fingers smooth a few stray strands of hair from her face. This is the child most like me and yet it is Dharma who, just lately, elicits in me a fear like a brooding knowledge of danger lurking just out of sight in the invisible future. I finger the papers folded in my pocket.

Maybe it's just that things are going so well lately, I can't help but worry. Dad has recovered from his bypass surgery. Bubba and I, having woven our way through my old, deeply-flawed relationship with Hawk, have created an intricate, fresh tapestry under which to warm ourselves. The girls are healthy, happy, and secure in this strange world of men and Bigfoot and love in which I am raising them.

So then, why does my throat close over a lump of fear, my eyes sting with hot, liquid worry? Why does my imagination create an image of a carefree girl-child splashing in sun-kissed waters while a predator of epic proportions glides just below the surface, already locked onto the sweet smell of innocence?

BUBBA SPRAWLS THE length of the couch, a hole at the big toe of one white sock. His discarded boots, laces open and tongues exposed, take up most of the space under the coffee table. Rufus, stretched at the foot of the stairs so I nearly trip on him at my entrance, unfolds himself and follows me to the couch. Bubba opens his arms and I settle along his bulk while the dog lowers himself along the front of the sofa with a grunt. It's like lying between two mountains. Living, breathing mountains. Bubba's left hand on my butt, he runs his right hand up my back, presses me into him.

For some reason I am crying. Quiet, almost peaceful tears wet my cheeks and Bubba's shirt. Sleep almost takes me then, but my husband's voice pulls me from the brink.

"Whatever's in that paper, it ain't going to go away just because you don't open it." His voice rumbles his wide chest, vibrates in my ear.

Getting up off Bubba is less than graceful. I end up tangled with the dog before settling on the rug, my back against the couch, my legs bent at the knee with just enough room for Rufus's head to make a wet spot on my thigh. The folded papers, now wrinkled nicely, crinkle in my hand. Bubba sits up, throws one leg over the dog so that I'm cradled between my husband's long, denim-clad legs. Calloused hands close over my shoulders.

He doesn't say a word.

I unfold the papers, read them all the way through. Quickly. Scanning over the legalese. Second paragraph in, my heart suspects what my brain refuses to process. A fluttery beat pounds in my chest. I keep reading. Doing my best to make sense of these black scriggles on white paper. The letters morph on the page, become indecipherable hieroglyphics. A code that, once translated, will rearrange my world, leave my perceptions in shards at my feet. All the way through three and a half pages, I make my eyes flow from character to character.

I pass the letter to Bubba. His left hand stills on my shoulder. Paper crinkles. He gets up from the couch, steps over the dog, pushes the coffee table and his boots out of our way, and sits flat on the floor against me. I take comfort in the warm bodies on both sides while Bubba reads and the dog whines softly. I don't have a single thought until Bubba folds the papers neatly and sets them carefully on the couch behind us.

I am suspended between a world I've always known, and another parallel universe just at the limit of my vision. The grandfather clock in the entrance, a gift from Dad on Bubba and my first anniversary, insists that time passes with each loud tick.

Sometime later, Bubba stirs beside me.

"You want caramel syrup and hot fudge?"

"Not quite yet. Don't think I can swallow right now."

"That'll pass."

He stands, pulls me to my feet and, as though I'm made of thin glass, lowers me to the couch where he covers me with a quilt that smells only slightly of wet dog. He cranks up the thermostat on his way to the kitchen and I let my mind fall into the rumbling and crackling of the furnace and then the lovely feel of hot air cocoons me in warmth.

Well, be careful what you wish for. Haven't I been moaning since the twins were born about finding out more about my mother? Seriously, God? This is your answer to that prayer?

Bubba hands me a heavy bowl. A mound of whipped cream tops my Cherry Garcia ice cream. I rest the bowl against the dog's broad head and spoon cold, sweet comfort into my mouth.

"You think it's her?" Bubba eases me into the moment.

"Ah, yeah." I lick caramel off my dripping spoon. "Rose Ambrose. Probably it's her. But who is Gloria Ambrose? And why are the two of them wanting to meet with me? The death of my sperm-donating dad's got nothing to do with me."

"Well, now. It'll probably make a heap more sense tomorrow after the meeting."

six

I STARE OUT into the night from my third-floor bedroom window. Hair still damp from the shower Bubba and I shared, my chenille robe covers ratty, gray sweats. Bubba's snores mix with those of Rufus behind me. Through soft drizzle, yellow light is fog-blurred at the high windows of Dad's room across the street—a homing beacon.

Bubba's cheek is bristly when I kiss it. The smell of his skin nearly pulls me down under the covers with him. In the girls' room, I untangle Dharma from her blankets once more, kiss her soft cheek, touch my mouth to Victoria's smooth forehead, and signal Rufus to lie between the beds.

There's no need to leave a note. Bubba will know where I've gone.

Downstairs I crumble the papers into my robe pocket, slip into my Carhartt, tuck my hair into my watch cap, and I'm ready to step out into the night. The grandfather clock chimes three times as I step out the door into cold, wet air.

I saw a good many wonderful places on my book tour. Kentucky, where locals occasionally spot the creature they call a skunk-ape, and the mountains roll away like blue waves in air so crisp and clear it sears your lungs. Nepal, where Sherpas encounter Yetis with regularity and the mountains rise steep and supreme. Mexico City, where locals have recently spotted hombre pelodo among the pyramids of their ancestors.

None of those places is more beautiful to me than this quiet, rain-blackened city street. The meager halos of the streetlights. Fishy, salty air gentle on my face. Every soul on earth I love protected by soft fog and within easy reach.

The keys rattle in the pocket of my jacket as I trot across the empty street. Once inside, I make one brief stop behind the bar before tapping on Dad's door.

"Come on in, Samantha." His voice is sleep-deprived, ragged at the edges.

"How'd you know it was me?"

"Heard the lid twist off the jar of maraschino cherries."

Ancient mold overlays the cozy smell of burnt popcorn. Dad's in his ancient recliner. The once-plaid chair lists to the left and is held together with assorted colors of duct tape. I kiss his cheek. Then I lower myself into the new recliner, the one that vibrates and rocks and swivels, the one in pristine condition that Bubba and I and the girls got him for Father's Day three years ago.

He marks his place in a paperback *Iliad* with a postcard of Bigfoot, lays the book carefully on the end table next to his beloved chair. In the glow of the pole lamp to his left, his deeply lined face is beautiful. The folds and crisscrosses and scars of a life well-spent mark him indelibly as the honest, hardworking outdoorsman he is. It was me who ranted, raved, and finally persuaded him to stop smoking so he could have his bypass surgery. I keep to myself how much I miss the comforting smell of Winstons that I grew up with and have always associated with love, acceptance, and comfort.

I hand him the folded papers. Only once does he look up at me. In his eyes I see my own confusion, fear, and anger—softened, reflected back. It takes him a long time to read the three and a half pages. He flips back and forth a time or two, runs his finger along a few lines.

The new recliner squeaks at each forward rock. Faster and faster it chants out my impatience.

"Dad," I say just to hear that word in this room. "I googled the bitch. It's her. And Gloria Ambrose? She's my... she looks... I have a twin. A sister the lying witch never even bothered to tell me about."

He rattles the papers on his bony knees, refolds them before handing them across the braided rug into my reluctant hand.

"Don't bad talk her." His voice is flat. The instruction mere rote. "She's your mother."

"Pushed me out of her body and never looked back. She's never going to be my mother." My voice cracks, comes out all stupid and scared when there's no reason for me to be upset about some woman I've barely even met.

He changes the subject. "I guess it must have been your twin Letticia and Lefty saw."

"Ah, yeah. I guess. Peculiar to think that all these years I've had a twin out there and never even suspected it. I can't even imagine how much different Victoria and Dharma would be if they didn't have each other."

I push myself out of the chair, head toward the door to the bar.

"Bring me a shot of Private Stock while you're in there, will ya?"

I nod and keep walking.

In the gloom of the bar, I stand for a moment and wonder how different my twin's life must have been from mine. How odd that this other person, this Gloria Ambrose, once formed and grew right beside me and now, the two of us raised in such completely different worlds, will we have any connection? Or will that turn out to be another loss I can chalk up to the selfish monster who birthed me?

I swipe at my eyes. Damn those old timers with their smoking in the courtyard. It's not like all that freaking blue haze doesn't float its way into my bar about two seconds after they exhale. I hate when people muck up my bar. It may not be much, but it's my inheritance.

I focus on the Bigfoot casts along the back wall arranged for tonight's earlier meeting. The white plaster of Paris glows eerily in the silence. A tiny, battery-powered tea light illuminates the photo of Patty over the bar. That's new. One of the hunters must have put it there tonight at the meeting.

Patty. The female Bigfoot caught by Roger Patterson's camera. Heavy breasts swinging, frozen in mid-stride, looking back over her shoulder at the man who stirred up a pot-load of interest, speculation and, finally, in a few cases, faith. For the ten-thousandth time, I stare into the eyes in the photo. She's like the Shroud of Turin. Faith doesn't rest on her authenticity and—someday—somebody somewhere may prove her to be a fake. In the meantime, for anyone who's ever come face-to-face with one of the creatures she epitomizes, she's a powerful focal point, a beautiful symbol of faith in that which we can never hope to fully understand, a lost past and a future unimaginable.

Back in Dad's room, the smell of spiced rum momentarily overpowers the popcorn. I lower myself back into the recliner, tuck my knees to my chin, and balance a highball glass of cherries on them. Dad rolls his heavy glass between his palms, sips at the rum. At eighty-three and after heart surgery, the drink is a prop and a comfort more than anything else.

"What do you make of finding out the identity of your biological father?"

My throat closes. The chunky, syrupy cherry burns my throat, chokes me. Through the coughing fit I sputter, "You… are always… my dad."

"I'm not threatened, Samantha. Or not much. It's part of your history. Good for you and for the girls to know these things."

I stagger from the chair to the sink, fill a water glass, and sip slowly, hoping to quiet the spasms of my throat. From the counter, looking back at Dad propped in his dilapidated, duct-taped throne, a circle of bluish light behind him throwing half his face in shadow, he seems, suddenly, old beyond reckoning and bone tired.

"You remember I told you your mom left just before you were born?" Back in the rocker-recliner, I nod, sip the water, and resist the urge to stuff my mouth again with cherries.

"She went to a Rolling Stones concert you said. 'Eight-and-half months pregnant and stubborn as a Missouri mule' is the way you told it to me."

He nods. "Well, reading those papers and thinking about how there was another baby all along. Maybe that concert was just a cover. A planned lie. Could be, looking back at how she never let me go with her to doctor appointments, never would answer a single question of mine about the pregnancy. I'm wondering now if maybe she knew all along she was having twins. Planned it from the beginning to split up the babies. To raise one child with the… with the father… and to come back up here and leave the other child, you, with me."

I've already come to the same conclusion but the big question is, how did she choose? Why was it me she abandoned? What fault or wrong did I do so that she walked away, never looking back, went on with her life with my twin, as though I didn't exist? I can't ask Dad any of this. Because the double-edged sword here is that, if she had not made that decision, if she had kept me and discarded the other baby, I would not have had this loving, wonderful man as my father.

"There's no changing history now," I say. "I've got zero interest in this… John Ambrose person who may or may not be my biological… father. And I've got no inclination to meet some stranger who has me followed and then announces herself through some private investigator."

"Honey, for a few months I loved your mother beyond good sense, but I have never been able to fathom her reasoning or her actions. For your own sake, I think you ought to give her a chance to explain herself. But unless she's changed since I knew her? You better bring your own lawyer to this here meeting tomorrow."

seven

"I HATE OATMEAL!" Victoria taps a spoon on her steaming bowl of mush.

I'm at the counter, doing my best to slice chunky peanut butter and blackberry jam sandwiches into triangles without my shaky hands cutting off a finger. "You want a few blueberries and a handful of walnuts to stir in?"

"No!" The tapping is louder, faster, more insistent.

Bubba, across from Victoria and to Dharma's right at the scarred oak kitchen table, sips his coffee, keeps his mouth shut.

The sandwiches cut, wrapped, and tucked into one Princess Fiona lunch pail and one Donkey pail, my now cold coffee in hand, I walk to the table and remove the offending bowl of oatmeal.

"I want Toaster Strudel," Victoria demands.

"People in hell wantin' ice water too," I tell her, "but they aren't any more likely to get it than you are to be wiping strawberry filling off your mouth this morning."

"Can I have blueberries?" Dharma asks.

Bubba pushes back his chair, heads for the refrigerator. His warm hand on my shoulder as he passes calms me not one bit. Still, I appreciate the gesture.

"Sister Martha Mary says breakfast is the most important meal of the day," Victoria informs me.

"I've heard that."

My coffee is cold. I hate cold coffee. Don't believe I've drunk a full cup hot since the twins were born. What about my own mom? I bet she never missed a beat once I was dumped with Dad. Lots of nice hot coffee and plenty of time to enjoy it for that bitch.

Oh God, what the hell is the matter with me? There's no way I'd rather have been raised by her than by Dad. She did me a favor walking away and never looking back. So, why am I so damn angry I could chew nails?

"Uncle Lefty came to see us last night," Dharma says. "Him and Daddy Hawk gave us horsey rides. And he told us a funny story about Princess Little Dove and Honey Girl Page."

Bubba sprinkles blueberries and chopped walnuts on Dharma's oatmeal, sets Victoria's equally decorated bowl back on the table. He bends to me as he passes. His mouth tastes of coffee and the Toaster Strudel he snuck when he came down to the kitchen an hour ago to get breakfast for the girls.

One warm kiss and, I gotta admit, the rest of the morning goes a little better.

Twenty minutes later, I watch from the kitchen window as Bubba loads the girls into the truck, heads for Saint Bernard's Elementary School. I scrape half-eaten bowls of oatmeal into the garbage, wonder if maybe it wouldn't be better to let the girls go to the good sisters hyped-up on sugar and fat. At least they'd clean their plates.

The round face of the kitchen clock reads 9:09. Time to make the call I decided on last night after returning from Dad's.

It takes twelve minutes to get him on the phone, inconveniences his secretary who, by the time I persuade her to get him out of the morning meeting, has convinced me that her possessiveness means she's sleeping with the big galoot.

"Robert Rossi, Humboldt County District Attorney." His voice is gruff. He doesn't actually say, what the hell is so damn important? But I get the idea.

"Hey, Bobby. How's your dart arm?"

"Sam?"

"Ah, yeah. Who'd your watch dog tell you it was?"

He laughs and I picture him with his feet up on his desk, wrinkled suit jacket draped over a chair, tie askew, big grin on his handsome Dago face.

"She said Missus Johnson. I guess I forgot you married that Georgia Bigfoot lookalike. How's your dad? The girls?"

"Everybody's good. Finer'n frog's hair, as Bubba'd say. We miss you at the weekly dart tournaments."

"I've been busy. Turns out there's a fair amount more work to being District Attorney than there is to being Assistant DA. That why you called? To entice me back to VD's?"

"Not exactly. I have a little problem I'm hoping you can help me with."

"You wondering if I'll leave Sheila, help you divorce your husband so you can run away with the best looking District Attorney in four counties?"

"Not today. Anyway, it seems like you've got your hands full, what with your wife and your secretary."

I hear his feet come down off the desk, thud onto the floor.

"What? Who told you... why do you say that?"

"I'm just rattling your chain. Listen, I do need a favor. Can you call an attorney for me and move a meeting, scheduled for about two hours from now, out of a suite at The Rarcet House and into VD's? I'd do it myself, but I'd like this guy, and his client, to know they're not dealing with some Humboldt County hick."

"Ah. So, I'm the hot-shot, impressive legal muscle. Oh, Sam, you are a sweet talker." His laugh is low and husky. God, no wonder this man has been getting into trouble with the women of this county since he's been old enough to get a hard-on. "Is this a local guy?"

"No. Or I'd do it myself. His letterhead says Merritt James Burke, Esquire."

"*Esquire*, huh? Gee. Impressive."

"Yeah. As in City Asshole."

"DID THE GIRLS tell you about my idea?" Lefty settles his skinny butt onto the stool next to me. He signals Carey for a beer. She keeps restocking behind the bar, does her best to ignore his increasingly insistent hand gestures.

"We're not open for another hour and a half," I remind him. "You know I don't cater to the breakfast drinkers. What the heck are you doing here this early anyway?"

The sun's out this morning, the temperature up into the 60s. A dead-fish breeze blows in through the back windows and out the open front door, sweeping the smell of flat beer and stale sweat in front of it. The plaster of Paris casts have been returned to the locked storeroom.

Bubba has pushed two tables together under the head of the one-eyed bear. He and Dad sit with their backs to the wall on two of the six gold-flecked Naugahyde chairs along the makeshift conference table. The third chair with its back to the wall, the one between them, is reserved for me. There's something expectant, nearly ominous, about the three empty seats arranged on the opposite side of the table. Or maybe I'm being paranoid.

Lefty goes behind the bar, roots around in the trough of crushed ice for the coldest beer. Before he can lower himself onto the stool beside me, I begin the process of throwing him out of my bar.

"Go," I tell him. "Take Carey with you and get some breakfast or a decent cup of coffee. We're locking up in about ten minutes for a meeting."

The bottle is half-empty when he lowers it. He squints at me, removes his ball cap, stares into its greasy depths as though contemplating the mysteries of the universe.

"I enjoy meetings," he tells me. "Plus, like I mentioned, there's an idea you need to hear. Make you a good chunk a change." He resettles his cap, adjusts the stained brim. "'Less you so high and mighty now you don't need money."

Bubba appears at Lefty's side, leads him gently to the front door where he slips him a couple of bills and motions for Carey to join our old friend in getting the hell out of VD's.

"Hey!" I call down the bar to Carey as she unties her bar apron. "Do me a favor? Take the credit card from the till and pick up the dogs and chili for tonight's dart tournament."

Lefty's empty beer bottle in hand, Bubba shuts the front door behind them and joins me at the bar. "You okay?"

"Nervous," I allow.

Scared half to death is more like it. All those years of staring at the one picture of my mother I have. Caught in mid-twirl, flowing Chinese dragon robe a silk ripple at her ankles, her hair swinging around her face like the first golden day of summer. And now, she's almost here. I'm a grown woman with daughters of my own, and, right this moment, feel like a god-damned abandoned child.

I hate this! Why on earth did I ever think I wanted to meet the woman who dropped me like a sack of garbage and skipped lightly away without so much as a backward glance? I'm happy with my life the way it is. The girls. Bubba. And Dad. God, Dad. I have no idea how to even begin to know my mother without feeling like I'm betraying a man who has loved and been there for me every single moment of my life.

"Are you certain this is the correct address?" A voice at the door that sounds like mine. They're not even inside and already I'm in one of those *Alice in Wonderland* dreams where reality stands on its head and laughs in your face.

The door swings open and, ready or not, here they are.

eight

IT'S THE SCENT of jasmine that assaults me first.

Three-inch heels on high, leather boots are loud on the bar's plank floor. The boots are the dull gray of a dead dove's breast. Her skirt dances softly around her legs, stops an inch below her knees, hugs the curve of her hips like the obscene hands of an illegitimate lover. I have no idea what fabric it is. Silk? Lamb's wool? The gossamer dreams of the innocent? Tucked into the waistband is a sheer blouse the color of pink rose petals floating in a champagne flute. Or maybe it's the peach tint of a discarded newborn's cheek.

I refuse to raise my eyes any higher, lean into Bubba who has, somehow, materialized at my side. Dad sits alone under the one-eyed bear, back to the wall, two vacant chairs to his left, three across the makeshift, coffin-sized conference table, his calm presence a blessing.

She can leave now. Rose Ambrose. My mother. Just knowing she's alive is enough. Now she can go. Far away from me. Maybe call once a decade or so. To keep in touch.

Those heels! Closer and closer.

Her scent. Stronger and stronger.

No escape. I raise my eyes to look into the face I've dreamed about for thirty-three years.

"Hello, Samantha Jean."

I hate, hate, that her voice sounds enough like mine to fool someone who didn't know us at all. Someone who couldn't tell the difference between me and this traitorous, lying, conniving bitch.

Her hair is a rich, glowing blonde, like gold spun by enslaved elves. Her eyes are a deeper blue than my pale ones, which, for some stupid, ridiculous, freaking reason are spilling hot tears onto my cheeks.

To escape her smell, and some kind of energy field that seems to be robbing me of years, sloughing off maturity at an alarming rate, I slide off the back of the bar stool, and flee to the chair next to Dad. Bubba's warmth remains a constant comfort at my side. With my back to the wall and wedged between Dad and my husband, my heart slows a little. I feel less childlike, more the adult I pretend to be.

Only now do I notice my twin.

It's the oddest feeling. Like looking in a skewed, fun-house mirror. Same full mouth as my own. Except, while mine makes me look like a large-mouth bass, hers is pouty, touched with coral pink, and calls to mind a particular sex act. I look into eyes the exact same violet-blue as my own, but she's done something with eyeliner and mascara and color so that, while mine are drab, pale orbs, hers seem to tilt up at the outside corners like those of the sexiest, most beautiful kitten in the world.

The apparition speaks, extends a soft hand. "Hello, Samantha." A rhinestone, hell for all I know it could be a diamond, set in the lacquered nail of her index finger, flashes in the dusky light from the back window. "I'm Gloria. Your… your sister."

I twist my calloused, cuticle-impaired hands in my lap. Breathe deep to anchor myself in Dad's Bay Rum and Bubba's comfortable, spicy scent. This aromatherapy helps. A little. But I cannot look away from my sister's lavender-kissed eyes.

"Hello, Victor." Mother's voice is husky, pitched low, with the hint of some drawl I don't recognize. The implied sexuality in the tone breaks the spell I'm under, draws my eyes away from my twin and focuses me on the older, jasmine scented woman. "It's been a long time." Her voice sounds as though she's whispering across a sex-wrinkled sheet. As if she and Dad are the only two people in world.

Did her eyes just cut toward the bedroom of my eighty-two year old father?

She bestows her manicured hand into his, a gift from a benevolent queen, palm-down, ready to receive the mandatory kiss of a subject. Dad shakes her hand briskly.

"Been a long time, Rose," he says flatly. "What brings you back now?"

She glides into the chair across from him, waits for her real daughter, the blonde goddess, to lower herself opposite me. In my peripheral vision some little guy in a gray suit, can't be much more than five foot, takes the chair on the end across from Bubba.

"Please, Victor Dear." That honeyed drawl again. "I hope you're not still angry with me for my little deceit."

Little deceit? Abandoning your six-week-old-daughter. Me. Disappearing without a trace. And, oh yeah by the way, hiding a twin for thirty-three years.

"Never was angry with you, Rose." Dad looks directly into those icy, glittering eyes. "You left the best part of you here."

Her eyes cut to me. She moves her gaze over my bare, makeup-free face, hair pulled back in a braid, my purple t-shirt, the only one I could find that didn't have a telltale stain on the front. She runs her tongue along the inside of her cheek. Her shoulders shrug slightly. She may as well say the words out loud. This? This plain, insignificant girl here, you think this is the best part of me?

"Yes, well," she says with no trace of the previous drawl. "It all worked out for the best."

The conflict between my fierce hatred and resentment of this woman and the pain at her dismissal tunnels my vision, sets me to shaking. Bubba wraps a warm arm around my shoulders. I yearn to close my eyes and pretend none of this is happening.

"The real question," Dad says, "is why you're here now."

From the other end of the table, The Little Suit clears his throat, opens a leather briefcase, distributes heavy, gold-edged folders to everyone. Dad and Bubba open the pages flat on the scarred surface in front of them. I am anchored to these two men. I squeeze tight to their calloused hands and try to remember to breathe. My folder lies unopened in front of me.

A refined male voice drones on about provisions and signatures and clauses. I watch the eyes of my twin. Gloria. Gloria Ambrose. Twenty-four hours ago, I didn't know she existed. She winks and that lovely mouth turns up. I can't help mirroring her smile. An opal and gold necklace circles her neck. Opals are my favorite gemstone. Well, okay. The opal earrings Bubba gave me for my thirtieth birthday are my only jewelry. But still. They are my favorite. She searches in her elegant clutch purse, slips a business card across the table like a confidence shared in the dark of a childhood bedroom.

"Is that arrangement to your satisfaction Miz Foster?" The Little Suit is talking to me?

"What? I wasn't... I didn't hear.... What?"

Dad squeezes my hand and translates the legalese. "Your biological father didn't know about you until just a few months before he died. Didn't know your mother had twins any more than I knew." A flash of anger tints these last words. "Evidently he became suspicious when he found some personal papers of your mother's."

"Yes, yes. The point being," Poser-Mother interjects smoothly. She flutters her graceful, bejeweled hand in a motion of dismissal. "Though we are under no obligation to be so generous, I am, after all, your mother. All I've ever wanted is to be fair. To do right by you... Samantha."

Did she just stumble over my name?

"Nonetheless," Dad says. "I can't help asking, once again, why you've shown up now. Your husband died a little less than three months past. I'd think you'd be busy as a spider with a new web, down there in The City. Arranging a life for yourself. Mister Ambrose was, if I'm reading the Internet right, richer than Midas. Must be a good many loose ends to tie off, money to spend. Instead, you drive all the way up here to throw money at a daughter you haven't seen in over three decades."

Dust floats in the morning light, a wet breeze from off the bay paints a vision of low tide, iridescent green kelp, temporarily high and dry on exposed rock and pier.

"I can explain," The Little Suit says. "After the unfortunate death of her husband, Miz Ambrose desired to travel to Humboldt County immediately for the purpose of informing her daughter, Samantha Jean Foster, of the death of her biological father. Unfortunately, my client's grief over the demise of Mister Ambrose made travel impossible at that time."

Salty air lifts the curtain at the window to our left. A shaft of pale salt-laden light momentarily illuminates the photo of Patty above the bar. Dry words buzz ineffectually in the fishy air and I am right back in that greening meadow above Bluff Creek, looking into red-rimmed eyes. Struck, once again, into joy and awe.

"Ah, yeah," Dad says. "I understand about grief for a loved one. But I still got a few questions. If I'm reading these documents correctly, you're offering Samantha money to sign off on, let's see if I got it right here. 'Any and all future inheritance due her from Mister Stephen Ambrose.'

"That don't sound like something you'd offer, Rose. Unless you thought there was a mighty good possibility that ole Stephen has left our girl here a whole lot more than what you're offering her. And here's the question I'm most curious about, since you never divorced me, how'd you legally marry Ambrose?"

Mother stiffens. For a split second a look of evil intent washes over her carefully made-up face. The shadow disappears, a shiver still racing up my spine. She leans across the table, gives us all a nice view of the curve of tan line along the top of her peach lace bra.

"Darling Victor," she purrs. "I'm doing my best to make amends for past mistakes. Now that I need no longer lie, I want to make it up to the daughter that circumstances took from me. Can you find it in that big heart of yours to give me a second chance to make things up to you and to Samantha?"

She winks and a premonition settles over me like a caul.

Bubba shifts his bulk beside me, removes his arm from my shoulders, and stands.

"I'd like my wife to have the opportunity to review all these here documents with an attorney of her own before she does any signing of papers." His deep voice is loud in the quiet bar.

The Suit makes a few protest noises, but Bubba isn't suggesting, he's done made a statement of fact. He escorts the trio out of VD's, locks the door behind them. The scent of jasmine continues to taint the honest smell of the bay. I run my finger along the embossed name of my twin on the card cradled in my palm, never turn loose of Dad's hand.

Bubba steps behind the bar then returns to sit beside me. He places an offering on the table in front of me—highball glass heaped with maraschino cherries, a toothpick like a flagpole on a mountaintop stuck into the top of the pile. We three sit silently until the glass is empty, my shaky hands are sticky with syrup, tears dried on my face.

nine

DAD HAS THE gold-edged legal folder spread out on a wooden table under the cauliflower-eared elk we call Rudolph. Early afternoon light pours thin through the window to his left.

Carey and I are on our final run from the storeroom. My arms extended in front, I have paper plates balanced precariously on the last four dart boards. Carey, right behind me, platform heels thudding on beer-marinated wood at each step, balances the scoreboard and an old shoebox of pencil nubs. The sound of scraping chairs and an off-key bass growling out the words to "Hunka, Hunka Burnin' Love" tells me Bubba's setting up in the courtyard.

A ringing cell phone stops everything while we all pat our pockets, ask at the same time, Is that mine?

I dump the plates onto the bar, fish my phone from the front pocket of my jeans. The display window warns Sisters of Saint Bernard's. The Hamm's Beer clock behind the bar reads 1:47. Not quite time to pick up the girls. I have a bad feeling about this phone call. Of course, that could be the residual shadow of the meeting with my mother, or it's possible it's just a remnant of fear of nuns from my catechism days.

I suck a deep breath of air spiced with rain-drenched asphalt, stale beer, and high tide, then flip open my phone.

"Samantha Jean." Sister Mary Martha's voice could cut through a sinner's best intentions. "Come to my office immediately."

My heart pumps adrenalin to every inch of my body.

"My girls! What happened?"

Tiny broken bones, bloody gashes on soft skin—more real than a flat screen, high definition 3-D—pictures of pain and mayhem flash before my eyes.

"Your daughters are fine. It's Jamie Farnsworth who's on his way to the emergency room."

"What?" I lower myself onto the nearest stool, wait for my heart to slow.

"Victoria and Dharma attacked a child. On the playground. Before Sister Joan could reach them, the girls had teamed up, and in the scuffle, Jamie's head hit the metal post of the swing set."

"Who's Jamie Farnsworth? He's not in the girls' class, is he?"

"Not that it makes any difference, but no, the young man is in Brother Paul's class."

"But… Victoria and Dharma are in pre-kindergarten. Brother Paul teaches the third grade. Doesn't he?"

"I'm not going to discuss this with you over the phone, Samantha Jean. Get in here to my office immediately."

At the moment, I'm not reacting well to older, mean, female authority figures. No doubt six to eight centuries will be added to my time in purgatory, but there is no way I can keep my mouth shut.

"My girls would not have started a fight, Sister. They know better, and it's simply not in their nature."

Well, okay, it's not in Dharma's nature. Victoria might punch somebody if they pissed her off enough.

"We will discuss the matter in my office, Samantha Jean."

Bubba, having heard my end of the call, stands at the door, jiggling keys in his pocket. Dad pulls his arms into the sleeves of his plaid coat.

"We'll be there in a few minutes," I say to Sister Meanie.

"There's no reason for the whole bunch of you to—"

I hit the red end call button.

THE PRINCIPAL'S OFFICE stinks of cheap floor wax and sour milk. Pale light from windows is infused with chalk dust and what's left of souls destroyed by too much authority invested in too weak a vessel. My girls sit on a bench made for adults. Their bare legs dangle a foot or more above the green-flecked squares of linoleum. Victoria smiles when we come through the door. Dharma, whose face is already red and streaked with tears, breaks into sobs.

I kneel between them, nuzzle my face into their soft necks, run my hands over their bodies to reassure myself they're not hurt.

"You okay?" I ask.

Behind me comes the creak of a heavy wooden door, the muted slap of hard-soled nun shoes on worn linoleum, and the heavy sigh of a woman well past her prime called upon to raise the children of others.

Sister Mary Martha clears her throat. "If we could talk in my office, please. I'll explain what happened and we can decide on the proper course of action."

God, I wish I had a bucket of water to toss. Instead I stand and face the old witch.

"I'll talk to my girls first, Sister. When I have a clear understanding of what happened, then we'll talk."

The girls each take one of my hands and we go out the door, down the hall, through double doors, and into the overpowering scent of incense, Johnson Wood Soap, and flickering prayers cupped in beeswax. Bubba and Dad are right behind us. The twins stand on tiptoe, dabble their fingers in holy water, and bless themselves like the Catholic school girls they are. I pull down the kneeling bench directly in front of Mary, Mother of God, settle myself in a semblance of piety, and pray hard to deal with this little crisis without making it worse. That seems about as much as I dare hope for.

The girls kneel between Dad and me. Bubba, good Baptist boy that he is, sits awkwardly beside me. When my heart rate returns to normal, I push myself back into the pew.

"What happened?" My voice echoes in the chapel, seems to bounce softly off statues and stained glass before coming back to me.

"Jamie Farnsworth is a big, fat poopy-head," Victoria declares.

A retired nun, dressed in the black habit of her youth and bent almost double with osteoporosis, glares at us from what I imagine are her fervent prayers for the return of pre-Vatican II days.

"Could you be more specific?" Dad asks softly, his voice pitched so low the sound drops through sandalwood-infused air directly into our ears.

"Stupid, stupid fart-face Jamie Farnsworth," Dharma whispers to me. "He poked me with his stupid, dirty finger and called you a Bigfoot Looney Tick."

Oh God, please no. I don't want my girls going through this the way I did. Loyal to Dad, ostracized at school because of his beliefs.

The girls fighting to defend me? This is my worst fear.

"Don't worry, Mama." Victoria pats my arm. "We fixed him. Got him in the super-dooper midget headlock, scissor hold. Just like Uncle Lefty taught us."

"Like Princess Little Dove and Honey Girl Page," Dharma adds helpfully.

ten

DART NIGHT AT VD's is winding down to its happy, buzzed conclusion. I balance eight longnecks on an aluminum tray, move fast for the courtyard where Letticia's Redneck Mothers, mostly through some complicated handicapping system that factors into account age and takes advantage of the male ego, are whipping the pants off the Swinging Dicks from the District Attorney's Office.

"I guess I owe you an apology," Letticia says when I hand her an ice-dripping bottle of Humboldt Brewery's Downtown Brown. "How was I to know you had yourself a twin?"

"How were any of us to know? Gloria Ambrose is her name by the by, and we look nothing alike. I got no idea how you could have mistaken her for me. *Je*-zuss."

One of the Swinging Dicks misses his shot. His dart hits the wall behind the board, and The Redneck Mothers dance a victory lap around the men, whoop it up a little.

"Three for three!" Letticia brags as the little circle of merry witches sashays its way back around to me. "Sam," she shouts loud enough to be heard over the celebrating behind us. "I'll be seventy-eight next month. I'm just about done listening to your nonsense about your looks. That girl is your twin. Your identical twin. Time for you to face the bitter truth." She throws an arm around my waist, walks with me back to the bar. "You. Are. Beautiful." She bumps me with her bony hip. "Always have been. Always will be."

I ignore her and focus on Lefty, who sits at the end of bar, one cheek of his scrawny, trouble-making butt balanced on the end stool.

"Don't give him any beer!" I call to Carey. My face inches from his, my voice as low as the growl of a mama badger about to kick the bejesus out of some mutt caught with his snout in the den. "You taught my girls wrestling moves. Midget wrestling moves no less."

"You're welcome." He grins, the rapid blinking of his eyes the only sign he knows the trouble he's stepped into.

"Jackass. They used the moves you taught them to send some third-grader to the emergency room to get three stitches in his head."

Lefty's grin is wide enough to display his missing molars. "A third-grader? Them little bitty girls tag-teamed his ass?"

Dad's been subbing all night for The Gnarly Nooners who've got two players out with the Humboldt Crud. He slips behind me, pulls two Buds from deep in the crushed ice. He waves a bottle above his head at Lefty, like enticing a dog to obedience with the bribe of a liver treat. Lefty slides backward off the stool, follows Dad out of my reach.

Bobby Rossi claims the vacated stool.

"We need to talk." The District Attorney sets his empty bottle on the bar.

I remove it and hand him a fresh one, signal across the room to Bubba that I'm taking five, and lead my old friend upstairs to my childhood bedroom. Bobby follows me into the musky smell of wood that never dries. When I flip the light switch, the room stays dark, reminds me that the bulb has been burnt out for a couple of months. The three large, bay-facing windows are salt-speckled, mute the corner street light to a soft, lacy glow. Bobby helps me to wiggle and force open the swollen wood of the frame until cold, wet, salt-infused air blows clean into the room.

My back against the headboard of the bed, I motion him into the only chair. As he lowers himself onto the cushion, I have a moment of *déjà vu*. An instant out of time when another body superimposes itself over this man's.

It's Hawk I see sitting in the streetlight's halo, one long leg crossed, boot-side resting on opposite knee. I blink away the double exposure. Take two seconds to convince myself the flashback is the natural result of entering my childhood room. The sanctuary where Hawk and I made love every chance we got from the time I was sixteen until I came to my senses, almost three months pregnant, and accepted Hawk for the undependable and wounded man he is.

"I looked over the papers you sent me." Bobby's voice slams the door on the time travel.

I breathe deeply of the mold and salt of the here and now.

"Thanks. Why do you think... Mother is pushing so hard for my signature? They're offering a lot of money. Jeez, I could pay back the advance on that damn book sequel I'm supposed to be writing and still have a good bit left over." I pull my legs up onto the bed, tuck them under me in a modified version of the lotus position.

"Or," he says, "you could write the book and hire yourself an estate attorney. It doesn't take a legal genius to decipher the probable motive for the offer of a quick cash settlement in exchange for you signing away your right to whatever it is your biological father has bequeathed to you. I'd be shocked if it didn't turn out your dear mother has knowledge that the man has left you a lot of money or control or something she doesn't want you to receive."

"I'm sure you're right, but they're offering cash in my hand, and I never have to deal with the bitch again."

He runs his fingers through his dark hair. "One thing we need to know is who she married first." He raises one bushy eyebrow when I blink at him in confusion. "If she was married before she met your dad, then you're legally the daughter of Mister Ambrose. If she was already married to Victor when she married in San Francisco, then your dad is the legal father of both you and your twin. That could make a difference in the distribution of the estate."

"What? But... we know Dad's not my biological father."

The buoy at the entrance to the bay mourns into the darkness, echoes in the fog, warns of danger, promises sanctuary for those who follow the correct path.

Bobby leans forward, plants his boots firmly on the wood floor.

"When a woman is married, her husband, whether or not he fathered any children of the marriage physically, is legally the father of all children born within the marriage."

These are not complicated issues. And I'm not stupid. And yet. I can't seem lately to transform words into coherent thoughts or ideas. Words like father. Mother. Sister. These words tug at me, block my thoughts like cross currents in a confused sea.

"Look, Sam." Bobby does his best to mark the channel for me. "Here's what you need to think about." He holds up his index finger. "First of all, don't sign anything until you've gotten in touch with the estate lawyer whose name and number I'm going to give you. My guess is your inheritance from John Ambrose, your biological father, is a hell of a lot more than what they're offering."

My head nods as though I understand. Bobby leans forward, taps my booted foot with his hand before popping up a second finger.

"Secondly, I think Victor is the legal father of both you and your sister, Gloria. Rose Ambrose? Your mother? It is my suspicion that woman never does anything without it gaining her an advantage of one kind or another. There was no reason to marry your dad if she was already married. I'm checking those records for you, but I'd be surprised to find that she was married when she waltzed into VD's thirty-three years ago."

Into my fugue, a vague suspicion, a distorted shadow, falls. Dark knowledge creeps at the edge of my vision.

"My twin? Gloria is Dad's legal daughter too?" My true fear almost swims out into the misty air around my head, but at the last moment, I manage to ride the wave of pain, turn it to anger and determination. My intent is as clear and bright as it is ridiculous and petty.

I'll be goddamned if I'm going to share Dad with some twin who shows up out of nowhere. If that makes me a jealous twit, so be it. I don't care how beautiful Gloria is, or how nice she seemed at the meeting, she's never going to be Dad's daughter. No way in hell.

Ten minutes later, when Bobby and I return to the bar, I'm confronted with the twisted nature of fate. Run face-first into God's intricate sense of humor. Stare, once again, into the knowledge that, no matter what my fear or hope, destiny will tweak the vanity just enough to surprise the living hell out of me.

At the back of the bar, under the poster of that bloody handprint across my very own belly, with their heads together like the lovers they are obviously on their way to becoming, sits Hawk and my beautiful twin, Gloria. My knees wobble. For a split, unguarded second I stumble. My stomach clenches as though I've taken a punch, my left hip bouncing off the wall. I forget how to breathe.

Instinctively, I search the room for Bubba. There. Behind the bar. I'm already in motion toward him when his eyes stop me, reflect a hurt I never meant to deal. Caught in a moment out of the present, transported to a time of bone-deep longing and false hope I thought I left behind years ago, my stumbling moment of jealousy has brought pain to a man who's never, not once, shown me anything but sweet, powerful love.

Muscle memory overrides ancient, heavily scarred wounds. My legs keep right on moving to the sanctuary of my husband's arms. Where, pushing my cold, trembling body along his warm, solid love, I lie. Quick as a snake, healing as a mother's kiss, up on tiptoe, I whisper into his ear.

"Seeing Hawk with her? Gloria. Her looking so much like me? I had a sort of out of body moment when this great crashing fear lit on my chest. For a second, I was afraid it was me with Hawk. That my life with you was all a dream."

He enfolds me in flannel and muscle and the lie becomes truth.

eleven

CHALK DUST FLOATS in the pale afternoon light filtering through the rain speckled windows of Saint Bernard's Elementary School lunch room/auditorium. I'm wedged between Dad and Bubba, three rows from the raised platform stage at the room's front. On the other side of Dad, Hawk whispers into the tiny shell-like and multi-pierced ear of my twin. Lefty, next to Bubba, perches on the edge of his seat, his back straight, in a semi-catatonic state brought on by death threats. From me. The squeals, whines, and giggles of seventy-three overexcited children are only partially muted by heavy, mustard-yellow stage curtains.

It's a huge privilege, our rowdy family being allowed here for *The Adventures of Carlos Carrot and Amy Apple*. I know this because, during the course of a ten-minute, extremely un-Christian phone call, Sister Mary Martha explained the original ban on our attendance to me in excruciating detail. In the end, I won the small battle by refusing to turn over the two pinto bean costumes so that some more deserving and better disciplined children might participate in the program. I did manage, by the skin of my gritted teeth, to hang up the phone before cussing out a nun.

Casting my girls in roles that require the simplest outfit in a cast of dancing carrots, singing broccoli, and talking cherries, oranges and peaches—this was Sister's little dig at my lack of skill with a needle and thread. The girls' bean suits required no more sewing than stitching a speckled rectangle of cotton fabric and slitting holes big enough for sturdy legs, dimpled arms, and adorable, round-cheeked faces to poke through.

The hard part was finding the required brown leotards and long-sleeved t-shirts to go under the outfits. Plenty of girl-sized clothing in pink, lavender, sequins, and even one stunning pair of leggings in a plaid of lime green and purple. But hard to locate plain brown. In the end, I took two pair of black leggings and a couple of old black sweatshirts and washed everything in bleach which produced a perfectly respectable mottled brown-ish. For the love of God. The girls are four and this is an elementary school play for parents who pay a small fortune for the privilege of tearing all over town on mandatory treasure hunts brought on by a nun's whim.

"This is what the girls will be wearing under their outfits?" Sister Joan asked when I brought the twins backstage thirty minutes ago. She held the sleeve of a splotchy sweatshirt between two fingers. "You know, Samantha, the other mothers spent days making creative and beautiful costumes for their children." Sister leaned into my space. "It's the way mothers demonstrate to their children that they care about them."

"No kidding," I said. "I like to listen to my girls. Spend actual time with them when I'm not frazzled from competing in some school-dictated mother-of-the-year competition."

Now, replaying the conversation in my head I can't help wondering if, by not having a mother in my life as a child, I may have missed some essential lesson. Am I short-changing my girls by inventing this whole motherhood deal as I go along?

"You think we're doing all right with the girls?" I whisper into Bubba's ear. "Running a bar. Named VD's. Their mother and grandfather Bigfoot Looney Ticks." The soft hair touching his collar tickles my nose, smells of damp woods on an early fall day. "The last thing I want is for Victoria and Dharma to grow up fighting the same battles I fought as a child."

This man has the best smile. Every time I see it, I fall in love all over again.

"What you got to remember is that happy, carefree children most often grow up to be vacuous adults." He kisses my forehead.

A giggle bursts from my mouth like a rumbling fart in a church pew, turns the heads of two nuns up on stage fiddling with the sound system, and earns frowns from the well-heeled parents seated directly in front of us.

"Still with the word-of-the-day calendar, huh?"

Too late, I stifle my laughter.

A change in the air, a shift in the energy of the room, a heavy whiff of jasmine-tinged perfume turns my head toward the aisle before my ears register the sound of spike heels on milk-stained linoleum.

Terrific.

Mommy Dearest.

"Oh, my Gawd!" the woman on the aisle seat behind us exclaims in a voice that reminds me of Victoria when she spots a new My Little Pony. "Are those Jimmy Choos?"

Mother's voice is as buttery soft as her suede sandals. "You caught me. From last year's collection, but I simply adore them and Jim-Jim is such a treasure, he reserves a pair of his favorites for me each season. It's a curse, really," she trills. "My abnormally tiny feet. Extremely challenging to find decent shoes in a size four and a half."

What? This bitch hasn't worn a size four and a half anything since she was four and a half. Does she pay someone to sew two or three tiny shoes together so they fit her size eights?

"*Excusez-moi.*" She pushes past Lefty, plants her stupid, giant high-heeled feet in front of me.

"Perhaps." Is she speaking to me? "This… person." She nods a carefully made-up and irritatingly angel-soft face at Lefty. "Would it be possible for… him… to give up his seat to a lady."

Most people have a delay switch between their brain and their mouth. That's my understanding. Must be handy.

I rise, stand solid on my size nine Wolverines. "It might. If there was a lady needed a seat. But, I don't give a rat's ass if you are wearing five-thousand-dollar shoes. You. Are. No. Lady."

The room is nearly plunged into a vacuum as every parent in the auditorium simultaneously sucks in their breath. Could be my voice was a little louder than I intended. Could even be I reached a volume designed to carry over thirty-three freakin' years of abandonment.

Rose Ambrose sways on four inch heels, lays a French manicured hand on my arm. Now what? Are those tears in her glacier blue eyes? She's pretending she has feelings? Her hand is a fire-hot brand burning its way through the fleece of my sweatshirt. I jerk my arm away before sympathy can sear itself under my skin.

"There's a seat down here." Hawk's voice.

I refuse to turn and look at the traitorous bastard. That man would do anything to get into a new pair of panties. With Gloria beside him, he'll follow his dick into whatever hornets' nest awaits. Mother sidesteps her way around me. For one long moment, we're close enough to kiss.

Two seconds after I'm back in my place between Dad and Bubba, the musky smell of the opening of a slightly mildewed stage curtain wafts over us. Jamie Farnsworth waddles on stage. The chubby third-grader is swaddled in carrot-orange satin. A snowy-white bandage is a sympathy-sucking beacon across his forehead. Tall, stiff, bright-green feathery felt protrudes from the orange hood of his costume.

Behind carrot-boy, the stage fills with children costumed in foam-filled cotton. Five red apples with curved brown stems protruding from their hoods in varying degrees of crookedness. Two redheads in banana suits complete with age spots. A head of iceberg lettuce with only the tips of her fingers visible at the rounded, pale green sides of the pillowcase in which she's entrapped.

Finally Victoria and Dharma skip onstage. They hold hands, search the crowd. Beside me, Bubba waves. Lefty's whistle damages my eardrum. Sister Joan frowns, glares at the source of this breach of stage etiquette. The lead carrot turns his bandaged head, glares at my girls, sticks out his tongue. Dharma ignores him, looks to me as if to say, You see. This is how the stupid-head behaves. Her sister is quicker, proves once again she has inherited my faulty safety-switch.

Victoria, still skipping to her mark, grins like a little demon and expertly lifts a pudgy hand into the air, extends one finger, flips off the carrot. Lefty cuts his eyes to me, shrugs his bony shoulders, confirms my suspicion of who taught my girls this latest example of redneck manners.

Bubba's warm breath tickles my ear. "Could be," he whispers. "Maybe our best bet might be to home school."

A shudder passes through me that has nothing to do with my fear of the lecture I know will be forthcoming from Sister Mary Martha. I turn in my seat, twist around to recon behind me while seventy-three children, hobbled in fruit- and vegetable-colored fleece and shiny cotton, stumble through a badly choreographed dance routine.

A man leans against the back of the auditorium, sinewy arms crossed high on his wide chest, pectoral muscles clearly visible through a navy blue t-shirt. One leg bent at the knee, the sole of a bright red tennis shoe pressed against the wall. When our eyes lock, he tips his black ball cap, throws me a grin that sends a shiver along my spine and raises goose bumps on my arms.

Bubba touches my shoulder to bring my attention back to the stage where Victoria and Dharma dance in a circle with six grains of brown rice and the unfortunate child of a granola queen in a lumpy wool outfit with the word *quinoa* sewn to the front.

When I turn around again, the bodybuilder is gone but the dark fog he projected remains like filmy gauze of fear over my spirit.

twelve

MARCELLI'S IS PACKED with hungry survivors of the workweek. Dharma and Victoria, still in disguise as pinto beans, wave to the line of regulars along the counter, slap high fives with Mario Cotaldi's construction crew draining beers at the table by the front window. Letticia hugs our necks before she leads us to a long table where, through the steel and brick at our backs, we can feel the reverberations coming from the other side of the wall. My mouth waters with the smells of garlic, olive oil, and the gunpowder that drifts in every time the door to the shooting range opens.

I successfully postponed the wrath of nuns by snatching the girls from backstage and hurrying them to the truck while other parents were still easing numb arms out of padded costumes and assuring Sister Joan that the twelve-minute production was s-o-o worth the hours of running around town for supplies, sewing until two in the morning, and taking off work to attend.

The decision to send the girls to Eureka's only Catholic school was based on my hope that the nuns would do a better job than poorly paid and over-worked public school teachers at protecting Victoria and Dharma from the Bigfoot detractors and tormentors that taught me early the tactics of avoidance and distraction, along with the art of occasionally popping some bully in his big fat nose. It now appears this was a vain and naïve hope.

The grandpas, Dad and David, anchor the table, one at each end. Dad lays his hands, palm down, on the red-and-white-checked oil cloth, winks at Victoria next to him. Kneeling on the red Naugahyde of the booth, a breadstick in each hand, Victoria conducts an invisible orchestra and hums the theme to Spongebob Squarepants. Bubba tucks a paper napkin into the neck of her pinto bean suit, whispers something in her ear that produces a giggle and causes her to sit still for almost a full half-second. Sitting between Bubba and Dharma, I have the best view of the restaurant door, where I know Hawk will be entering shortly.

Across the table from Victoria, who has transformed her breadstick batons into light sabers by dipping them into a saucer of olive oil and balsamic vinegar, Lefty, armed with his own baked arsenal, raises one arm above his head in classic, moronic, en guard pose, smacks his breadstick into hers.

"These are not the droids you're looking for," he intones while the two of them scatter breadcrumbs over half the table.

"Luke," Dharma chimes in, "I am your father."

Something about this line, spoken in childish fun and innocence, raises goose-bumps along my arms, causes me to shiver.

Bubba wraps his arm around me, whispers in my ear, "You copacetic?"

I bump gently against him, run my hand along the smooth muscles of his thigh under jeans as soft as the ears of a child's favorite bunny. "Please. No more with the vocabulary words."

He growls in my ear and sends warmth all the way to my toes. "So, y'all are finer'n frog's hair, huh?"

At this moment—my toes curling, Dad narrowly rescuing a glass of water bumped by Victoria in her oil-dripping saber fight with Lefty, Dharma's warm body pressing against me smelling of strawberry shampoo and elementary school auditorium—the front door opens. Hawk, in jeans, hand tooled cowboy boots, a long-sleeved white shirt, and a black western-cut jacket, holds the door for two women.

The glare I aim at the father of my children ought to peel the skin off his face.

Ten flannelled backs at the counter turn in near unison. Crew cuts and shaggy heads stare at the apparitions stepping, one elegantly-heeled foot at a time, into Marcelli's Restaurant and Gun Range. Rose Ambrose enters first. I've done the math. My mother has to be fifty-five. So, how does she look better, younger even, than me at thirty-three?

Long legs rise on thin ankles out of those nude-suede Jimmy Choos, but don't disappear under a swirling cloud of lavender until well above her shapely knees. The filmy dress scoops low enough to display high breasts where a long gold chain dangles a sparkling diamond pendant, draws the eye deep into their rounded softness. Hair almost the exact color of the necklace is swept up in something like a Gordian knot and tucked against the back of her neck.

Her wintry-blue eyes sweep the room, don't stop until they settle on me. I run my hands through lank hair. Bite my lower lip. Press teeth together to stop their shaking. Force my fingers away from caressing the silverware. Order hands to my lap where I twist a paper napkin in a knot. The dichotomy of wanting to plunge a stainless steel fork into those freakishly high breasts while aching to bury my face in their softness freezes me in a moment outside of time—a horrible wood-between-the-worlds where drooling beasts pursue and long shadows claim every patch of sun.

Behind this vision of cold loveliness, Gloria strides through the front door. My twin has the good sense to strut past Hawk and Mother, leaving them behind. In platform heels, low-rise skinny black jeans, and an ice-blue blouse—like a hot knife through cold Bigfoot shit—my twin cuts a swath directly to me.

"Who… are they?" Dharma, her little butt flat on the leatherette, stretches herself as tall as she can along the padded booth, looks from me to Dad, and then settles her gaze on Bubba.

Victoria, a mangled breadstick in each small fist, looks down the length of the table to her grandpa David for explanation. At four, she knows David is her Daddy Hawk's father. Her little girl mind seems to have decided that David must be in charge of his son's actions in bringing these oddly familiar strangers to this, our weekly Friday night dinner at Marcelli's. I take credit for keeping her fooled so that she still thinks parents have control over their children at any age.

My outspoken daughter drops the remains of her light sabers onto the oilcloth, slams tiny fists on pinto bean hidden hips. "Ooh. She's like mama," she announces at the same moment that Gloria arrives at our table. "Except… she has too much gunkie stuff on her face." Victoria turns to me, wrinkles her nose, and proclaims, "She's not bee-u-te-ful like you."

From the corner of my eye, I see Dad and Bubba close ranks on either side of Victoria, know they are reminding her of what little manners I've managed to teach.

"I'm sorry, Samantha." Gloria lowers herself into the chair next to Lefty, directly across the narrow table from me. "Mom wanted to come. I don't want to intrude on your family dinner, but I would like to get to know you."

Like a dumb animal confused by its reflection in a mirror, I am knocked speechless by her voice, her face. It's like looking at myself in a dream world. An imaginary universe where I'm pretty. Pretty hell, bee-u-te-ful.

My twin's smile is tentative, hopeful. "It's why I came up from San Francisco with Mother on this little mission of hers. I didn't know you existed any more than you knew about me. Not until just before Dad died and then, when we found the will…."

"Sweetheart." Mother's smooth hand is a claw on my twin's arm. She floats downward into the chair beside her daughter. She cuts her eyes sideways. A woman forced by necessity to enter a roadside Mexican toilet. "Certainly not the place for private talk. Besides…." Her voice rises, takes on that shrill tone used by ineffective animal trainers. She extends her arms across the table, the diamonds in her tennis bracelet sending flashes of light into the greasy air. "After attending such a marvelous theater production, I simply had to meet the two little stars. My lovely granddaughters."

This is not the way I meant to reveal to my babies that they are related to this well-heeled Wicked Witch. I'd like to slam the meddling bitch against a wall and explain to her that she knows nothing, zero, crap about children, and that I don't want her anywhere near my girls. Except Victoria and Dharma are right here. Looking to me for denial or confirmation. So. No recruiting Lefty for a little tag team action where we wrestle my interfering bitch of a mother to the floor and drag her out of the restaurant.

I force a fake smile, but before I can open my mouth, Victoria slips off her chair, crawls under the table and up into the lap of her new grandmother. Chubby, olive-oil-slick hands pat a face frozen in surprise while a confetti of hard bread crumbs fall over lavender silk.

"How come, if you're my Grandma, I never met you?"

My daughter twists around in the slippery lap. Looks across the table at me and then peers again into the eyes of her newly-discovered grandmother.

"And how come Mama don't like you?"

I'm hoping Victoria outgrows the bluntness she inherited from me. But not just this moment.

A sort of magic happens now. Gloria, on hearing Victoria's question, glances quickly to me. For a moment, so fast it's hard to believe in its existence, a look passes between us. A nearly telepathic link of amusement tinged with a hint of fear connects us, joins us together in league against our mother.

thirteen

I AWAKE IN the dark, a weight like a young elephant pressing me into the lumpy couch cushions. My left arm and both feet are numb. There's a wet spot the size of a dinner plate on my chest. But it's the dog fart that pulls me from sleep. I fight my way up through the exhaustion of a full Friday night shift at VD's, breathe shallowly through the canine-manufactured methane. The clock in the entrance hall chimes three times.

Oh crap. Now I remember.

"Get off me, Skunk Ape."

With my one good arm and both flailing feet, I force Rufus to the floor where he groans and moans and in a slow series of movements ends with his butt on the rug in front of the couch, front half still anchoring me to the sofa. A knock at the door comes before I can sit up, wiggle out from under the dog, and run my fingers through greasy hair in preparation for the arrival of my twin.

I stumble over Rufus, make it to the door before she can knock again. I don't want Bubba or the girls to wake and wander downstairs.

"You sure it's all right? Me coming over this late?" She's scrunched under the wide porch roof, squeezed against the purple door by homeless Oscar and John curled in blue nylon mummy bags at her feet.

Gee, Lord, just this one night you couldn't have arranged for these two to sleep at the mission?

67

"Come on in." I yawn. "Sorry about the living welcome mat here. Try not to trip on 'em."

She turns once, waves to a dark-haired figure in a black Chevy SUV—Hawk masquerading as a gentleman.

"When you run a bar, early morning dark is your wind-down time. Let's go on into the kitchen."

The dog heaves himself to his feet, lumbers after us trailing his essence behind him.

"Well, anyway, I'm glad you agreed to see me." She's wearing jeans, a red Abercrombie and Fitch sweatshirt, and matching Converse high tops. Her gold-streaked hair is pulled back in a loose braid the way I wear my washed-out blonde mess most of time.

In the kitchen I switch on only the small light over the sink, hope the glow of the streetlight softens the look of peanut butter and jelly and bread crumbs on the counter, a sink half-full of the plates and smeared glasses accumulated tonight while the sitter stayed with the girls.

"You want a cup of coffee? Decaf? Tea? Diet Cherry Coke or Cherry Seven-Up?"

I turn toward her then, slow my mouth enough to take in her makeup-less face, the look of nervousness that tightens her jaw. Exactly like the expression I assume is on my face.

"You have wine?" She sits at Bubba's place at the table.

I swipe at the pudding puddles, milk spills, and Oreo crumbs, set two fat bubble glasses and a half bottle of Rutherford Hill on the table.

"It's left over from my… our… birthday two weeks ago." I fill the delicate glasses half-full with the thick, blood red wine.

"I love this merlot. It's my favorite." She lifts the glass, her smile tentative.

It is the oddest feeling, this reflection of myself. There is an immediate kinship and bond that almost overrides my natural instinct for caution and cynicism. Almost. I raise my glass, watch the streetlight's glow turn the surface of the contents to a reflection of shadow and light.

"To our birthday," I say and the clink of glasses hangs suspended in the room's soft light.

"May we celebrate them together from now on?" Her question is almost a whisper, the toast a soft hope.

The glasses of thick, warm wine barely touch, but the image carries deep into my center, rattles my fears, and leaves me hollowed, fearful of losing something I didn't know I had until a few days ago. Rufus plods across the tile, lays his head in my lap, and offers comfort with bloodshot, droopy eyes.

"I've always wanted a dog." Gloria leans forward, tentatively runs her manicured hand over wavy, brindled fur. With his head in my lap, the dog's wide butt is wedged between the table and Gloria's chair. She strokes his rump and activates the giant club he thinks is his tail.

"You want this one?" I ask as we narrowly rescue our wine glasses. "He sort of adopted me when I wasn't really in the market for a dog as big as Sasquatch."

"I read your book. *Touched by Bigfoot.* You explained the role Rufus played in your encounter with… the… Bigfoots."

There is something with pheromones or energy fields or auras going on here. Some link between us triggered by a power deep in our joint psyches. Some twin thing. Both survivors of our mother's womb, we're joined in a way I can't quite figure out. Tied together in a kind of twisted knot of blood and destiny.

My voice is low. "I understand the whole Bigfoot thing is difficult to believe. For years, I was a sort of a hopeful agnostic. Not willing to come right out and say the whole deal was a hoax perpetrated by the bored or the insane. I sure as hell never expected to find any proof that there really are strange beings about whom we know next to nothing wandering around in our forests."

In the familiar shadows of my own, ordinary kitchen, the flashback is vivid. Eyes watching in the dark. Me, falling through thin air. Waking, cradled in soft ferns with a bloody handprint three times as big as any human's stamped on my belly like a brand. Or a blessing.

I press my hands flat on the table to ground myself in the here and now.

"Still," I confess, "if it hadn't been for that handprint and the second daylight encounter, I might have been able to rationalize my way out of belief."

We lean toward each other across a corner of the table, simultaneously as though drawn by some invisible thread. Gloria's eyes are wide, her lips part just enough to reveal the tip of her tongue tracing the bottom of her front teeth. That running her tongue over her teeth deal? I do that, too. Usually, I'm touching smooth enamel seconds before I excuse myself and get the hell away from whoever I'm talking with at the time. God, I need to change the subject before she walks out of here never to be seen again.

Think of something else to talk about.

Do I have any normal thoughts to share?

"Now, Rufus here was different." My voice is too loud. "One whiff of the smell of Bigfoot on me and the dog attached himself to my side. No hesitation on the part of ole Ruffy. But me, I fought against believing."

That's great. I'm a varietal virtuoso of normal, everyday conversation.

The smell of Bigfoot?

Well, fuck it. This is me. Either my twin and I will be friends or we won't. I don't have the energy to pretend to be somebody I'm not just to win her approval.

The streetlight flickers, creates surreal flutters of weak light and gray shadows that skip and stutter on the amber wood of the table top. Gloria moves her hand a few inches closer to mine. I don't close the distance between our fingers, but I resist the need to fold my hands in my lap, twist my fingers in a knot of fear.

"It wasn't until that family of Bigfoots, the female in particular, looked across that meadow directly into my eyes," I whisper to my twin and the memory prickles the skin on my arms, sends a shiver through me. "After that personal encounter, there was no way I could deny their existence."

Her eyes hold curiosity, empathy maybe. If there's judgment there, I can't find it. And, as Bubba tells me, I'm right good at spotting criticism, real or imagined.

"In essence, the encounter changed me from a back-pew member of the congregation, Dad's tag-along, to a washed-in-the-blood believer in Bigfoot."

For the first time, she touches me. One butterfly light brush of her fingers on the back of my hand. My eyes spill salty tears down my cheeks, my body betrays my best intentions to act like a normal human being. I tear a paper towel from the roll on the table, wipe roughly at my eyes.

"Your dad loves you so much. What was it like growing up with him?"

I luxuriate in the homey smells of my kitchen, anchor myself in the tang of lemon dish soap, the rainwater scent of my girls and the spicy, woodsy-green smell of Bubba.

"Raised above a bar known as VD's? Dad a Bigfoot hunter? It had its peculiar moments. But I always knew, every moment of every day, that Dad loved me." I swirl the last inch of my wine. "Looking back I wasted a lot of time and energy grieving for a mom that walked away instead of being grateful for a dad who was always there for me."

"Let me tell you," Gloria says flatly, "being raised by Mom was no picnic. Dad was a great, but he was rarely home. I… I envy your childhood. I'd have given up the sterile, ostentatious house and every one of the ballet and art and music and poise and modeling lessons Mother forced me into for one quiet week with a parent who looked at me the way your dad looks at you. Like you're some priceless treasure more valuable than any multinational company or object of art or charity event."

I have no idea how to respond to that observation.

"It's stuffy in here, huh?" I stand, blow air out my nose like a winded horse. "Let's take a walk. Rufus needs to go out and I need to stretch my legs."

Belly pack in place, Rufus's leather leash snapped onto the pink rhinestone collar the girls picked out, I lead the way to the front door. Cold, salty air instantly curves my mouth up at the corners when I step outside. Even though I know damned well what's coming, I pick my way carefully around the elongated lumps under the blue nylon sleeping bags on my doorstep. Gloria follows like a soldier stepping in the footfalls of the point.

The dog waits, butt wiggling, at the doorjamb. He'll not step outside until I give the all clear. Rumbling snores issue from the mummy bags. I give a slight tug on the leash and Rufus, never one to thread his way lightly around anything, tangles his saucer-sized feet in both sleeping bags. Slurred expletives and a few sharp cries of pain ring out into the dark, wet street.

In the bluish glow of the street light, Gloria looks startled. Her blue eyes wide, she steps quickly down the sidewalk, away from the sleeping homeless.

"Wha' the fuck?" John sits up, his hair a swirl of matted gray, electrified by the nylon. "Get that damn beast away from me."

My laughter bounces off the brick wall, dances gaily across the street, and touches the wood shingles of VD's where a yellow light glows from the high, narrow windows of Dad's room.

"You don't like the accommodations on MY front porch? Forego the afternoon hooch and sleep at the mission."

Grumbling and the flopping of cold, wet bodies on hard concrete scooting away from directly in front of the front door follow us out into the night.

"See," Gloria says when I get to her side. "That right there. I could never do that."

I unclip the leash from the flashy pink collar. Tap the dog's nose to tell him to heel.

"Do what?"

"Aren't you afraid? I mean, most of those people are, like, insane."

The calm night waters of the bay are blanketed in pale gray fog. Ghostly fingers creep silently over the pier, inch along the black, wet asphalt of First Street.

"Those people? John and Oscar?" I walk across First and out onto the wooden pier. The hard heels of my boots make a muffled thump at each step, Gloria's tennis shoes barely raise a whisper into the night air, and Rufus's padded paws contribute no sound at all as they carry his massive weight over the bay.

"You know their names?" Her eyes are wide, pale orbs in the diffused light of the fog-shrouded lights of the pier.

"They live here." I lean on a wet rail, stare out at the mist-haloed lights of the boats at the marina across the bay. "Hell, I know the name of the Bigfoot whose picture hangs over the bar."

My laughter is tainted with nerves. I hate that I want so badly for her to like me, to approve of who I am. She stands beside me at the rail, glances back over her shoulder.

"You sure we're safe here? At this time of night?"

A two-hundred-pound, overprotective dog pressing against my leg, the solid weight of a .38 resting against my belly, and the knowledge that every living soul within ten blocks knows that, if anyone ever dared to harm me, Dad would gut shoot them, after Bubba skinned them alive. All this in preparation for me beating them to a bloody pulp.

"Ah, yeah. I'm sure we're safe."

The nostalgic bass of a ship's horn conjures an image of a boat creeping along the coastline on the night sea, coming from God knows where and headed to a destination equally unknown. I turn away from the mysteries of the dark ocean and look into the eyes of my twin.

"I dated a guy from your world for a week or two." I say. "Things got complicated. But, I think I know what you're saying. How you feel. It's hard to be in a situation you have no clue how to deal with or what behavior is required or expected."

Her wide mouth smiles, white teeth flash in the night. "I'm outside my comfort zone, that is a certainty."

The horn moans into the night again. She reaches across the damp railing, lays her soft palm over my rough knuckles.

"One reason I wanted to see you tonight," she says softly. "Don't sign those papers Mom and her attorney are pushing at you. Dad talked to me a few weeks before he died in that car crash. He'd found out about Mom's bodybuilder boyfriend. And, he knew she'd given birth to twins."

A single star appears between wispy clouds, hangs suspended, and then is swallowed by the night, returning the sky to pressing darkness.

"He was changing his will. He meant to cut Mom out and split everything between his daughters. His two daughters. What I don't know is whether he made those changes before his Ferrari went off that cliff on Highway One."

I am an emotional mummy, swathed in gauzy bandages, but one particular revelation penetrates the numbness.

"Bodybuilder boyfriend?"

"Tommy Joe Lyons is one scary piece of work." Gloria says. "It wouldn't surprise me if he had something to do with Dad's car going over that cliff."

"You think this Tommy Joe killed your father?" My tone brings a low growl from the throat of Rufus. The soft leather of my belly pack is a reassuring warmth under my hand.

"I do. Yes. I think Mom found out about dad's plans to cut her out of his will. She told her boyfriend and the bastard did something to sabotage the Ferrari in the hope of killing Dad before he could rearrange his finances."

Prone to vague premonitions for as long as I can remember, shivering warnings of danger to those I love have fallen on me for years. Since the encounter in the woods with the female Bigfoot, these pictures in my head, like the silver-tinged washes of old photographs, are more acute. Standing on the pier, lights from the marina reflecting in the rippling surface of the dark bay, a shimmering vision of my girls, sleeping unprotected under their warm blankets, propels me toward home.

"Let's go."

My legs stretch out in long strides as I close the distance between me and mine. Gloria trots beside me, does her best to keep up. Rufus reaches the house while I'm still on A Street, his deep barks echo back to me along the rain-darkened streets.

The first thing I see, when I round the corner, is the homeless Oscar. He stands, arms folded over bony chest, leaning against the brick wall next to my front door.

"You need to lock your door in this neighborhood."

The Colt is heavy and cold in my hand.

"What happened?"

Oscar scratches his head, points down the empty street where Rufus stares trembling, his barks shaking the windows along First.

"Beefy fucker in a ball cap thought he'd prance on into your house unin-vited. Didn't expect to find John and me protecting your doorstep."

"He didn't get inside?"

I'm already moving in the direction Rufus is pointed. John's assurance that the house is safe catches me as I turn the corner onto Bay View. The dog's rump disappears in darkness seconds before I hear an engine cough to life and the deep baying sound of a frustrated canine. I arrive at Rufus's side in time to watch a black Jeep Wrangler disappear into the night.

fourteen

"NICE ROOM." I use the words to delay looking at her, keep glancing around, let my eyes dart over the carefully arranged pillows disguising the hotel bed as a Persian lounge.

I don't want to be here. Fought hard to avoid sitting my denim-covered butt in this butter-soft, high-backed chair. In the end, I overcame my terror, suppressed my best instincts, and here I sit. My stiff back presses hard against the padded leather, across from the woman who gave birth to me. I suck shallow breaths of her expensive perfume and do my best to distract myself by focusing on the muted light diffused through layered curtains and falling in a narrow slice across the thick rug under my Wolverines.

Her voice is cultured, soft, about as genuine as a three-dollar bill.

"I am pleasantly surprised at the accommodations available in this... um... little... town."

"As I understand it, you didn't have any trouble finding accommodations the first time you were here either. Let's see, I'm thirty-three, so that would be what? Thirty-four years ago, huh?"

She rises elegantly from the brocade chair across from me, sways her way to a small, round, linen-draped table, and pours herself water from a silver carafe. The ice tinkles like imprisoned raindrops in the rarified air. A

French-manicured nail points to the second glass. She raises one carefully arched eyebrow and I shake my head at her offer.

Which is stupid. I actually am thirsty. Dad would accuse me of cutting off my nose to spite my face. I'll die of thirst before I take anything this bitch has to offer. All right, realistically, I'm not going to die of thirst. But, still. I don't want a fancy glass of her damn water.

The seat across from me is the green of a newly opened leaf with sparkles of silver like insidious worms woven into the brocade. She settles into its cushion, brushes an imaginary speck from the chair's arm.

"I can't change the past," she says. "I'd like us to make a fresh start."

"Why?"

"I'm your mother. Isn't that reason enough?"

"Not by a damn country mile."

She doesn't even blink at my vehement rejection. Seems simply to re-group mentally, prepare her next angle of attack.

"Let's talk about your boyfriend," I say, "and just what role he had in the death of your husband. Oh, wait now. Mister Ambrose wasn't actually your legal husband, was he? Since you're still married to Victor Foster. You re-member Victor, huh? You tricked him into marrying you and then dropped off one of your newborn babies with him when you couldn't be bothered to raise both girls yourself."

Which turned out to be the best thing that could have happened to me. But still. This bitch abandoned me!

A thin slice of sunshine leaks from the edge of the curtains, cuts across the carpet for less than a minute before the light dims, vanishes as mid-morning clouds roll in from the Pacific and the sun disappears. I stomp across the plush carpet, pour myself a glass of water. If I want water, I'll damn straight get it myself.

"You've grown cruel, Samantha Jean. I'm your mother and a grieving widow. I'm disappointed in you, speaking to me in that manner."

The depth of my rage rattles me, transubstantiates my knees from strong bone to watery ache. The elegant room narrows, vanishes into a red mist. A primal scream pushes its way up from my exposed center. Two full, deep breaths. Into the rage Dad's voice whispers his love. Bubba's spicy scent floats on cloudy memory. Dark eyes look into mine from across a meadow, newly greened with the season's first rain.

I remember why I'm here.

My legs carry me back to the butter-yellow chair.

"Your boyfriend, Tommy Joe Lyons, tried to break into my house. Why?"

My voice shakes at the edges but the core holds solid. I force myself to stare into hard turquoise eyes.

She studies her pointy-toed shoes, draws a gold-rimmed thumbnail along the underside of her firm chin. Finally she meets my eye, attempts a smile.

"Mister Lyons is an admirer, Samantha Jean, not a boyfriend. That's a difference I'd think you'd have deciphered by this time in your life."

"Cut the shit and do not call me Samantha Jean." The only person on earth who uses my full name is Dad. Not this witch. Not ever.

"What on earth would make you think Lyons tried to enter your home?"

She maintains eye contact but her crossed legs give her away. The right high-heeled foot bounces like the needle of a polygraph.

I wait.

"Oh, all right," she admits as though confessing to indulging in one too many bonbons. "I asked Tommy Joe to keep an eye on you. Because I was worried, okay? My goodness, Saman... I don't know what on earth I'm permitted to call you if I can't use the oddly androgynous name your father insisted on giving you.... The point is, I am concerned about the company you keep. I admit, I wasn't thrilled with you being raised Catholic. It's such a messy religion, dear. All those saints and its emphasis on blood is just bizarre, and now, of course, this celibacy thing has come back to just haunt the entire church. Still, I told myself, we even had a Catholic president. But, my Lord, above and beyond the Catholic issue, Victor has just sunk into this ludicrous Bigfoot miasma.

"I never dreamed the man would continue that nonsense once he had a child to raise. And you, Samantha Jean... sue me. It's your name. You appear to have allowed yourself to be manipulated into the middle of the entire mess. What on earth were you thinking? Writing that book? Making up that ridiculous lie about actually seeing one of the creatures. Honestly, Samantha, you just get as angry as you want! I am disappointed in both you and Victor."

My boots are still flat on the elegant carpet, my arms folded across my chest, but part of me now watches this entire exchange from across the room. I resist the urge to wink at my psychic-self posing there calmly by the window, a confident grin on her face.

"Ah, yeah. A man turning wine into the blood of another man, dead over two thousand years, that's more believable than the possibility that an undiscovered primate roams in what's left of our world's wilderness."

"Don't be deliberately obtuse, Samantha Jean."

"No, I understand. It's not about which belief is more absurd, it's about what's acceptable in our society. If I lived in India, you'd expect me to worship the three thousand plus gods of the Hindu religion."

She actually stamps her pointy-toed shoe on the plush carpet, gives me a look of such frustration that joy momentarily reunites my mind and body.

"It's about correct choices." She spits the words across the two feet that separate us. "Another example of your inability to stay within the lines of conventionality. Like your buffoon of a husband. That gorgeous, charming Hawk? A PhD. The real father of your twins? Him, you throw out. And with whom do you then connect? This ridiculous joke of a Southern hillbilly."

My heart keeps beating. Breath continues to enter and leave my lungs. My gaze has not left her face. Something, though, has gone wrong with my ears. Or maybe my brain. Or some connection between the two. I stare at her mouth. It moves. Forms sounds that explode out into the air of the room. Her lips are a soft bruised peach. She's lined the edge of the top lip with some slightly darker, rotten-plum color.

"…you've seen your sister I understand."

"What?"

"Gloria? Your sister? The two of you have spent time together?" She doesn't say "behind my back" but the arched spine and narrowed eyes project the thought adequately.

"You get that information from your boyfriend?"

"Gloria and I do speak, Samantha. She tells me you two are planning a camping trip. Some creek place. Buffalo Creek?"

My Timex insists I've been inside this room for the longest twelve minutes of my freaking life. I stand. Enjoy the sensation of looking down on her. My knees hold. My voice only hints at shakiness. My fists meet, hard knuckles touching deep in the front pouch of my hoodie.

"Call off your watchdog. Mother. Before somebody gets hurt. Anybody, I mean anybody, comes near my girls, I will kill them dead and bury them in a grave as dark and cold as your soul."

At the door, I turn, the crystal knob already biting into my palm. "And if you ever again say anything against my husband, I am going to forget you're my mother and kick your wrinkled ass from here to Sunday."

fifteen

RAIN BLOWS SIDEWAYS off the wind-scoured bay this morning, washes the bedroom window in salty spray. I stare into the accusing blankness of the computer screen. Not a single black letter to mar all that white. Just that damn blinking cursor demanding Words. Words. Words. What could be so hard about writing a memoir? All that's required is to tell the truth about growing up above a bar known as VD's and being raised by a famous Bigfoot hunter. The truth though, keeps shifting on me. Tracking the golden beast of truth has become more difficult than hunting the elusive Bigfoot.

I had the first two chapters. Choppy and inadequate though they may have been, at least I had something on paper to show for all the time I spent sitting on my widening butt, staring into a computer screen. My problem is, now I've met my bitch of a mother and am getting to know my twin sister, my need to rewrite history is a dull, numbing compulsion.

I can't force the words onto paper until I've sorted them out in my swirling brain. It's not as though I didn't know, growing up, that Dad loved me. Of course I did. But, looking back from this distance, it does seem that I wasted a lot of time staring out windows, studying the fog and rain, aching for a missing mother, and feeling sorry for myself that Dad wasn't like other kids' fathers.

A clear, bitingly crisp memory like a shard of blue ice keeps popping into my head.

I must have been six or maybe seven. No older than that. Between rain-storms, I was pacing the wet sidewalk in front of the bar. Wearing my pink denim jacket, I kept opening and closing the front snaps in a rhythm. Ten steps, unsnap. Ten steps, snap. Letticia bought me that girlie jacket at JCPenny to wear on my first day of second grade, so I must have been seven.

The air that day smelled of dead fish and seaweed with an occasional whiff of boiled shrimp from the fishery two blocks down. Dad was in the bar setting up for Dart Night. I wasn't allowed to cross the street, and back then there was no pier along the bay, so I just kept pacing from A Street and back to B. One foot in front of the other. Snap open that pink jack-et, stride ten steps, begin the process of unsnapping, bottom to top. Nod my head at the rain-speckled window of Smoky Joe's Barbeque where, each and every time I passed, Joe's developmentally-disabled son, Jason, grinned a jack-o-lantern grin and waved a pudgy hand. Smile politely, but keep my distance from the men in army green fatigue jackets lined up at the Salvation Army Mission for a meal that must have included tomato sauce that day because I remember a craving for spaghetti each time I came within sniffing distance.

I was begging God for a different dad. That's what I was doing that day. Snap. Pace. Unsnap.

"Please God, if you could just have Dad make it through the whole school year without writing a letter to the editor about Bigfoot or having the news team come to the bar to interview him about a new cast or sighting. Is that so much to ask? Please, don't make it be like last year when Dad showed slides at the Clark Museum and Timmy Martin called me Sassy Squash and all the kids knew I was weird and made fun of me and then I punched Timmy in his big-fat-stupid nose and Dad had to go to the principal's office where he got in a feel-o-soft-e-call discussion with Mister Bradford and then, for the rest of the year, Miz Connor called me special."

Here's what I remember vividly about that day of pacing when I was seven years old.

A whisper in my ear that, even then, I understood meant my prayer had been heard and I did not like the answer. Knowledge, like a heavy winter blanket settled over my seven-year-old self. If Dad stopped talking about Bigfoot and maybe even changed the name of the bar—which, while I did not know why, I knew the name VD's raised eyebrows and wrinkled foreheads when I said it at school—if God would just make those two teeny tiny changes, well then, Dad would no longer be the man I loved. He'd be a different parent altogether. That's a hard and beautiful truth for a seven-year-old.

When I returned to VD's, my face was wet and the pink sleeve of my jacket was smeared with dried snot. And I knew that I did not really want God to intercede. I loved my daddy just the way he was. That feeling of acceptance and privilege only lasted until the next day when dumbass Timmy Martin called me Miz Sassy Squash again while we stood in the lunch line for beanie weenies and apple crusty.

I hit him with my fist doubled up around five quarters and broke his fat nose.

Unfortunately, over the years, I fear the satisfaction I felt standing there in the smell of burnt molasses and sour milk, watching blood drip in gooey, hanging threads and accumulate on the front of Timmy's striped t-shirt, I'm afraid I remember that happy feeling way more than I recollect the earlier insight about acceptance and love.

Bubba's footsteps on the stairs break my reverie. I conceal the happy, nostalgic smile from my evil face and swivel the chair around so I can watch his entrance. He brings the sticky sweet smell of maraschino cherries into the room with him, sets a tall, napkin-wrapped glass of iced Diet Cherry Coke on the TV tray next to my chair. The offering is decorated with, not one, but two, long skewers of cherries.

His mouth is warm at the hollow of my throat as he bends, enfolds me in his bulk. I am overcome with the knowledge of how close I came to prancing right past this soft-spoken, warm-hearted giant of a Southern man, missing his worth entirely. Wrapped in his hard arms, my face pressing eagerly into the spicy scent of flannel, desire sparks, flares up quickly.

"How on earth did I ever trap you into loving me?" I wrap my stocking feet around his calves, lean into his love.

A long, slow kiss makes me forget my name.

"Well, now." He nuzzles the tops of my breasts. "You mean 'sides the little ole fact that you was cuter'n a spotted pup and could suck the pit outta a ripe peach without bruisin' the fruit?"

Only Bubba can make me laugh like a hyena while desperate to replace plaid flannel with bare skin against my own.

"Where are the girls?" My fingers fumble with the last button of his shirt, my mouth already working its way down his wide chest while his hands slide my t-shirt over my head.

He pushes me gently away as a long, wet dog tongue slaps the side of my bare belly, a cold nose presses between us, and the sound of small feet, like icy rain on steamy, thirsty ground, pound the stairs.

The door swings open. Both girls have stripped down to their underpants. Victoria's are pink with The Princess Somebody-or-Other stamped into the cotton. Dharma sports plain black panties that can only be found in her size at JCPenny. It's her one vanity. Black underwear is the only color she'll step into. Today, just above the panties, is an old leather belt of Bubba's, threaded four times through a wide oval of cardboard decorated with gold stars and about two gallons of glitter-glue. In wide block letters someone, whose handwriting looks suspiciously like Lefty's, has printed *WWF Champion*.

"You're not working!" Victoria accuses me.

Rufus claims my lap as his pillow. Bubba stands at the window buttoning his shirt.

I smooth my hair, adjust my t-shirt.

"You don't know that."

Dharma, naked chest already reddened by the hard edge of the cardboard belt buckle, her one-eared elephant, Pete, firmly in hand, climbs over Rufus to displace his head on my lap with her small, hard body. The dog collapses like warm Jell-O at my feet.

Victoria stomps directly to Bubba, eyes him suspiciously. "You said Mama was working. You said we wasn't to disturb her."

"I remember saying that exact thing." He nods toward Dharma. "What's that belt you got there?"

"We're wresslin'. I won the cage match against African Pete." Dharma waves the defeated elephant in the air over her head.

Lefty is a dead man.

"I don't like you girls fighting," I say. "We've talked about this. Remember what happened at school with Tim...."

"Hey," Dad's voice calls up the stairs. "Anybody up there like to go to the Fresh Freeze? Grandpa David and I have got us a craving for a double chocolate-dipped soft serve."

It's 52 degrees, spitting rain, with fog so thick the bay is a hidden mystery, but the girls' enthusiasm for ice cream is undented. The cadence of two sets of eager footfalls descending wooden stairs assaults my ears before I can get my feet out from under the dog and stand up.

Dad's voice floats up the stairs. "Whoa. Lookee here. You two aren't very big birds without your feathers, are ya?"

"We don't got feathers, Grandpa." Dharma I think, but even for me, it's hard to tell their voices apart.

"Well." David's voice now. "If you're sure you don't have a suit of feathers, go put on some ice cream eatin' clothes."

"Let's see what you've got in the way of sweat shirts and fleece...." Dad's voice fades away.

Bubba, silhouetted in the dull light of the window, grins, wiggles his eyebrows at me. "I'll go. Make sure one of 'em doesn't wear that wrestling belt with their clothes. But...." He drops his hand deftly in passing, cups my left breast. "I'll be back," he promises. "And right soon."

sixteen

MY BENT LEG is stuck to his naked thigh. I shift my sweaty body from his in a move that makes an audible sucking sound. The rug burns on my knees are bright red, warm to the touch. Bubba's curly chest hair tickles my face. Rufus, stretched beside us on the heavy braided rug, opens one bloodshot eye. The dog seems disturbed by our encroachment of his floor space.

I stretch my right arm out, pat Rufus's brindled head. "Sorry boy. We couldn't make it to the bed. And just for future reference, I'm not that all-fired fond of an audience."

"Lord Almighty, woman. You are hotter'n a wildcat tucked in a wool sock come July."

A fit of giggles leads us back into the ring for a second round when a phrase flies out of my mouth that, even as I hear the words, I struggle to take back.

"We need to use some of our time to talk."

Bubba lifts his head and my left nipple cools in the dog breath air.

"It don't take that long to eat an ice cream cone. That's for certain." He settles beside me. "We might ought to talk before the girls get back."

My palm strokes the goose-bumped skin of his belly. "It's cold in here. Maybe we ought to get dressed." Neither of us move.

"How you doing with your mama and sister?"

He gets right to the point. A good attribute in a man when our "quality" time together is limited to short bursts grabbed between running the bar, my writing, raising the girls, and now this mess with my newly-discovered family.

"It's my mom's boyfriend that worries me. Muscle man. Tommy Joe Lyons."

The sun makes an appearance. Light pours in the window, falls suddenly in a sharp slice across our middles. I automatically respond to the warmth with a small moaning from deep in my moldy core, sprawl into the sunlight. Rufus thumps his feathery tail against the wood floor.

The musical theme to Spongebob Squarepants leaks into the room. Bubba jerks his head off the rug. We're listening to the second verse before I return from my blissful state, back into the reality of life, and identify the sound as the ringing of my cell phone.

"Victoria must have changed my ringtone again." One leg of my jeans is wrong side out when I find them under the computer desk. I fumble in the pants pocket, retrieve the cell, and snap the damn thing open.

"Sam?" Dad's voice with what sounds like ten thousand screaming monkeys in the background. "We're at Sequoia Park Zoo."

"Ah, yeah. I hear that. How are the gibbons?"

"Loud. Listen, honey. We got sunshine here."

"Here, too."

"David and I are keeping the girls till it rains."

"Good deal. Have fun and we'll see you in a little while."

Hmm. An hour or so to kill. Bubba and I already butt naked. What to do? What to do?

A grin stretches my face. I lower myself onto my husband.

He lifts me bodily from my position straddling his hips. "Nope. Not yet. First we talk." His voice is a little froggy, but he seems determined.

I stretch out beside him, let my hand float down over the evidence that he's lying about his desire for conversation.

"How long do we have?" He groans, firmly imprisons my wrist in his hand.

"They'll be home when it rains."

"After, then. First, we talk." He releases my hand and I lay my palm quiet and still against his hard chest.

I prop myself up on one elbow. "The other night, Friday. When Gloria came over?"

"Uh, huh. You said you felt some kind of twin connection." His eyes leave my face, track downward. His grin sheepish and adorable, he sighs heavily, returns his look to my face.

"Well, remember I told you Gloria and I took Rufus for a little middle-of-the-night stroll?"

He's focused on my words now. Knows me well enough to understand that what's coming is the heart of the story.

"Did I mention that John and Oscar were camped on our front step that night?"

"Nope. But that don't make it any different from most any other night of the year."

My hand inches downward from his belly. Sunlight illuminates a trillion dog hairs floating in the air. How many do I breathe every day? Ingest in my coffee and food? I close my eyes. It's a dead cinch I'm not going to be vacuuming any more than once a week. Maybe we ought to get one of those air filter HEPA deals.

Bubba stops my creeping hand, returns it to his belly. "No fallin' asleep now. Talk to me. Your mama? That woman has me spooked. Something not exactly natural there."

"Ah, yeah. Well." I yawn. "Okay. So Gloria and I took Rufus for a walk that night." The dog opens both sleepy eyes. His tail thumps once against the floor. "When we got back to the house, John was awake and standing guard. He said a beefy guy in a black cap had been fiddling with the front door."

Under my hand, Bubba's body tenses. I can almost feel the adrenaline charging his muscles for action.

"He didn't get inside. I chased after him but never saw anything but his taillights."

For the first time, it occurs to me that my husband is going to be pissed as all get-out that I didn't tell him any of this. But it seemed like nothing I couldn't handle myself and, until that night, I didn't even know the stalker was Mom's boyfriend. Why worry Bubba for nothing?

His voice a whisper. "You think I haven't noticed how jumpy you been? Didn't see that dude at the back of the auditorium the other night? I don't like when you hide yourself away from me."

I was raised to be tough, handle my own problems. Then spent twelve years, formative years I might add, with Hawk, who was always clear that he didn't want to become involved in my personal problems.

"I'm not good at sharing every little concern that pops into my life," I whine like a little girl.

He rolls away from me, gets to his feet so that all I see is his wide back and that nice, firm ass. Which I've evidently seen for the last time today. He retrieves his briefs and steps into them. Bundles his jeans and shirt in a wadded mess of denim and flannel.

His voice is low, growly with controlled anger. "You have me confused with someone else, Samantha. I'm your husband. Ever' little concern that pops into your life is my concern. It hurts that after all this time, you don't know that."

He closes the door gently behind him. Rufus whines, thumps his tail twice.

"Ah, yeah. I hear you," I say to the dog. "Sometimes he is such a girl."

seventeen

MY COFFEE IS cold. Again.

Rain blankets the kitchen in shimmery silver, the windows fog-wrapped and speckled with rivulets of water. Rufus is stretched like a lumpy rug between me and the counter where I lean over him, mix concentrated orange juice in the purple Fiestaware pitcher. Bubba is at the stove, flipping a bunny-shaped pancake and humming "You've Lost That Lovin' Feelin.'" Even when I could happily beat the holy crap out of this man, he is irresistible.

The girls have dressed themselves for mass. Veronica's legs are covered in pink denim, last year's Halloween fairy skirt a stiff blossom of organdy around her little waist, a V-necked purple tee with the words Early Dawn stenciled across her narrow chest. The shirt was a gift from Lefty and I'm suspicious of that *Early Dawn* deal, but I'm saving this morning's fight for that fairy skirt which is going to draw fire from the nuns like an ACLU lawyer at a meeting of the Daughters of the Confederacy.

Which reminds me. My drawling husband hasn't touched me since our little misunderstanding yesterday afternoon. That's a problem for a couple of reasons. First of all, Gloria and I are going camping next week, and I haven't told him yet. He is not going to react favorably to me wandering off into the woods with a stalker on my heels. Now see, to me, the middle of the forest with only one easily evaded witness? That is exactly where I want to meet this Tommy Joe jackass. But Bubba's not going to see it that way. I can feel it in my bones. Leastwise not unless he comes along to help bury the body.

The second reason our little tiff is problematic is that just the smell of the big galoot as he passes me, pancake balanced on a shiny spatula, makes me want to rip the buttons from his shirt, unbuckle that silver bulldog belt buckle, open those jeans, and have at him.

Dharma dances into the kitchen. Oh God. Really? Dressed in black tights, a black sweatshirt over a black dress, she has hung a heavy silver cross around her neck. The chain pools in her lap when she seats herself at the table, the cross dangling between her knees.

My mouth is clamped shut against commanding my beautiful daughter to get that stupid thing off from around your neck and for God's sake, you're not a vampire, find some touch of color to go with all that black, when Bubba's voice purrs, "Wow! Nice. Where 'bouts did you find that interesting chunk of bling?"

"Uncle Lefty's friend gave it to me yesterday at the park." Dharma smears butter and dumps a half cup of maple syrup on her pancake.

My heart actually stops in my chest. A warning of what will happen if anyone ever harms this child. Bubba's eyes are as wide as my own. He turns off the burner under the griddle. I leave the lumpy orange juice in its pitcher on the counter.

"What friend of Uncle Lefty's?" I lower myself into the chair to her left, Bubba already seated at her right.

"He was nice." The swinging of her legs against the chair rails has stopped. Shit. Now we've frightened her. How many times have I lectured the girls not to ever, ever take anything from a stranger? And where were Dad and David when this new friend gave her this lovely gift?

"I'm sure he seemed nice, honey," I say. "Just tell Daddy and me what happened."

"I told her she was gonna get it," Victoria chimes in. "And, plus, she knew she was bad. Else why did she hide the stupid ugly necklace thing from our grandpas?"

My heart is making up for lost time. It pounds fear against my chest like a drummer in a bad garage band.

Bubba lifts Dharma from her chair. Once she's settled on his lap, her dark head against his chest, he turns to Victoria, touches her cheek, puts one finger against his pursed lips, raises his eyebrows to confirm she understands the instruction he's given. Victoria squirms in her chair, zips her mouth with a dimpled hand, grins at him.

"You're not in trouble, baby," I say to Dharma. "Just tell us what happened."

Tears spill from blue eyes, her lashes already wet against her cheeks. If that son of a bitch touched her, one hand on any part of my sweet child, I will chop him into tiny chunks.

"Grandpa David had to go to the bathroom." The words tumble out of her mouth.

Bubba pushes her hair behind her ears, rubs little circles on her back.

I force myself not to make too big of deal out of this. Maybe nothing happened. Lefty does have peculiar friends. Maybe one of them recognized Dharma and gave her the necklace for his own odd reasons. Could be this whole deal will turn out to be nothing but a bad sense of children's fashion.

My hands, sticky with orange juice, sandwich Dharma's. "Where were Grandpa Victor and your sister?"

"The bears were drinking." Victoria interrupts. So much for that mouth-zipper. "She wanted to keep watching the stupid monkeys. I was gonna miss the bears!" She lowers her voice to a loud whisper. "Mama, they drink from their paws. Did you know that? Not like Rufus. He gets his whole big face wet when he drinks. The bears dip water in their paws. Grandpa said that's what Bigfoots do, too. Is that right, Mama?"

"We'll talk about the bears later, Victoria. Right now, I need to hear what your sister has to say."

So David was with Dharma, left her for a few minutes in front of the monkey cage which is within sight of the bathrooms. How long does it take an eighty-six-year-old man to pee?

Bubba's eyes are hooded. "What did Uncle Lefty's friend look like?" My husband's not good at subterfuge. He's talking all nice and gentle, but the tightness of his muscles, the set of his jaw make it plain that, once we have all the information, he's going to flip quietly into assassin mode.

Dharma shrugs her shoulders. I hold a paper towel under her nose and she blows. The tears have stopped. She seems to be getting control of her fear at our bumbling interrogation.

"Was he as tall as me?" Bubba asks.

Dharma giggles. "Nobody is big as you."

"Ain't that the truth." I force myself to laugh. Hope the noise escaping my mouth sounds like gaiety and not hysteria. "Was the man wearing a hat?"

She brightens. "Uh-huh. A hat like Uncle Lefty wears, only black."

A black baseball cap. My stomach clenches with this information. Did I endanger my babies by keeping Gloria's suspicions about Mom's boyfriend to myself, by not telling Bubba until yesterday about the attempted break-in?

"What did he say to you?" Bubba asks. He winks at Victoria over Dharma's head, does a damn fine job of pretending nonchalance until he asks, "Did he touch you baby? This friend of Uncle Lefty's?"

"Noooo!" Dharma's denial is adamant. "He was nice. Uncle Lefty and him go to World Wressling Fed-ration matches together. One time they even saw The Undertaker and Hulk Hogan."

"You're so stupid." Victoria's on her feet, hands on stiff, pink organdy-tufted hips, fully prepared to throw her twin under the bus. "The Undertaker is like a hundred. He don't even wressle no more."

"Victoria, how would you like to spend some time in your room? Alone."

"How come I'm in trouble? Dharma's the bad one that talked to some man she didn't even know."

Bubba smoothes Dharma's hair. "Your sister is not bad. Never has been. And nobody's in trouble."

"However," I say to the irate Victoria. "You, my good and lovely child, are getting on my last nerve. So sit here on my lap and be quiet, or go to your room. Last chance. No more warnings."

She wiggles onto my lap, her little body a gift of comfort. I squeeze her against my chest, sop up the warmth and normalcy of the weight and feel of her. The dog heaves himself to his giant paws, lurches across the tile floor to fall at my feet like he's been shot.

"All's he did was put the cross on the bench," Dharma whispers. "I couldn't take it from him. 'Cause you and Daddy always say not to take things from strangers. Not even when he was a really, really good, good friend of Uncle Lefty. But then Grandpa David came back and Tommy put the necklace on the bench and walked away and I wanted it real bad and so… I… put it in my pocket… before Grandpa could see."

Tommy?

The inane theme song to Spongebob Squarepants shatters the red rage of mist forming in my head. I pull the cell from my pocket, think to turn off the ringer when I see that the screen is lit, announcing who is calling us this fine morning.

I turn the phone to show Bubba the caller ID. He lifts the necklace over Dharma's head as carefully as if handling a viper, signals with a nod for me to give him the phone. It goes against all my instincts to lay that blinking, cheerily ringing phone in my husband's calloused palm.

Then again, my gut hasn't led me plumb-line straight here lately.

eighteen

THE ONLY WINDOW in the District Attorney's office faces Fifth Street, which is highway 101 North, with a bleak view of the block of concrete that is the courthouse and county jail. This quiet Sunday afternoon, the tires of vehicles on 101 make a soft hissing on the wet asphalt. From where I stand, staring dully out the rain-speckled window, a curved line of head-lights are pale auras in the heavy fog.

Behind me, Dad and David sit stiffly in high-back leather chairs the color of old blood. Both men are shaky with shame, fear, and anger. It was on their watch that Tommy Joe Lyons got close enough to Dharma to hand her the necklace.

Bobby Rossi leans forward. His narrow butt barely touches the seat of the swivel chair behind his desk. He clears his throat, pushes Bubba's statement about this morning's phone call to the side. Too antsy to sit, I pace the carpeted floor—window to door and back again. Twelve steps each way. The movement does nothing to ease my desire to find and kill this Tommy Joe scum, feed tiny bits of him to my bitch of a mother.

"Bubba stayed home with the girls?"

I nod in answer to Bobby. "I'd have asked you to the house, but there's no way I want the girls any more upset by this than they already are."

"No. You were right to meet me here. First thing, before I have a fatality on my hands, I spoke with Lefty and let me assure you that he and Lyons have never met. My guess is the piece of scum overheard our scrawny little friend spouting off about his scheme to bring wrestling to the courtyard of VD's and then extrapolated from there. The second thing. Bubba was right. The necklace had a bug secreted in the cross. Cheap. Probably from Radio Shack. Didn't have a radius of more than fifty feet."

Bobby watches my face as this information sinks in. The son of a bitch was right outside the house this morning. If I'd gone hunting right then, no waiting around, this whole meeting might have been avoided. Bubba and I might right now be happily digging a hole in the woods off some dirt road.

The leather under David's skinny old man butt squeaks in protest when he shifts back in his chair. "I still don't know what this guy said when he called your house this morning."

Bobby taps Bubba's statement with the flat of his wedding ring. "Looks like his phone call was meant as a gotcha. His way of implying he could get to the girls any time he wanted. It was good thinking on Bubba's part to record the bastard."

"How'd Bubba know the necklace was bugged?" Dad looks older than I've ever seen him. Even worse than right after his open heart surgery.

Watching the shame Lyons has caused these two honest, loving men makes me envision a half-dozen more ways to torture the bastard's damnable hide when I find him.

My voice is shrill, pitched higher than I intend. "He knew details of our breakfast conversation. Listen."

I push replay on the cell phone. A voice with a hard, Midwest twang scratches through the tiny speakers.

"I hate to disturb your cozy family breakfast, but your wife needs to sign those papers for her mother. Lot of bad people out there these days. Be a real shame if something unfortunate happened to one of your little girls. Me, I'm real partial to Dharma. Can't help myself, I like 'em soft and sweet. There's folks who'd prefer the spunky one though. Victoria. Hell, couple of twins, cute as coon dog pups. My man, you need to keep a real close eye on those little girls. There's some baaad people out in the world. "

Into the cold rage and fear flooding the district attorney's overheated office, my husband's voice through the phone is a rumbly growl. "How's it feel, Mister Lyons? To be a walking dead man? Here's a promise you can take with you back to whatever filthy hole you crawled out of. I will find you, and when I do, y'all will beg me to kill you."

Thinned through the cell's speakers, a high-pitched giggle raises the hairs on the back of my neck. "Tell the old guy, I think it's real nice him teaching those little darlings about the watering habits of some hairy-assed monster. Nothing like passing the insanity down from one generation to the next."

My hand shakes so that it takes two tries before I push the correct button to shut off the recording. The opposing desires to race home and wrap my arms around my babies, feel their little bodies safe against me, and my visceral hunger to find Tommy Joe Lyons and beat him to death with my own two hands are conflicting rip currents in my belly.

The DA holds his hand to me palm up. "That last part, Bubba's threats, is liable to muddy the waters for a judge."

I stop midstride, stare calmly into the eyes of Humboldt County's DA. "You get this guy, Bobby, or we will. Couldn't be any simpler."

Bobby claps his hands, maybe an attempt to break the tension in the room.

"Good news and bad news. Let's start with the good." He opens a manila folder, spreads several papers in front of him on the redwood burl desk. "I called in some favors in the San Francisco area. Had a buddy do some checking. This Lyons is a grifter, but he's no child molester."

"You mean he's not been caught molesting a child." My voice sounds like it's coming from deep in a tunnel. My hands, fisted in the front of my hoodie, twitch and jump. The pocket must look like some fanged animal is fighting its way out into the muted light of the office. "And let's not forget that my mother and her boyfriend are all about the money. It's a dead cinch this guy knows other scumbags who would pay for just the kind of sick shit he hinted at when he talked with Bubba."

"Well then," Rossi says, "so much for the good news. The bad news is this...." His eyes skid over mine, refuse to make contact. The rain begins again, taps lightly at the window. "About all I can do for you is to pick him up, lock him in a room for twenty-four hours, and do my level best to intimidate him into leaving town. Now that Connors died, I don't have a judge on the bench in this county that will let me hold him any longer than that on what we've got."

Two steps and I lean across the fancy redwood desk, my hand reaching for the DA's loosely knotted tie.

"Calm down, Sam." A trio of male voices echo in the small office, all with the same exact message.

One step back so the edge of the redwood desk no longer bites into my thighs, I reach for Dad's hand, wait for my vision to clear.

"This animal stalked my child. Threatened her life. And you're telling me there's nothing you can do about it?"

"I said no such thing, Samantha. First of all, with no priors for kidnapping or molestation, this guy is just jerking your chain. He's not going to grab the twins. But he wants you to believe he will so you'll sign off on that inheritance from your biological father. It's as simple as that. He's all about intimidation. That's his MO. He intimidates until he gets the money."

"It's simple all right." Hands flat on haphazard piles of paper, I lean across the desk. To his credit, Bobby doesn't flinch, takes my words as hot breath on his face. "But it ain't you or Lyons making the rules anymore."

nineteen

CAR EXHAUST HANGS low and heavy in the morning air. The drop-off zone is edged with a long, slow-moving row of vehicles. Small children in oversized backpacks and ugly uniforms clamber from giant SUVs, wade through thick, ozone-stealing air, trudge up wide, stone steps, and disappear into the maw of the beast that is Catholic education.

But perhaps my mood isn't the best this morning.

Bubba steers the Ram past the line of waiting SUVs, turns into the lot at the back of the building, wedges the truck between a yellow school bus and the football coach's Navigator. It is unequivocally forbidden—against the law, punishable by death with a metal-edged ruler—to carry a firearm into a school. The familiar weight of my belly pack calms me some. Bubba rolls his shoulders under the weight of his jacket, specially tailored to hide the Glock.

Our fear and tension has tainted the girls. Neither child has said a word since we left the house. The equivalent in rarity of an entire January in Humboldt County without a drop of rain. Bubba holds the door of the king cab for Victoria. Dharma's hand is warm and moist in mine. The twins be-tween us, we stride across the parking lot toward the back entrance to Saint Bernard's Elementary and High School.

Less than ten steps from the truck, Sister Mary Theresa scurries toward us. A Chihuahua with the instincts of a pit bull, her calf-length black polyester skirt flaps against her short legs.

"You're not allowed to drop-off students anywhere but at the designated area in front." Her voice scratches at the base of my skull, like the pointy nails of an inconsequential rodent clawing its clueless way into my free-fire zone.

"Not today, Sister." My voice is casual, matter-of-fact. A listener could barely tell at all that I'm holding on by a thread here. Anyone gets in my way is likely to get chewed up badly. Neither Bubba nor I slow. The girls, their small hands trapped in our larger ones, hesitate but are swept forward with us.

Sister Theresa follows along at our heels, yapping into her cell phone. Her bark is a steady yip. "Yes, Mother Mary Martha. I understand. I've explained that to them, Mother. Yes, Mother."

At the push-levered backdoor the good Mother Superior herself appears, the wicked witch preparing herself to demand the ruby slippers, flying monkeys on call.

"Mister Johnson." The principal nods to Bubba, speaks remarkably clearly while grinding her teeth. I suppose she's had a good bit of experience. "Samantha Jean. As always, a treat to see you."

"Good morning ma'am… sis… Mother Superior." Bubba says. Nothing like a celibate nun to elicit fear in a good ole Southern Baptist boy.

"Sister Theresa," the principal says, "thank you for your diligence. I'll take it from here."

Behind us the heavy door bangs shut with the soul-deadening sound familiar in all schools and prisons. Our little troop is strung out across the locker-lined hall, hands held, heads high. Chalk dust, cheap floor wax, and melting beeswax infiltrate the air like Superman's kryptonite. God, I went to public school, came here only for catechism each Saturday morning and yet, each breath saps my resolve, weakens my faith in the good Sister's ability to listen and respond to the situation.

Mother Superior's office is directly behind the admissions desk. Four elementary school kids are a single line of boredom waiting for the minimum-pay secretary to look up and fulfill their need for a readmission note or a dentist-appointment-inspired permission slip. Three girls and a lone boy with dark hair spiked into some kind of gel-hardened mess shuffle their ugly, school-required oxfords, stare like zombies at the black and white clock on the wall.

We seat Victoria and Dharma against the wall in the corner of the outer sanctum, as far away from the exposed windows as we can manage. Bubba squats in front of the girls, whispers something that calls forth two bell-like giggles. I lay my hand on his shoulder, the stiff wool of his jacket rough against my palm. He covers my hand with his, turns and looks up at me, one knee resting on the linoleum floor.

"I got this," he says. "You take all the time you need."

My throat aches with fear and love. I nod, lay my hand against his fresh-shaved cheek, know my babies are safe. For the moment.

He stays with the girls. I follow Sister Mary Martha into her office, sit in one of the two wooden chairs.

"Well, Samantha Jean?" Sister arranges herself behind her desk, strokes her black skirt over her knees. A half-empty cup of coffee is balanced on a neat stack of papers, a bowl of soggy Cheerios beside the cup.

"Someone is stalking the girls." Saying this out loud, here in this ordinary, official place makes the situation more real to me. I want to snatch the words back the minute they're out of my mouth.

Sister's right hand flutters up, rests on the simple, silver cross at her throat. Though it hardly seems possible, her back straightens even more than usual, like something has tightened the steel line that runs from the top of her head to her tailbone. The words hang in the air while I focus on the picture of Mary, Mother of God, above Sister's head. Mary's arms are at her side, palms facing me, a pose that is unnatural as a soft-pelted porcupine and yet manages to convey a sense of comfort, openness.

Mary's sad, smiling face blurs. I swipe at my eyes. What the hell is the matter with me? Why am I crying in front of this nun? The principal comes around the desk in one practiced, fluid movement. She scoots the hard chair next to mine sideways, lowers herself onto the seat, leans forward, and, in one deft move, cups my wet face in her hands.

"Tell me." Her breath is warm on my skin.

I lean into this warmth, ache to luxuriate in the care this woman offers. Instead I wipe roughly at tears, lay my hands carefully on the belly pack in my lap and explain to the principal about my mother's return to Humboldt County. By the time I get to the part of the story where Bubba and I discover the bugged necklace, my tears are nothing but track marks.

Sandwiched between Sister's warm palms and the heavy comfort of the belly pack, my hands are steady. "So, we don't want to remove the girls from school, would like to keep their lives as normal as possible while this mess gets settled, but we don't know, Sister. Will the girls be safe here at school?"

She rolls her thumb along the top of my hand, sits back in her chair, and fingers that silver at her neck again.

"You know," she says, "I have a prayer list I work my way through each morning and every evening. People I hold up to the Lord, as well as individuals for whom I am thankful. You and your family are on both lists. Have been for years."

From the other side of the door Bubba's deep rumbling laughter makes its way to me. God, talk about things to be thankful for. I wipe at my eyes once more.

"Your father is truly what we in the religious community call other-centered. Has he ever told you that he and my mother attended Eureka High School together?"

The surprise of her words pushes me back in my chair like a force of nature, a mighty wind. That this seemingly rigid woman has ever given my family a moment's thought that didn't begin and end with her begging the Lord for permission to backhand me, well, it's a shock.

"I talked your father into promoting Saint Bernard's as the school of choice for your girls, Samantha. Do you remember it was me, and this was in my novice days, who so often lingered in the back of your catechism classes, kept an eye on you when the other, less well-brought-up children taunted you about your father's Bigfoot beliefs?"

"By the slide that time?" I ask. "When that sixth-grader called Dad a Bigfoot fucker... sorry, he made fun of Dad and I coldcocked him? That was you that pulled him off me once he got back up?"

Her laughter seems natural enough, doesn't appear to be forced or false. Sounds, in fact, like she does this sort of thing quite often.

"Yes, dear, that was me. I got a sprained wrist and a scar on my shin for my efforts too. Not from the sixth-grader either. It was you who fought like a wildcat to get in one more lick before I pulled the two of you apart."

"I guess Victoria and Dharma sort of come by it natural."

"Indeed. So, back to my prayer list. I thank the Good Lord twice each day that you did not attend Saint Bernard's as a child. Give praise that it was only on Saturday that I was forced to deal with your unquenchable intellect, misplaced hatred of female authority figures and, most of all, your ferocious anger when your father's name was slandered."

My mouth remains open in a small flytrap of surprise. At the drop-off zone out front someone loses patience and leans heavily on a horn.

"I also prayed each day that Jesus, Mary, and all the saints watched over you as you grew up among all those men. Your father. Hawk's dad, David. The dozens of Bigfoot hunters who bounced you on their knees, filled your head with wild stories. Loving men to be sure, but Samantha, your childhood was anything but ordinary."

"Bubba tells me ordinary can be extremely boring."

Again her clear laughter bursts into the room, knocks some of the dust off the *World's Best Principal* plaque, the pictures of past graduating classes.

"Your Bubba, my dear, is one of the best answers God could have given to all my prayers for you."

"Dad calls him Saint Bubba."

"Well. As the kids say, it takes one to know one."

The bell rings for the start of classes and Sister holds up a pointy finger to me, steps to the phone on her desk and instructs the secretary to read this morning's announcements as she's busy and won't be able to do so. She comes back around the desk, sits beside me again.

"Here's what I can assure you," she says. "In this day and age, sad to say, we at Saint Bernard's have experience dealing with this sort of thing. We've never had a stranger stalking a student, but we've had our share of custodial fights between parents and a few issues with grandparents who have some problems of their own." Her sigh seems both prayer and exasperated plea for mercy and, possibly, the begging for permission to strangle the life out of some adult without the ability to properly love the child in their care.

"We will do our best, and our best is very good, to ensure that Dharma and Victoria, while on these school grounds, are never out of sight of a responsible adult. I'll put an extra aide in the classroom. Call the police department, alert them to the situation and request they beef up patrols in the area."

"Very good isn't a great assurance, Sister. These are my babies."

"Truth be told, Samantha? None of us, not even you and your wonderful Bubba, can protect those precious girls from all the evils in this world. We must do the best we can and trust in the Lord."

twenty

THE AIR IS heavy with the threat of rain, rich with the spores of sword fern and the musk of a forest older than Jesus, or Mohammad, or Buddha. Columns of light filter through tall trees like sun through the stained glass of a European cathedral. My Wolverines crunch thimble-sized cones from the redwoods that tower around us. Bubba and I walk through the only patch of virgin forest remaining in the Eureka city limits.

"What d'ya think?" I ask. My hand hasn't left Bubba's since Sister Mary Martha escorted us to Dharma and Victoria's classroom, pried our fingers from theirs, and sent us on our way.

"I don't have me a good feeling about any of this." There's a low vibration in Bubba's voice I've never heard before. Somewhere between anger and fear is my best placement of the tremolo.

About halfway down the first canyon between the zoo and the duck pond, the patter of rain on the upper branches of the forest begins a slow, building symphony. I peer inside an old lightning-struck tree trunk, careful not to disturb the local wildlife—homeless humans, not bear or cougar here inside the city limits. No stashed sleeping bag or shopping cart. I edge on into the protection of the hollowed stump, pull Bubba along behind me. The hollow is high enough even he can stand upright in the shell of the dead tree.

He unbuttons his coat and opens his arms. I lay my head against his chest, his heavy jacket, already warmed with his body heat, he wraps around me. Enclosed in a layered cocoon of protection—the ancient redwood stump, the scratchy wool of his coat and the thick arms of a man who loves me—a sketchy, tentative calm settles over me.

"There's no way Lyons has a stake in my signing that paper except through Mother." The words are whispers in a church, a shameful secret shared in a dark confessional. "She has to be involved in this stalking."

Bubba's wide chest rises and falls slowly under my cheek. The air infuses with ozone or whatever energy it is that constricts the spaces between molecules the instant before a storm hits. Tension seems to pull the air itself tighter for a split second before thunder rolls a warning and the clouds release their burden. I turn, press my back along the length of his front so we both look out the narrow, vertical slit of the stump.

He crosses his arms around me, manages to lightly cup my breasts in his hands in a pose that makes me feel so very married—cared for, cherished, and loved. I do my best to sink into this feeling, draw what strength I can from the moment even as a brooding premonition whispers darkly in my ear.

"A person wants to see the best in folks." Through three layers of cotton, his warm hands are busy. "But, darlin', no amount of love and need on your part is gonna change your mama. Even you can't turn a sow's ear into a silk purse."

Softened by a canopy of layered branches, the rain falls in patchy showers outside our sanctuary. Soon, very soon with this downpour, the branches of the redwoods will be saturated and the wind will throw green-tinged water in veritable buckets onto the forest floor. We are going to be very wet by the time we fold ourselves back into the Ram and head home.

The front pocket of my 501s vibrates with the ringing of my cell. I flip the phone open and a shock of fear trembles my hands when I see the glowing readout across the little screen.

"It's Sister Mary Martha," I tell Bubba.

"Probably nothing to worry about." His arms stay tight around me.

"Samantha?" Sister's voice is all wrong. "We are certain the girls are here on the school grounds. There's no way they could have gotten off the property. But it might be best if you returned to the school. Samantha? Are you there?"

My throat has a vise grip on my words, mind blank of all thoughts but one. I am halfway up the side of the hill, jeans soaked, breath coming in short, hot gasps before I realize Bubba is clearing a path for me. We race across the zoo playground and some part of me knows mothers are scooping up children, staring in surprise at this wild-eyed couple tearing a path to the parking lot. A dog barks frantically. A horn honks as we clear Maple Street, throw ourselves in the truck.

The noise of the diesel can't cover the pounding of my heart. Through the half-circle of windshield the wipers clear at each swipe, Duck's Market, the old water tower, the emergency room entrance to Saint Joseph's hospital—it all appears and is left behind. Important only as markers of our progress toward my babies. Bubba makes the turn from Harris unto Henderson Street and there are flashing blue lights, a line of cars, a patrolman leaning into each window as the vehicle passes Saint Bernard's school.

I open the passenger door before the truck stops. Fall. Get up. Run the last two blocks on numb legs. Dad and David pace under the wide overhang of the school's front porch. An inhuman wail echoes in the air and a circle of cops, a gathering of nuns, and a group of parents turn and stare toward me. Dad and David reach my side at the same time Bubba overtakes me. The wide front doors of the school open.

"Mama!"

The most beautiful sound in the world.

I don't so much kneel as collapse to my knees in the pouring rain. Victoria reaches me first. Her little body is hot and wiggly and glorious against mine. Dharma slams into me a second later smelling of incense and old candle wax and that wonderful, heavenly strawberry shampoo she loves. Bubba squats beside me, enfolds us all three in his arms.

"A new janitor approached them with a question about the location of a classroom." Sister Mary Martha's voice comes to me from somewhere unimportant, somewhere outside the presence of my babies. "The girls took fright, ran, and hid in the old confessional at the back of the chapel."

Somehow, I'm on my feet.

Bobby Rossi strides across the rain-black asphalt, his suit wet and rumpled, his brow lined.

Victoria is all but hidden in Bubba's arms. Dharma's mouth breathes hot against my throat.

The cell phone, still clutched in my shaky hand, vibrates like the tail of a rattler. It takes three tries to flip the ominous little device open. I stare at the green-tinted words.

Unknown Caller

A numb finger presses the speaker symbol and the wet air is permeated with maniacal laughter that leaches from the little speaker, turns the head of every cop, quickens the step of the DA, and chills me to the bone.

twenty-one

OVERLAPPING, MISMATCHED BLANKETS hastily nailed to the frame block the third-story window. For the first time since moving into this house, I sleep in a bed without a view of Humboldt Bay. Dharma's *Cars* nightlight throws two thin beams of illumination into the pitchy darkness—Tow Mater the tow truck making a meager attempt to pierce the heavy blackness. The light is yet another half-assed gift from Lefty. It's equipped with a motion detector. I'm afraid to move for fear of activating the voice of Larry the Cable Guy as the tow truck.

Bubba and I face inward on the king-sized bed, the girls snugged between us. Our arms thrown over our sleeping daughters, his hand is warm in mine. Dharma flounces, pumps her legs against the heavy comforter, flips in one complete circle, faces me, belly down, flips, faces Bubba, then onto her back again. Rufus pushes himself from the floor on my side of the bed, lays his slobbery head on my pillow, his nose presses wetly against the back of my neck.

Bubba's silent laugh bounces the bed. "You awake?"

"Ah, yeah. Maybe taking the girls to bed with us wasn't our best idea."

"We've had worse. You saying you wanna move 'em back to their own beds?"

"God, no." I pull Dharma against me. Bury my face in her silky hair.

"Good. 'Cause I don't believe I can sleep on one of those twin beds and there ain't no way I'm letting either of 'em out of my sight right now."

"Feels like Lyons has already won in a way though, doesn't it?" Do all voices sound lonely whispered in the dark? "Blankets on the window. Huddled here together on the bed, afraid to leave the girls alone for one minute."

Rufus sneaks one front paw up onto the bed. I shouldn't let him up here. There's barely room to breathe now. But I like to think he's worried about the girls too. Besides, his warm, breathing bulk at my back wouldn't be such a bad thing.

"It's temporary." Bubba shifts backward on the bed, lifts Victoria with him. I scooch Dharma toward her sister, slide in another foot to make room for the dog.

"Get 'er done! Get 'er done!"

God damn that Lefty! Rufus has activated the motion detector on that freakin' nightlight.

This is not the first time the dog has heard this voice in the night. He ignores the interruption, heaves himself onto the bed, settles against me, lets loose a fart like a mountain rumble. I push my head under the covers, wave my free hand in the air. It's a sad fact when even a dog fart comforts, provides a homey, if God-awful smelly, reminder of all things normal.

"Y'all still copacetic with the plan?"

I smile into the dark, poke my head out from under the covers. Copacetic? Bubba's been trying to improve himself since he and I hooked up. Word of the day calendar. Business classes online. Hell, he even started tucking in his shirt until I put a stop to that. The fact is, on his worst day, he's twice the man I deserve. I know there are folks out there who would agree with my mother's assessment, judge I traded down when I walked away from the handsome, well-educated Hawk and joined hands with this farmer's son from rural Georgia with a degree in agriculture from the home of the Bulldogs. Well, they can all go fuck themselves sideways. It turned out to be my good luck when Hawk refused to accept my pregnancy as a blessing. His rejection freed me, and about damn time, to see Bubba clearly.

I stretch my arm across the girls, lay my palm on the stubbly cheek of my husband. "Did I tell you there's no one I'd rather have with me in this mess than you?"

He kisses my lifeline. "Goes without sayin', that sentiment flows both ways. You talk to your sister?"

"Ah, yeah. We're set for Wednesday. Is that enough time to get everything organized do you think?"

"VD's is covered. Carey's working overtime. Your dad and David can pitch in if need be. Lefty and Caroline agreed to make the big sacrifice and hang out at the bar every open hour until we get back. They'll fill in if it gets busy. Nothing for us to do but load the guns and leave a trail of bread crumbs."

NOONER'S IS CROWDED with locals stretching out a lunch hour and tourists slipping off their shoes, sipping from bottles of Mexican Coca-Cola and moaning over the restaurant's famous Greek salad. A golden aphrodisiac of sunlight filters through the wide front window, bathes the tables up front with a dreamlike warmth, pours a wavy river of light over the murals of old Greece along the side wall.

Mother waves from the far back table, the only red-and-white-checked surface without a hint of sunlight. I breathe deep of olive oil, red onions, and feta cheese, turn my face in profile to the window, and receive one final blessing before my shaky knees take me to the dark zone.

It is the oddest sensation. As though two people stride step-by-step across the black and white tiles of the floor. One a confident, logical young woman, the other a small, frightened child, whimpering in the dark for her mama.

God, I hate this shit.

"Thank you for meeting me, Samantha." The shiny red heels of her open-toed shoes make her almost exactly my height. Not expecting her to stand in greeting, certainly unprepared for her to grab my stiff shoulders and attempt to pull me into the scent of a French countryside layered lightly over burning brimstone, I step back. Don't know whether to push her away or cling to her like a damned trained monkey.

"Well." She flips her rhinestone sunglasses up so they all but disappear into the crown of her carefully streaked blonde hair. "Too soon, perhaps." She fusses with the crease of her pants, lowers herself gracefully into the wooden chair.

For distraction, to allow my heartbeat to slow and remind myself how to breathe, I speculate on the color of her trousers. Not pink. Maybe mauve? Or taupe. What the hell is taupe anyway? Rosy cream? Got it. Her pants are the color of expensive champagne tinged with a tiny drop of the blood of the innocent.

The waitress, Tiffany, a VD regular, pours me a glass of ice water, buzzes my cheek.

"Crazy busy today. The sun's brought 'em out. Know whatcha want?"

I push the menu away, do my best to control my breathing. God help me, part of me wants to squirm in my seat, clutch mother's hand and squeal, "Tif, I want you to meet my mommy." The other ninety percent of me yearns to jerk handfuls of dear Mother's coiffure out of her deceitful head and beat her to a bloody pulp with her over-priced shoes.

My voice comes out all froggy and odd. "A meatball sandwich with a salad side."

One manicured nail, painted today with what looks like a palm tree and inset with a flashy red stone, taps the tabletop, lets me know that, by ordering first, I've breached etiquette. "A Greek salad. No onion. Feta and dressing on the side, of course. A glass of pinot grigio would be lovely."

"Wine would be nice, but we don't carry it. How 'bout an ice cold Downtown Brown?"

My laughter is obnoxious and rude. That knowledge only makes me laugh louder. It's a nice tension breaker. For me.

"Beer," I explain to Mother's blank stare. "They have beer or iced tea or soda. Pick one."

"Perhaps just the water." She watches Tiffany hurry away with our order. "Really Samantha. We couldn't have met at the Ingamar?"

An exclusive men's club, where women are allowed to visit the outer ring of power only by express permission from an elite male. No power on earth could drag me into the belly of that beast.

"No. We could not meet at the Ingamar Club. Who do you know that bestowed the privilege of entry? And did you have to fill out a form swearing you weren't on your period? You know, to be sure you didn't inadvertently contaminate the chairs?"

Ah. So, after all these years, I've discovered what it is I inherited from my mother—her bitchiness. Damn. Snarky really does feel good. Empowering, that's what it is.

She looks down, brushes at the napkin in her lap, removes her sparkly sunglasses, and fits them gently into her shiny red clutch purse.

"You're not making this easy," she says.

Delicate tears spill from eyes the blue-green of the Caribbean Sea. The color is deceptive. Gazing into them, others may think warm waters on white sand beaches. I'm waiting for that toothy gray shadow to appear from out of the depths.

"Here's the thing." A sip of ice water soothes my tight throat. "Your boyfriend stalked my daughter. Invaded the privacy of our home with an electronic bug." I put my hand up to stop her from interrupting. "And here's the kicker, Mom. To try and force me to sign that fucking piece of paper of yours, he called my house and threatened my babies and, when the girls got temporarily lost at school, the son of a bitch knew and gloated about it. So, if this is your idea of starting over with each other? I'm not liking it much. In fact, your technique for reestablishing yourself in my life has thrown me into a sort of murderous rage."

At the edge of the black tube into which my vision has narrowed, I see Tiffany start this way, pitcher of ice water in hand, hips swinging in the way of all good waitresses threading their way through a crowded restaurant. The tension emanating from our table stops her progress three feet away. Tif turns, sidles away, leaves us to our misery.

"I have nothing to do with anything that awful man does. How could you think I would endanger my own grandchildren? Honestly, Samantha Jean, your attitude just cuts me to the core."

Never trust anybody who says *honestly*, or *to tell the truth*. Dad taught me that. Not to trust this bitch? I learned that from her when she abandoned me at six weeks of age. I relearned it every night I traced my finger over the one and only picture of her I had, cried myself to sleep trying to figure out how I could change myself, make myself lovable, convince her to come back.

"Ah, yeah. Well, see, but the thing is, you're the one who stands to benefit from my signature on that piece of paper. I may live in the sticks, but I ain't stupid. My biological father left an estate worth millions. Now, maybe he didn't leave me a dime. No reason why he should. I never even met the man. Thanks to you.

"But, then again, all this fussin' and fumin' and carryin' on about me signing over my rights to anything he may have left me? It's got me curious. Makes me wonder just why you're so desperate to get my signature you'd threaten your own grandchildren."

The smell of marinara sauce turns my head a second before a red plastic basket is placed in front of me. A salad, its collection of sides perched precariously along the plate's rim, is balanced on Tif's elbow. She deftly settles the order onto Mom's side of the table, squeezes my arm gently, strides quickly away.

"You know, dear." Mother glares at her salad. "You could try and see this from someone's point of view besides your own. That would be a novel approach, wouldn't it?"

The meatball sandwich is warm and gooey with the exact right combination of spice and garlic and cheese. It takes a long time to chew that first bite. God, this woman can ruin the taste of even a Nooners lunch. I set the leaking sandwich carefully on its paper-lined basket.

Time to get on with the job of dropping the first bread crumb. What sounded like a decent idea, our only option really, in the dark of our bedroom fortress, has morphed now, sitting across from this woman who makes me shake and quall like a child. Now I'm not so sure using my babies as bait for this monster and her trained gorilla is a good idea. In fact, it may be the worst idea ever in my long history of bad ideas.

"You know we're taking Gloria camping?"

She keeps sliding spinach around with her fork, but her whole body stills for a split second before she raises her face to me, does her best to hide the predator lurking in the shadows of those blue eyes.

"I was under the impression it would be only you and your sister out there in the woods on your little bonding trip."

"That was the original plan. But, now, after that awful man whose behavior you are in no way responsible for has threatened my girls—now we're all going."

She dips the merest tip of the spinach leaves in the dressing, pauses with the fork resting against her plate. "By all, who do you mean exactly, darling?"

Darling my tiny ass. "Bubba's going too." I almost miss the momentary curving of her lips, the way her eyebrows lift ever so slightly.

"And what of Victoria and Dharma? Will the girls be staying with Victor?"

"The girls are coming camping with us."

"You're bringing those children with you into the wilderness? With wild animals and… dirt… and my God, Samantha, medical attention miles and miles away. What can you be thinking? Wouldn't it be better to leave them here? With Victor?"

Sure, that'd be great. I'll let my eighty-six-year-old father be responsible for defending my babies against you and your mutant boyfriend.

"Really Mother? You're going to give me advice on parenting?"

She brings her fork to her mouth. Christ. The woman even chews elegantly. Come on God. Spinach caught in the teeth? A little salad dressing dribbled onto the silky blouse with the lacy bra clearly visible beneath? You got nothing for me here?

I push my sandwich around, wait for the shark to take the bait.

She swallows, rises to the enticing offer floating on the surface, on the border between one future and another.

"Perhaps I'll go with you." She dabs her clean mouth with a napkin, sips daintily from her water, reaches a manicured hand across the red-and-white-checked cloth, taps the top of my wrist with one painted nail. So brief is the contact I'm not sure she really touched me.

"I may not be good at showing it, but I do care about you, Samantha."

I blink, feel as though I'm waking from a dream already forgotten, the memory sinking down into the realm of deep night and lost hopes.

"Now, where exactly will we be going, dear?"

"Really Mom? You'd actually go with us? Camping in tents. In the middle of nowhere?"

And the hook is set, easy as catching fish in a barrel. Though for a moment, I'm uneasy about which of us just leaped from safety to swallow the bait.

My mission successful, I study my sandwich to hide a small smile. But, before I can sink into the muddy sea of success and complacency for even one goddamned second, a premonition flashes behind my eyes. Triggered by fear, or God forbid, instinct, a vision like a subliminal message robs me of my next breath.

Primordial forest in the dark of a cloud shrouded night. A child's scream. An empty tent.

twenty-two

BEER BOTTLES CLINK in the midst of whooping male ruckus like giant howler monkeys on a happy rampage. We've got the fiftieth birthday celebration of one of our regulars going on in the courtyard. Earlier, Bubba wheeled the portable cooler back there with a hundred pounds of ice and four cases of the birthday boy's favorite beer, Bud Light.

Coming up on midnight and I haven't left my position behind the bar since I got here just after seven. Victoria and Dharma are directly behind me, in Dad's room, under the care of the grandpas. Both Dad and David pack Colt 1911s under their flannel shirts and any predator who thinks those two octogenarians are the weakest link in this ring of protection is going to be in hell about four seconds after making that mistake.

Besides, the only path to that back room is the narrow door to the far left of the bar. There never has been an exit door to the street from what used to be the working girls' room. When Aunt Mandy built the cribs, it was necessary to ensure a customer didn't sneak out the back without paying or sneak inside and snatch a quickie from one of her working girls, robbing Auntie of her fair share of the profits while she was busy entertaining the likes of Tom Mix.

Lord, I am constantly reminded of the good stock from which I come.

Bubba wipes clean a table in the back, his reach straining the green plaid flannel across his wide shoulders and back. The shirt tail hangs loose around his waist, covers the bulk of the Glock. He returns with the empties, cups the back of my neck with a thick hand on his way to the front table with a refill of lime-laced mineral water for Hawk.

"So," I say to Lefty, whose scrawny backside hasn't yet fully settled onto the bar stool. "Couldn't keep your mouth shut, huh?"

He's been avoiding me all night. Ever since I told him I googled Early Dawn and discovered just who that t-shirt he gave my daughter is advertising. He scratches under the brim of his ball cap with an index finger, ducks his head, and throws me the same look Rufus gives when I catch him chewing one of the twins' favorite toys. And there's just about as much chance that he's truly contrite as there is that the dog is ever going to quit stealing and destroying property.

Every table has two men seated with their backs to the wall, watchful and unblinking as the one-eyed bear, mangle-eared buck, and bedraggled elk above their heads. Bubba and I. Dad and David. The DA and Lefty. No one else knew about the electronic invasion of our home, the gift of the cross, the threat to the girls. Only one of that group embraces the theory that a roomful of weapons in a crowded bar is a safeguard and not a menace.

My face is close enough to Lefty's to kiss his acne-scarred cheek.

"What were you thinking? Larry over there has been itching for a fight since the last helicopter lifted off the roof of the embassy in Hanoi. Jonesy's been pissed since Baghdad," I whisper, referring to a former Marine, and a First Cav Gulf War vet—both sporadic regulars.

"You ain't the only one worried 'bout them girls." He tilts his chin, looks defiant. And a little scared. I do, after all, control his beer supply. "And I don't know what your problem is with that t-shirt. Early Dawn's the number one lady wrestler in the whole damn country. You always bitchin' about how them girls don't have enough female role models. Think you'd be grateful."

This is like a liberal Democrat debating a Tea Party affiliate. Well, except that in the case of Lefty and me, the opposing individuals grew up together and love each other beyond reason. Still, there is no way in hell Lefty and I are going to find enough common ground to even begin this discussion.

"Look." What I intend as a heavy sigh filled with poignant frustration mingles with Lefty's beer breath. "Just knock off the wrestling crap or…."

My head jerks up instinctively. The air in the bar is charged with the magnetic pull of a half-dozen itchy hands drawn to the warm reassurance of a pistol butt. The former Marine and the First Cavalry vet both sport smiles as sweet as a child's on Christmas morning. Oh yeah, their grins project. The wait is over. Finally I get to open my gift.

I study the man who's just brought cold air and a near electric charge of testosterone into my bar. The stupid jerk is wearing the same black jacket he wore when he presented me with those papers. The door swings open again and the sweet, wet air ushers in my sister. Like a sudden calm in the midst of a building storm, there's an instant of pause. The room waits to see what this new presence portents.

"Does it ever not rain here?" Gloria asks cheerfully. With no apparent clue as to what she's walked into the middle of, my twin slips out of her rain slicker, stops to kiss Hawk with enough tongue that half the men in the bar are now packing two hard pieces for me to worry about.

The private investigator, Joe Stanton, stands perfectly still in the near middle of the bar. "Is this bar not in California?" he asks. "Where it's just about illegal to even own a gun, let alone carry one."

"Ah, yeah. They tell me Humboldt County hasn't managed yet to secede from the Golden State. You see any guns?" I keep my voice flat, watch Bubba behind our visitor turning in a slow circle to face the posse, do his best to employ his size and presence to calm everybody the fuck down. "I don't see anything but a bunch of people sittin' around on a rainy night enjoying each other's company over a few beers."

Gloria, in a V-necked, powder-blue sweater, her skin-tight jeans tucked into calf-high boots with some kind of sparkly crap going on with the three-inch heels, parks her little ass on the stool directly across from me at the scarred wooden bar. I really do like her, I do. But, it's disconcerting when she shows up out of nowhere, brings a man whose very presence is guaranteed to rattle the cage of every gun-toting adrenaline junkie in the bar, and then, if that's not enough, manages to look just like me, only about a hundred times prettier.

I do my best to ignore her for now, keep my concentration on the piece of trouble in the black jacket, motionless in a cloud of adrenaline.

"What are you doing here?" My eyes never leave Stanton's.

It's Gloria who answers my question. "He's with me. Don't be mad. I asked him to come because I didn't want to walk alone through the, you know, the… street people around here." Gloria reaches across the bar and squeezes my arm in what I assume she means as both greeting and apology.

Which makes it hard to explain the fact that her touch causes me to jerk to the side. My right hand, already warming the butt of my .38, leaps with the pistol half out of its belly holster, the Colt light as sin against my palm.

It's like watching one of those picture-in-a-picture TV screens. In one frame, my twin is twittering about our upcoming camping trip and on another, much more sharply focused screen, an incompetent private investigator stands flatfooted, caught between bad judgment and misplaced accusation. While on an out of focus but no less compelling third television, Hawk struts across the bar.

Long denim wrapped legs, the heels of his pointy toed boots tap a nostalgic song on the beer-soaked wood floor as he positions himself next to Bubba, the two of them flanking Mr. Stanton. Some broken, jagged, but no less visceral edge of me is pulled toward Hawk in this instant. It's not as though I forget Bubba, more like I psychically drag his six four, two-hundred-forty-pound frame with me into the comfort of my misremembered past.

Peculiar what the brain does when fear, confusion, and rage overpower the conscious mind. This moment, the entire populace of the bar caught between one breath and the next, hangs suspended in time. I force air into my lungs, am struck with a near uncontrollable and totally idiotic desire to instruct my uninvited posse that this is not the droid you're looking for.

Bubba steps forward, slips one mighty arm around Joe Stanton and leads him to a bar stool. God, my mind is not functioning at all well lately. Fear, anger, confusion over my feelings toward my mom, tentative happiness at the discovery of my twin, blood-red rage at some muscled-up moron threatening my girls—I am a steaming mess.

"Sam?" Gloria's voice comes from somewhere at the edge of the blackness in which I'm standing—heartbeat steady at reptilian pace, breath slow and deep—at that peak of an adrenaline rush when nothing exists outside the perceived threat.

"Did you hear me? Sam? It's okay isn't it? If Hawk comes with us?" Gloria's voice, tentative, tinged with pleasure.

The smell of her flowery perfume is the first pinpoint at the entrance back to a larger world. The heavy, rich scent mingles with one of Lefty's beer belches and then Bubba's voice pulls me all the way back to this ratty bar, my girls safe in the back room, surrounded by my tribe.

"Darlin', it's all good now. Nothing to fret about. Mr. Stanton, he's dumb as a post, but he don't mean no harm to our babies. Man just escorted your sister down here to our big, scary part of town for a little sit down."

I haven't cleared the belly pack, the nose of the revolver hides snug in its little holster, but the fact that the scored butt of the .38 is warm in my hand snaps me out of my trance, carries me completely into the light. I replace the pistol in its seat, zip the pouch closed, and rub my numb face with hands that shake just a little.

God. Bubba's right. As risky as our little plan is, we've got to do something to bring this threat to a head or the poison is going to burst, cover everyone, innocent and guilty alike, with the green pus of greed and rage. And given my mental state, it could well be me that pops the blister.

twenty-three

STARS ARE HARD-edged, the sky moonless and bereft of clouds. The narrow, floating pier shimmies slightly under Rufus and me. My boots create a short downward movement with each step followed by a quick upward recovery of the planks against the surface of the water. The dog's swinging gait pushes the planks from side to side rhythmically. The sound of Jonesy's heel-first footfalls come from behind me and above. He's pacing, standing guard from his position on the stationary pier. Bubba, home with the girls, insisted I bring the Iraqi vet with me on Rufus's nightly walk.

"You ain't just yourself here lately, darlin'," my husband drawled, his hands firmly on my shoulders, his brown eyes lit with that golden glow that means, no matter what, he's not backing down.

"I can handle myself just fine. Don't need a damn guard in my own front yard." It's not like I thought the argument was winnable, but there was still no way my mouth was going to stay shut.

"Ah, huh. You might could. But, just for tonight, humor me. Jonesy's gonna follow along and give you that little extra margin of safety."

Each exhale, mine and the dog's, hangs motionless in air like the inside of a fish freezer. The scratchy wool of a watch cap makes my head itch. I hate that my safe world has been invaded by my bitch of a mother and her fucking predator boyfriend. I hate that my sister seems a perfectly lovely person, and yet each time I see her it's as though I've fallen down a rabbit hole into some weird wonderland where everything I ever believed about myself is false, everything I take as gospel is wrong.

Most of all, I hate that the me that can handle drunks and bar fights, survive anything the Pacific Northwest woods can dish out, walk away from a harmful, enabling relationship and recognize a good and loving man when he presents himself—that woman has somehow regressed into a frightened child, hiding under the quilt and praying for her mommy to love her, drawn once a-damn-gin, to the beautiful, wounded Hawk.

What in the hell is wrong with me? Every ounce of my attention needs to be on protecting Dharma and Victoria. Especially now, with the plan in place, Gloria, and now Hawk accompanying us into the woods. God, what am I thinking? Using my own children as bait. Even with Bubba and me right there, can something go wrong with our plan? Have we thought of everything?

Last time I tricked a city boy into the woods, events took a turn nobody had envisioned. This time, if plans go awry, my babies are at risk. Maybe we should just call off the whole camping trip. I'll phone Mother in the morning and sign the paper, put the money she's offered in the bank, and that will be the end of it.

Rufus's whine reminds me of what I'm supposed to be doing out here in the early morning calm. The floating dock rocks and sways as I step, Rufus pressing against my left leg, along the wood planks and back to the pier where the light from Jonesy's cigarette glows orange in the violet-gray of the predawn light. At the grassy field behind Saint Iggie's Mission, the warmth of the dog's body disappears from my leg and thigh. I can just make out Rufus's humped-up shape as he quickly goes about his business before returning in a lumbering gait to press, once again, against my side.

"Whataya think boy? Shall we set the trap or wait for the bastard to find us at the time and place of his choosing?" I bend and whisper in the dog's ear.

The dog growls deep in his throat, makes a sound like a mountain-shaking earthquake.

"Jonesy? You're worryin' the dog, man. Back off before he trots over there to see just what you're doing following us."

Rufus, his back to my guard, stares across the littered field, intent on some unseen threat. I move casually toward the source of the dog's worry. Behind me, Jonesy's movement into position is revealed by the swish, swish of his long legs through the thigh-high grass off to our left. A shriek and a dash for freedom incites Rufus to break into his rendition of a trot.

The dog returns from out of the dark at a swagger, head up, fanning tail sweeping the tops of the grass stalks. The cat was three blocks up Second Street before the dog had cleared the field. I stand in the dark, Jonesy's chuckle a peculiar hymn behind me.

"Ah, yeah. Good boy! You saved me from the big, bad old cat. Good dog."

The short, ordinary incident is a balm somehow, a tiny slice of everyday life that reminds me that soon this entire mess will be over, gives me confidence that Bubba and me and the girls will survive to once again be a normal, happy family. Okay, happy—normal is stretching the truth a bit.

Back at the house, I step over Oscar and John, unlock the deadbolt Bubba installed yesterday afternoon. It takes a few minutes to go room to room downstairs, belly pack unzipped, hand on the butt of the .38. God, if this doesn't end soon I'm going to be as crazy paranoid as Jonesy out there. One flight up I check the girls' room. Nothing but empty beds and messy closets.

I open my bedroom door cautiously, check to make sure the damn talking nightlight has been unplugged, remove my sweatshirt and boots, and step out of my jeans. My bra unhooked, right hand snaked up the short sleeve of my t-shirt, the second strap already hanging loose, I pull the second strap free and remove the bra from under my shirt.

"I always enjoy that magic trick." Bubba's propped up on his elbow in his holly berry-red Christmas pajamas, the girls tucked beside him on our bed. His grin is wicked, his voice throaty.

"Abracadabra." I slide in next to him, the sheets warm against my bare legs, slip my arm over his middle.

"You always was good at enchantment." He rolls toward me, wedges his arm under me, tucks my head under his chin.

"Ah, yeah, well. I hope our luck or enchantment, whatever you want to call it, I hope it holds." When I rise up slightly, peer over his thick chest,

Victoria and Dharma sleep face to face, each with one arm thrown over the waist of her twin. Physical mirror images, yet separate and different in so many other ways, one from the other.

My whisper is loud in the dark. "What do you think of Gloria's request to have Hawk tag along on the camping trip?"

"The man's entitled to be there. We gotta talk with him. Bring him up to speed."

"I suppose you're right." It would be so much easier to avoid Hawk altogether until my soul settles back into its rightful place in my center.

"Some tension t'ween you two lately?" His hand strokes my side. "Hawk and you."

How bad would it be, really, to lie? "I don't know what's going on with me."

"Mmmhmm. Seems right obvious to me. You and Hawk were near inseparable when you were kids. Right up until you and I got together."

Right up until I got pregnant and Hawk walked, no ran, in the other direction and I finally saw both men clearly.

"So? That was a long time ago."

"'Cept the heart don't always tell the same time as the head."

"What are you saying? That you and I have been together over four years, you're the best thing that's ever happened to me, and yet deep down, in some hidden crevasse of my past, I still love the man?" Fuck. Anger destroys what little delay exists between my brain and my mouth.

"I'm sayin' you feel like a frightened child. Because of your mom showing up here. Some idjit threatening our girls. And the last time you truly was a scared little girl, Hawk, not me, was your companion and your good friend."

I have one quick second to envision a messy tangle of multicolored yarn, a shiny pair of shears snipping the exact right thread, the perfect cut to free the knots and twists, the bits and pieces scattering into the wind. My throat closes, sobs rise from my belly unrestrained. I cling to my husband, empty myself onto his deep chest.

Rain taps a benediction at the window. Thunder, like a housewife shaking a heavy quilt, rolls in slow ripples far out over the dark Pacific. Bubba slips from his place beside me, teases my mouth with his warm lips, moves over me on his way downstairs. I scrunch over next to our girls, breathe deep of their peachy, yeasty innocence, beg a blessing from God and Jesus and every saint remembered from catechism.

The smell of Cherry Garcia precedes Bubba's return to the bedroom. He hands me a bowl and I scooch over against the girls, prop the pillows up behind us.

"This here ain't maybe the best comfort I can generally offer. But tonight." He nods his chin toward the sleeping twins. "It'll have to do."

"Ah, yeah. A far distant second." I kiss his cheek, snuggle back into his shoulder.

"You see me talking to the PI tonight?" He plucks a whole maraschino from his bowl, drops it into my waiting mouth.

I chew happily, swallow. "Stanton? What did he have to say?"

"Your mother took the bait. She's all set to come with us on this great trek into the woods."

"I've got a bad feeling about all this." My raised voice invades Dharma's sleep. She flings her arm sideways, connects with her sister's cheek. Victoria startles, rolls away, presses herself against my leg.

"Do you feel it too?" I whisper once the girls settle back into dreams. "A sort of shimming, silver veil rubbing against itself, sending shivers up your spine?"

"I don't feel nothin' but the desire to put this behind us. Your mom going with us makes sense. We can keep an eye on her better if she's with us than if we leave her back in Eureka to stir up whatever trouble she can come up with while we're gone."

"Maybe. But, I don't see her as a hiker. A broken fingernail is liable to disrupt the entire trip. More important, can we control her? What if she interferes with our plans?"

"The girls won't ever be more than two feet from us." He kisses my cheek. I leave the sticky ice cream imprint right where it is. "If she helps lead ole Tommy Joe right to us? So much the better."

"Maybe. But this whole trip feels like it's spinning out of our control. And we haven't stepped in the woods yet. I think I should just sign the damn papers. It's only money. Not worth risking the girls over."

"Problem is, that little ole piece of paper is worthless and your mama knows it. And your buddy the DA says about all he can do is pick this Tommy Joe bastard up and hold him twenty-four hours. Then he's back on the street."

He turns into me, traces my cheek with his thumb.

"Both he and your mother know that little signature won't hold up in any court in the country. No, sooner or later we're gonna have to face this head on and if I'm gonna protect my lambs against a wolf, I'd much rather his foot was already in my trap when we faced off."

twenty-four

"YOU SURE YOU know what you're doing?" Dad asks.

He's stretched out in his plaid recliner, light from the pole lamp reflecting from the silver duct tape that holds the molting mess together.

I lean forward in the other recliner, turn away from him to stare out one of the narrow, fog-curtained windows. Three o'clock in the afternoon and visibility is as limited as it will be twelve hours from now. Dad hasn't smoked in six years and yet, here in his room, the smell of tobacco is a rich perfume of memory. Hard to be an adult when so much of me wants to return to the safety of my childhood.

"No," I tell him. "I got no natural idea if we're doing the right thing. But this Tommy Joe threatened my girls. No way I'm going to let that stand. The whole damn bunch of us. Me and Bubba with the girls. Hawk and Gloria. My ever-so-charming mother. We leave tomorrow at dawn-thirty and, for better or worse, the whole deal should be settled by the time we get back here on Wednesday."

In this light Dad's eyes are ebony dark, with deep grooves at the corners paler than the rest of his face. I'm reminded of the floor of an ancient sea bed. A desert now, dry and very nearly barren, a place that was once the birthplace of all life.

"To some folks, let's call them a jury of your peers, it might appear that you're deliberately luring this Tommy Joe into the woods. Away from witnesses. For an armed confrontation."

"Ah, yeah. Well, first of all, I'd hardly say we're going to be away from witnesses. The entire damn family is traipsing along with us. But I can see how a misguided individual might get the idea we're setting a trap. Except. I haven't told the muscle-bound son of a bitch that we're even leaving town, let alone that we'll be camping at Bluff Creek. Bubba certainly hasn't let our destination slip. Hawk would never reveal our travel plans. So, if the bastard follows us, how is that our fault? If a predator is never heard from again and some tiny patch of forest is just a little bit richer in organic content, I can't see how we'd be legally responsible."

From the other side of the bedroom door leaks the ebb and flow of the noisy welcome of a regular returning to VD's beery fold. Bubba's deep bass southern rhythms intersect with a high tenor voice that can only be Lefty's. Victoria and Dharma, set up with a sixty-four pack of crayons and a pad of scratch paper, are ensconced at a table in the far back corner of the bar. Or they were when I left them in Bubba's care. From the high-pitched squeals coming through the wall, my guess is they're now mobbing Uncle Lefty who is, no doubt, already regaling them with stories of the midget women of wrestling.

Dad pats the arm of his recliner. I move across three feet of braided rug to balance on the duct-taped arm of his chair, lean gently against his frail frame. He lays a scrawny arm against my middle, paints slow circles with his hand at the small of my back.

"You remember David and I served in Korea?" Lately his voice carries a deep, abiding tremolo.

"Yeah. Joined the Corps, went in on the buddy system."

His voice in the fog-darkened room, the smell of old smoke and Bay Rum, the feel of much-washed flannel against my palm. All of it. Time folds in on itself and I am a child loved beyond reason and with total acceptance. Safe. Home.

"Did you never wonder why all those dead animal heads out there in the bar, they're all old and mangy and fur-bare?" Inches from my ear, his voice is a throaty whisper.

"Where did those heads come from anyway? You and David don't hunt."

"We damn sure hunted before Korea. Every chance we got. Between the two of us we killed every one of those animals. But not once have we taken a life in the woods since we made it back home from that cold damn hellhole of a country over there in Asia. Killing a human being, even one who's doing his damndest to kill you and your friends. It changes a person. I don't want that burden on you, Samantha Jean."

The melody of voices from the other side of the door, the soft, gray aura of the room, the smells of childhood, Dad's arm around my waist—I want to sink into this cradle of comfort. Instead I kiss the top of his downy head, straighten my back.

"Ah, yeah, but Dad, if it comes to that, I believe I can live under that weight. What I would not survive is standing by and letting some madman hurt my babies. That would kill me."

We sit in silence, the noise filtering in from the bar like gentle waves lapping a sandy beach. Dad's breath slows, becomes more and more shallow. I don't move until a quick glance confirms he's fallen asleep. Then I slip his arm away from where it's draped along my back, pull the twelve-patch quilt off his bed and tuck it around him, ease out into the bar.

"Mommy, look!" Victoria wraps herself around my right leg like a monkey on a denim palm tree. Dharma attaches herself to the other leg. I'd tell them to get off but lately this is about the only exercise I get. One shuffling step at a time, I drag them with me to the back table.

"See. Mine's Honey Girl Paige. Victoria got Princess Little Dove."

Dolls. Like Barbies. Only different. Instead of tiny designer dresses and pointy toed shoes, these have capes and wrestling suits. Well, really. Their parents own a bar. Their grandmother is a world class bitch and their mother is the Bigfoot Whisperer. Could wrestler dolls really do that much more damage to their little psyches?

The pocket of my jeans shimmies with the vibration of my cell phone. The girls, still attached, push their dolls at each other, make, for reasons unknown to me, growling, grunting noises.

The caller ID quickens my pulse just a little.

"Bobby." I press the cell tight to my ear.

"Where are you? Are those miniature badgers I hear?"

"Ah, yeah. Pretty much. What's up?"

"Listen. Sam. I, uh, talked to a buddy of mine in the San Francisco DA's office."

"Hang on just a second." Bubba peels the girls off my legs and I take the stairs two at a time. "Okay. Thanks for holding on." The stale, wet, moldy air of my childhood bedroom chills me.

"How are the twins holding up?"

"Loving the vacation from school, and eating up all the attention. Lefty's trying to induct them into the Midget Wrestler's union."

My old friend's laughter calls up an image of Bobby in a striped t-shirt sitting beside me at Alice Birney Elementary School. Even then he was a troublemaker who could talk and charm his way out of any situation. In times of stress, I seem to cling to the most mundane of images.

His laughter dies and an ominous premonition raises a shiver of goose bumps along my arms.

"Your sister's right. The police think Tommy Joe may have been involved in your dad's death. Your... biological dad. They can't prove it. Yet. But it looks like this scumbag might be a more serious threat than we first thought."

Than you first thought, maybe. He's been a walking dead man since the instant I heard his voice on that cell phone recording, threatening my girls.

"I don't know what to tell you. We're taking every precaution we can. Pulled the girls out of school. They're never out of our sight. We're even thinking of getting out of town for a while. Leaving the bar with Dad and David and taking off."

All through my childhood, this room, with its view of the bay, was my sanctuary. Today, the unused, abandoned feel of it gives me the willies.

"Ah, huh," Bobby says. "See now, that's the rumor I'm somewhat worried about. It does not sound like you or Bubba to run from a threat."

"I can't help what it sounds like, Bobby. As I understand it, all you and the law can do for us is to pick Lyons up and try and scare him. Which is going to accomplish exactly nothing. Except to tip him off that we're on to him."

I force cold air into my lungs. Breathe from the belly. Wait until my vision widens, the world seeps back into view.

"We've got the girls to protect. My mother and sister, even Hawk, are going with us. Nice peaceful trip. Hopefully things will calm down by the time we get back."

The bay is choppy, lead-gray water tipped with mottled white. I can't see it through the swirls of silver fog, but somewhere out there is the horizon line.

The DA's breath comes clearly through the cell. I wait.

"The last time you disappeared into the woods with an agenda, as I recall, your buddy Bigfoot showed up and things did not go as planned."

"What are you saying, Bobby? You think Bigfoot is my trained companion? We're getting out of town for a few days. Nothing more."

"Ah, huh. How many Bigfoot sightings have there been up there? At Bluff Creek."

"I have no idea."

"The hell you say. How many sightings, Samantha? Just over the last, oh say, ten years."

A halo of light makes a path through the pearly fog of the bay. 3:47 on a weekday afternoon. I don't need to see the boat to know the *Madeket* is making its way back from Samoa, the tiny island at the entrance to Humboldt Bay, ferrying tourists who've shelled out hard cash for a fog-dampened tour.

"Sixty-four sightings. In a twenty-mile radius with Bluff Creek as the center of the circle." How did I get to this? Standing in my old bedroom, my babies downstairs under guard, talking in code to the local law about a plan to kill another human being?

"How many when you discard the incidents that involve drugs, alcohol, or known liars?"

"Thirteen."

His laughter does not sooth me this time. Not for a moment.

"Well, whatever happens, Sam? Take care to clean up after yourself. Don't leave garbage lying around the woods for a goddamn hiker or some freaking boy scout to discover."

twenty-five

DAWN IS AN orange glow in a flat, cloudless sky, the bay's calm gray-blue surface broken only by the sleek brown head of a harbor seal. The animal rolls, disappears into the depths. The ripples it creates quickly surrender to the emptiness, leave no visible trace of its existence. On the floating pier, Rufus's heft is a solid warmth against my left leg. I'm beginning to think I may end up with that leg permanently curved inward. Persistent, steady pressure mutating bone and muscle.

I need to get back to the house. The vehicles are packed. A simple drive along isolated roads, a quick turn at the nearly hidden entrance to an old logging site, and we'll set up our tents, drag the coolers into the shade, hunker down, and see what fate brings our way.

Gloria, my beautiful twin, confided last night over a Downtown Brown that she's never been camping unless a picnic in Golden Gate Park counts. I served her a second dark local beer and assured her that deli sandwiches enjoyed anyplace within walking distance of concrete did not count as camping. No matter how beautiful the park might be.

Even with everything going on—luring Tommy Joe Lyons into the woods, setting a trap for a predator that had the stupidity to threaten my babies—even now, the promise of spending time with my sister puts a small smile on my face. And this worries me, for the precise reason I did not want her on this camping—

Ah, hell, who am I kidding? On this *hunting* trip.

Distraction is the enemy.

The *Prowler* pulls out of her slip in the marina across the bay. The air so quiet this morning I can hear the voice of the drag boat's owner, Pete Crowley, talking to the young boat puller as they motor out of port. Fishing's been bad this year. Hell, fishing's been bad for two decades. Maybe today's calm will bring enough fish into the hold to pay off Pete's bar tab. Maybe pigs will sprout wings and shit gold down on my head.

My mood's not great. We are carrying far too many distractions with us into the woods. I am the most worried about Dear Ole Mom. The woman is about as trustworthy as a rattlesnake. Less so actually, since at least a rattler will shake that tail tip, warn you some before she sinks those hollow fangs into you. I suspect my mother will talk around a mouthful of my flesh, protest that she has only love in her heart and good intentions even as she's pumping poison into my bloodstream. Still, Bubba has a point. Keep your friends close and your enemies closer.

Could be I'm making her out to be worse than she is. Maybe she's telling the truth and her muscle-bound boyfriend really is acting on his own to try and force me to sign away my inheritance by threatening my girls. Being around my mother creates a thick, twisted length of scratchy hemp in my belly, the rope pulled in a tug-of-war between my furious anger and my primal need for her love or, at least, her approval.

Another dangerous distraction on a critical mission.

The seal has resurfaced on the waters of the bay. His dark eyes stare up at us from less than six feet away. The dog and I stand on the shifting wood planks of the floating pier and look into the face of an animal that lives in an entirely different dimension from ours. Rufus's body tenses along my leg. But he isn't going anywhere. The big dog hates water. As long as the seal stays in his own world, he's got nothing to fear from ole Rufus.

Bubba and I played the cell phone recording for Hawk late last night.

Be a real shame if something unfortunate happened to one of your little girls. I'm real partial to Dharma myself. Can't help myself, I like 'em soft and sweet. There's folks out there who'd prefer the little spunky one though. Victoria. Hell, couple of twins, cute as coon dog pups. My man, you need to keep a real close eye on those little girls. There's some baaad people out in the world.

Hawk is the wild card in this venture. In all the time I've known him, and the two of us shared a cradle, he has never displayed a moment's anger. Until last night. His eyes, as he listened to that recording, transformed from those of a spiritual shaman to the hard, flat windows into the dead soul of a bloodthirsty warrior. Which might be a real asset, except for one detail.

Gloria's going to be on this trip and Hawk has been led around by his penis since he was a toddler. Seriously. Hawk is eight months older than me, but Dad and David potty trained us on the same summer backpacking trip. There are a dozen pictures of the two of us exploring the shallows of Redwood Creek, streaking through the redwoods and rhododendron, nothing on but tennis shoes and little t-shirts, naked from the waist down. In at least half of those old Polaroids, Hawk has a hand on his little erect penis, leading himself from one adventure to another, with me close behind. A clear omen of what followed for the next twenty-six years of our lives.

I turn my back on the preternatural quiet of the mercurial, flat bay. It takes a moment for the giant dog to execute the turn. Three steps closer to home, Rufus's weight is again warm against my leg. At the corner of A and Second, two heavily laden vehicles come into view, both parked at the curb of my front door. Bubba's king cab Ram 4x4 pours a fat tube of exhaust into the morning air. Hawk's borrowed a Suburban from somewhere. A black passenger door stands open. As I watch, Victoria climbs into the backseat of the Chevy SUV.

"Hey!" I yell, already trotting toward my house. "She's riding with us!"

Victoria stops, turns toward me. Even from here I can see her little jaw set in a hard line that, if I had a mirror, would look nearly exactly like my own.

"Your mom wants to visit with Victoria on the ride up," Hawk explains when I arrive, reach inside, and scoop my daughter's rigid body against my own.

"No. Gloria and my mother ride with you. The girls, both girls, ride in the truck with Bubba and me."

Hawk walks around from the street side of the Suburban. Puts his face nearly against mine. I don't have to turn to know that Bubba, Dharma on his shoulders, has my back, he and the dog flanking me.

"You don't trust me to protect my own daughter?" Hawk's voice is a low growl.

There are moments in life when truth is revealed like the sun suddenly breaking from behind a cloud, a beam of brilliant light illuminating some hidden treasure among the smooth stones of a slow moving creek.

"Until this is settled, the girls stay with Bubba and me."

The words hang in the still air. I'm convinced all three of us—me, Hawk, and my beautiful husband—each one of us hears the real truth behind these simple words. In this time of danger, my old attraction for Hawk is vanquished. I choose Bubba. For now and for always. I can almost hear a million little metal shards of childish need clinking to the gray sidewalk around my feet.

"Oh, for goodness' sake." Mother sounds disapproving, possibly even disgusted with this display of maternal protectiveness.

For the first time since I rounded the corner and saw Victoria disappear into that big black SUV, my focus opens to encompass the others standing in the cold dawn of this rundown street. Two-hundred-year-old houses, a thin façade of respectability painted and tacked onto their exteriors. Homeless hunkered under porch roofs or snuggled up to the vent in the alley behind the Mission Laundry. Dad and David, still in the worn sweats they slept in, their faces sleep-pressed, eyes worried, here to say good-bye before I lead posse, spectators, and outlaw into the heart of the ancient forest.

twenty-six

BUBBA BUILT THE fire. Which is why we sit in a wide circle, our faces licked by the warmth of blue-rimmed devil tongues reaching for the pale crescent moon. Hawk, still pouting about my insistence that the girls stay with Bubba and me on the ride up the mountain, refused to carry so much as a piece of kindling for the bonfire. He sticks to Gloria like… well, like a horn dog hot on the trail of his latest prize.

Someone who didn't know him well might even miss the way his dark eyes scan the perimeter, the fact that he instinctively took up a position at this white-man fire to back up Bubba and me. Each of us watch a portion of the woods, protect each other's backs. Close ranks against a predator who dared to reach for our girls.

"How can you be the proprietor of a bar and not have brought alcohol?" Mother fidgets in the blue canvas chair Hawk set up for her. She slaps at one of the biting flies buzzing lazy circles in the bonfire-warmed air around our heads. "And who invites somebody on a camping trip and then doesn't supply some sort of lotion to protect their delicate skin against these insidious insects?"

Dharma's silky hair is soft under my chin. The two of us sit flat on a scratchy army blanket folded into quarters. I lean back against the warm bulk of Rufus, my daughter's body cupped by my folded knees, her small back pressed along my belly and breasts.

"Far as I know, you invited yourself," I tell Mother.

Victoria, cuddled on Bubba's lap, the two of them stretched across a length of downed maple, sticks out her tongue at her sister before asking Mother, "If you really is my grandma, where were you all this time? Why was you hiding from us?"

"Ah, yeah. Mother Dear." A small ornery smile curves the edges of my mouth. "That's a great topic for discussion around a campfire on a dark and quiet night. Why were you hiding from us?"

It's not an attractive inclination on my part. Nonetheless, I've had this happen before. Once wrapped snuggly in the forest, cradled in deep woods and the cycle of life—I lose whatever censor I have on my emotions. Three years ago, on our first hiking trip since the twins were born, Bubba and I caused an avalanche with our lovemaking. A smallish tumble of granite boulders. Nothing more. But unfortunately, the rock pile came close to blocking the mouth of the cave where we bounced off rock walls and howled into the night.

Six years ago, in the midst of a monster storm, on the way to that same cave, I nearly killed a writer who had slandered my dad. Walked him up one muddy mountain and down another until the man came close to succumbing to hypothermia and exhaustion.

I get real on this mountain.

Since arriving a few hours ago, my maternal protectiveness has swollen to Shiva proportions. Back in town, standing on the pier gazing into the dark round eyes of that harbor seal, I knew I'd do what I had to do to keep my girls safe. But I was uneasy, guilt-ridden, or something close to that affliction, by the idea of luring a human predator into the woods and killing him. Now? With wood smoke in my lungs and primeval forest as comforting as a warm quilt? Now I'm praying for the opportunity to kill the son of a bitch who threatened my babies.

And as for my lying bitch of a mother. Well, that tug of war between desire for her love and anger at her abandonment has been won. Childish need dropped her end of the robe and ran screaming into the woods. The twin named Anger is now clearly in command.

Bubba's voice soothes me some, like earth tossed on a new blaze.

"Maybe," my husband whispers sotto voice into Victoria's ear. "Mama might could tell us how, last time she was in these here woods, she ran smack dab into Bigfoot."

"We already know that story, Daddy." Victoria slides from Bubba's lap, but does not escape the circle of his arms.

Sitting there next to Hawk, Gloria smiles across the campfire, directly into my eyes.

"I know your book told about that encounter, but I'm not good with topography maps. How far from here did all that happen?"

Mother rolls her eyes so far back in her head I have a moment of glee, thinking she's having some sort of bitch seizure.

"Really?" I ask when her eyes roll back into view like cherries in a slot machine. "You'd rather tell your story?"

Neither Mother, nor I, blink. We glare at each other, flames with cores as red as rage heat the air between us. And still, we stare.

"Well, for goodness' sake." Mother drops her eyes. "Hawk, dear, surely you brought something for us to drink."

There's an idea. Solicit booze from the recovering alcoholic among us.

Hawk leaves the circle to fetch and carry a soda for the woman with the downcast eyes. My grin is malicious. I know this. Am proud of it.

"On a topography map," I say, "we'd be gathered at the lower left corner of a lopsided chunk of reservation and forest service land known as The Bluff Creek/Blue Mountain Hexagon."

"That's where it all happened!" Gloria squeals. "The bloody handprint. The meadow you wrote about. Right here?"

"Ah, yeah." I confirm. "This is where Bubba, Hawk, and Lefty were held captive in that very Ram four-by-four parked over there. The three of them couldn't make it the quarter mile through the woods to me and Mark, the guy writing a book about Bigfoot. The writer and I were holed up in a cave above Bluff Creek."

"Stupid Head Mark told bad lies about our grandpas," Dharma announces.

"The Big Poopy Face said our grandpas killed some Bigfoots a long, long time ago," Victoria chimes in. "And 'cause of that, a real looney tick, not the kind like the kids at school call my mama, but a real for true looney tick, he shot Grandpa Victor. Right, Mama?"

"That's right, honey. But you're getting ahead of the story." I do my best not to cringe at the lunatic reference to myself, pray Bubba's correct and the girls are growing up strong and sure instead of twisted beyond the scope of normal.

"If I recall the tale correctly," Mother says. "You, Samantha, your rough-edged husband, and even the charming Hawk, all three of you were involved in an elaborate hoax that backfired."

"Did you just call my husband rough-edged?"

Dharma twists around on my lap, wraps her arms around my neck. Her breath smells like cherry lifesavers. "Don't be mad, Mommy. Victoria, and me, and Daddy will protect you."

Someday I'm going to get my mother alone and tell her exactly what I think of her. Someday. But not tonight. Not with my girls here. And not with Tommy Joe Lyons out there someplace, possibly eavesdropping on our every word.

"Nothing wrong with being angry," I tell Dharma.

Victoria eases her way around the edge of the fire and pushes into my lap. I swallow the moment whole, like a magical draught. I drink in the feel of both my daughters pressed against my breasts. The alchemy of the moment—wood smoke, no-more-tears shampoo, and a shaman's blend of cherry and butterscotch lifesavers—sweeps me into a sense of wholeness.

Moments later, like the shock of an unexpected, full-eclipse of the sun, I am stunned by a foreboding of loss so deep my breath catches, my heart pauses, another reality falls upon me, wipes away my world. For just a moment, or maybe for all time, I fall into a deep black hole in the earth. Sometime later my eyes focus on the face of my husband across the licking flames of the fire between us.

"Samantha?" Bubba's voice comes to me—summer sunlight at the entrance to a cave where I've wandered lost, given up all hope of finding my way home. "Come on now, darlin'. Tell the story 'bout how you met those Bigfoots."

I blink my eyes. Breathe deep of smoke and the artificial flavoring of hard candy. Rufus shifts behind me, lifts his head from the blanket, and applies his wet tongue to the side of my face.

"What on earth is wrong with her?" Mother's voice asks. "Is she having some kind of Bigfoot seizure or what?"

Huh. Well. That's as good an explanation as I've ever come up with. Maybe that is what happens to me from time to time. Since the encounter with a family of Bigfoots in these woods, I've thought of my occasional premonitions as a blessing something like an early warning system, but a Bigfoot seizure is as good a way to explain the phenomena as any.

My arms tight around my girls, fully returned to this world, I smile through the leaping blue flames and into the eyes of my twin.

"All right," I say. "Here's the tale in a nutshell. Mark Neilsen was writing a book about Bigfoot. He interviewed a lot of locals and seemed like a nice enough guy. Then Bubba found a blog where Mark claimed that Dad and David had killed a family of Bigfoots during the taping of the Patterson film."

Hawk adds his sidebar. "You forgot to mention the part about how you fell all over yourself helping this handsome writer," he says looking directly into my eyes. "Might say you bent over backwards doing your best to satisfy him."

The vehemence in Hawk's voice shocks me. This all happened a long time ago. A long, long time ago. And wouldn't have happened at all if he hadn't fallen off the wagon and, in a drunken attack of sexual idiocy, fucked some sweet young thing directly under my nose. He's right. I turned to Mark out of anger at him, but, Holy Christ, that was six years ago. Time to move on, ole Buddy.

My mouth is open to ask Hawk if he really wants to talk about who bent who over backwards when Bubba's voice cuts through the smoky night air.

"Was my idea to play the trick on the writer," my husband confesses. "Seemed like a right fine idea at the time. See, Lefty had just started dating Caroline and she had this here dog near 'bout big as Bigfoot."

"Rufus!" Victoria calls out from my lap.

"Ah, yeah," I confirm. "Rufus. Our plan was for me to take Mark around the long way to a cave about a mile from here, telling Bigfoot stories the entire way. Bubba and Lefty and the dog would drive in here, meander over, and prepare the cave by planting a turkey carcass in a crevasse and making sure Rufus knew that dead bird, his favorite food on the face of the earth, was there."

"Rufus loves turkey!" Dharma sings. The dog, hearing his name so many times, lifts his weight to a sit, peaks over the top of my head, and then rests his heavy head on my shoulder as though balefully studying the motley assortment of folks around the campfire.

"The plan," I say, "was for the guys, Bubba, Lefty, and Hawk, to plant the carcass, then wait for me to get the writer settled in the cave. Once it was dark they'd stroll the short distance through the woods, throw a stink bomb into the mouth of the cave, and release the dog, who'd charge straight for the carcass planted directly behind Mark's head."

I leave out the part about feeding Mark a marijuana-laced brownie to sort of get him in the mood for the prank. I did fess up to this trick in the book, but right now, with the girls right here, it's a little detail my sister and mother will have to do without.

"Except that's not what transpired, is it?" Gloria's blue eyes are wide, her blonde hair a nimbus around her beautiful face. How can she look that damn good on a camping trip in the middle of the woods?

"Mommy fell." Dharma is holding her sister's hand, the two of them still as sun-warmed statues on my lap.

"I did fall, yes, and hit my head. A family of Bigfoots carried me through the night and laid me gently in a bed of five-fingered ferns."

"Oh Lord, Samantha." Mother can't keep her mouth shut. Huh. Maybe I did inherit something from her after all. "You have no idea what happened once you fell and hit your head. This entire hoax, book and all, is just the result of growing up in that horrible bar with Victor and his insane Bigfoot stories."

"Mother." My teeth are clenched so tight I feel like a ventriloquist. "That bar is my inheritance. A gift from the only parent I've ever known. A man who loves me beyond reason. A man I adore. Did I ever tell you about what I used to do to the kids in high school who were stupid enough to talk bad about Dad in my hearing?"

In my lap, the girls are suddenly alert. The tightness of their little bodies reminds me of Rufus the instant between the time he sees a cat and the moment he releases that energy in pursuit of the fleeing creature.

"Now, darlin'." Bubba's voice is honey warm, laughter laced at the edges. "Might be good to hold on to that story for another time."

Somewhere outside our circle of light a vigilant owl screeches an eerie triumph into the night. I lift my head instinctively, nose held high like any well-equipped mammal, sniff the air for hints of the doings of the dark world all around me. For the briefest of instants I lean into a whiff of the overpowering sweetness of warm decay. Next inhale, the smell is lost, like the details of a dream upon waking.

"You're right," I concede to my husband. "Another time perhaps, Mother, we'll discuss the dangers of bad-mouthing Dad in my hearing."

"Back to the Bigfoot story!" Victoria and Dharma bounce like pinballs against my chest. Joy sweeps through me, flows into contentment, banishes all but this moment. My babies safe in my arms, Bubba watching me from across a dancing campfire, forest wrapped around me like a cloak. A still small voice whispers in my ear. Whatever comes, you have this gift. Outside of time. Forever.

I wrap my arms tighter around the girls, breathe in the indefinable smell of happy children already dusted with a fine film of the dirt of the woods. "Let's back up in the story just a little. Before I fell, I was flashing my flashlight into the night looking for Bubba."

"And Daddy Hawk and Uncle Lefty!" The girls push happily against me. Having had an encounter or two with the top of a little girl's hard skull against my chin, I keep one hand on the top of each head. A bloodied tongue isn't the end of the world, but it's an experience I don't care to duplicate tonight.

"Yep. Lefty were supposed to be there too, I didn't know Daddy Hawk was with them."

"But they was having they own adventure. Tell that part Daddy," Victoria intones solemnly. Maybe I should just let the girls tell this story. They know it as well as any Bigfoot tale Dad ever told me around a campfire.

"The way I recall...." Bubba's bass overlays Hawk's tenor saying, "The situation was interesting in that...."

This awkward confusion is cleared quickly by Victoria who innocently clarifies, "No, Daddy Hawk. Our real daddy tells this part."

The pain on Hawk's face stabs me with a jolt of sympathy. But, really, what does he expect? Call it karma, call it consequences. Whatever label you stick on the outcome, when you walk away from children, refuse to meet your day-to-day responsibilities to them, when another man steps up and claims your babies, loves them unstintingly as his own, well, you forfeit your right to be the real parent.

Bubba clears his throat. He and Hawk have been friends a long time. From the look of his downcast eyes, the way he's shifted his body slightly more toward Hawk, my husband isn't enjoying this moment.

"Me and Daddy Hawk and Uncle Lefty, we was all held prisoner right here," Bubba says. "It was right peculiar. We never saw nothing of the creatures but their eyes. But, Lord, did we hear them and smell them. We knew there was more than one because once they'd herded us into the cab of my truck, it was right clear that the growls and bellows came from at least two directions. Plus, they rocked the truck like it was a matchbox car and we could see them eyes. Lord those eyes. Made me shiver way down deep in my belly."

"Odd," Mother declares. "These giant creatures managed to chase you to your truck like school girls running from the class bully, but, once there, none of you actually saw your attackers. Seems almost like maybe you were, I don't know, dreaming or, perhaps, making the whole thing up as an excuse for why you sat over here and drank a few too many beers instead of sticking to your part of the big hoax."

Hawk looks like he'd snatch back the warm soda he fetched earlier for Her Ladyship if the can wasn't already empty lying on its side in the dirt at her feet.

"Those privileged to be visited by spirits from another dimension have been ridiculed since the coming of the white man," he says in his best professorial voice.

Mother rolls her eyes. Someone ought to tell her that little gesture overrides every bit of Tommy Choo, Wang, and Niemen's from her façade. Like a dollar store raincoat thrown over a designer outfit, that eye roll is a big *R for redneck* stamped on her Botoxed forehead, exposing her roots for all the world to see. She may have married up, but that don't change who she is in the center of her little black heart.

Hawk ignores the eye roll, misses the wide grin on my own face.

"People have a variety of reactions to these visits," he says. "Some seem to fall into a sort of fugue or dream state and wake with a feeling of having been changed, with only patchy memories of the actual experience. Others appear to black out and, once the encounter ends, through denial or some more instinctual and primitive response, they truly do not remember anything of what has happened. These are the individuals who often come up with the most outlandish and peculiar stories to explain the footprints, tipped concrete pipes, and even the photos of these visitors from another world that show up in the aftermath of the encounter."

The fire has died down, a deep orange bed of coals the result of the earlier leaping blue flames, the coals burn hotter and throw more heat. Hawk looks through the waves of the ebbing flames, directly into my eyes.

"Then there are the few, the chosen, who seem able see these creatures clearly. Who emerge changed and with distinct, life changing memories of the encounter. Those for whom the details often come back slowly, as though these shamans or carriers of the spirit, must prove first their trustworthiness, before being fully gifted with the knowledge of the visitors."

"I haven't heard this much nonsense since I fled Victor's bar thirty years ago." Mother rises from her canvas chair, brushes the seat of her pants. "Time for bed. Gloria, shall we turn in?"

"I'm visiting with Samantha," my twin says evenly. "You go ahead, Mom. Hawk set up the tent for us and our sleeping bags are all laid out. I'll be there later."

Mother squints into the inky dark in the direction of the tents.

"Well." She settles prissily back into the low-slung canvas chair. "Perhaps I'll wait just a bit longer before retiring for the night."

"Come on!" Victoria demands. "Tell what happened with the Bigfoots."

"Okay," I say. "Your dad... Bubba, and Hawk, and Uncle Lefty were trapped in the cab of the truck. Right here at this campsite. But of course, I didn't know that. I left Mark in the cave and went out into a storm to signal them to call off the hoax because the writer who slandered your grandpas, he was in bad shape from the hike to the cave."

"Wait, please." Gloria scoots her chair closer to the fire. "Isn't the cave just over that hill? How did this Mark get so banged up?"

"Well. See, I didn't bring him to the cave from here. Instead I walked him over two mountains and down a bear trail."

Gloria raises her eyebrows.

"My plan was to soften him up. So, by the time the guys released Rufus, Mark would be susceptible to the idea of a Bigfoot charging into the cave. Except we walked right into the first major storm of the year. The cold and the mud made the hike much more difficult than I intended. Plus, we all knew Mark had over-packed for the trip. I kept throwing things out of his pack, discarding pots and pans and these ridiculous pieces of technology along the way."

Dharma wiggles like a puppy against me. "But the Bigfoots gathered everything up. You'd throw it out of the pack and one of them would pick it up. Right Mama?"

A ragged wisp of cloud tears loose, exposes a narrow strip of black night studded with the reflected light of stars so far away they may already be dead, their light still racing toward the seven clawless creatures huddled around this campfire.

"Well now," I say. "We're getting ahead of ourselves with the story again. When Mark and I made it to shelter...." I nod to the left. In my mind's eye, I see the dark mouth of the den, a vertical slit in the cliff face above Bluff Creek. Memory of the sweet smell of decay floods me with an ache of longing for the creatures whom, I've come to suspect, come and go at will through that opening in the face of the mountain.

"Once I got Mark inside and warmed a little, I went back out into the storm to signal the guys to call off the hoax. By then I was afraid we had gone too far already with the prank. Mark was in bad shape from the hike over the mountains and I'd just about convinced myself he hadn't deliberately set out to harm Dad or David, he was just a selfish wannabe famous man without much honor."

"Grandpa David says honor is the most important at-tree-boot a person can own," Dharma shouts. The sound of her voice seems to startle her with its volume. She shudders slightly, tips her head up at me, and whispers, "Mama? What kind of shoe exactly is a at-tree-boot?"

"This is the kind of confusion that results when people insist on speaking to children as though they are adults." Mother's chin is high, her voice stiff, one might even describe it as judgmental, if one gave a flying crap about her opinion on child rearing.

Hawk arranges three chunks of wood on the orange embers of the fire, seems intent on forming a precise pattern only he can see.

Bubba grins across at me as the wood catches and blue flames dance between us. "The at-tree-boot of honor is like a steel-toed Wolverine work boot, darlin'," he tells Dharma. "'Cept you wear it inside, in your soul, and you don't even know it's there till you need it."

"Finish the story Mama." Victoria yawns, her head heavy on my breast. "Tell how you saw the family."

"That night," I say, "a storm roared through the woods. I couldn't find the guys. Bubba and Lefty and Hawk. But I did hear Rufus howling and I knew something was wrong. Then my flashlight beam picked up three sets of eyes in the night. Huge, wide-spaced eyes way too high above the forest floor to be human. And I was sort of enveloped in a smell like sweet rot. I was so startled I fell, hit my head, and didn't come to until the next morning when I woke on a carefully prepared bed of ferns just a few feet from the mouth of the cave where I'd left Mark the night before."

"You don't remember anything else about that night?" Gloria asks.

"That night came back to me in bits and pieces." I shift Dharma and Victoria's weight against my shoulders. Both breathe even and slow. They're not going to hear the ending of this story. "Eventually I remembered being carried through the woods by the female Bigfoot. Recovered a memory of her running her hands gently over me. That part came back in one clear flash a few days after it happened, while I was still in the hospital."

Mother shifts in her canvas chair, crosses and uncrosses her long legs, does another one of those eye rolls. My guess is the woman is unused to not being the center of attention for such an excruciatingly long time. All of these signs of boredom I pretend to ignore.

"I must have known, at some level, exactly what happened because one of the first things I did when I woke up on the fern bed was to lift my clothes and search for the handprint. I thought, at first, the brownish print was mud, but it turned out to be blood. And not just any blood either."

Off to my right, just beyond the circle of light from our flickering fire, the sound of a large animal stepping on a dry twig carries in the night air. Bubba, Hawk, and I stare at each other. Is this our moment of reverence before the trap is closed around prey? A few quiet, listening minutes later, Hawk shakes his head. Something is out there, but I have no sense of danger, no ripple of fear down my spine, no hair standing up on the back of my neck. No, if anything, I am reassured by a feeling of well-being. Just some common creature out there going about its ordinary business.

"Let's finish this story tomorrow," I tell Gloria. "The girls are already asleep and I think it's time for bed."

Besides by first light, we'll have a new story. Though, if all goes as planned, this one will be a secret tale the woods will keep forever.

twenty-seven

FLICKERING FLAMES FROM the campfire where Hawk and Rufus sit sentinel create chimeras of shadow and light on the inside of the nylon tent. I snuggle against Bubba and the girls in a cocoon made of two zipped-together, king-size sleeping bags. My legs stretch across the stocking feet of my daughters, my cold feet planted firmly between the warm denim covering Bubba's thighs. The tickling odor of mold-tinged air melds with wood smoke, the heavy mulch of the forest floor, and the unique smell of strawberry shampoo and little girl sweat that catches my heart, brings tears to my eyes.

"You think he'll come tonight?" My voice is low, pitched to carry over Dharma and Victoria nestled between Bubba and me and go no farther.

"We done set the trap, darlin'. Nothing for us to do now but wait."

His heavy arm is intertwined with mine. We pin the girls between warm layers of red plaid flannel, soft fleece, and the layered smell of hundreds of past camping trips into these woods. I am swept with a sense of contentment, a feeling of being in the right place at the right time, a surrender of events to the karmic powers of the universe. Or, possibly, I simply love my husband and daughters and sleeping in these woods, with these exact smells, triggers a memory of simpler times when Dad and this forest were my sanctuary.

"Tonight," I whisper, "talking about what all happened five years ago, when I hadn't even realized yet I was pregnant with the girls?"

"I knew." Bubba is a dark, solid form on the other side of the twins. He speaks the truth. The youngest in a family of six sisters, he recognized the signs of my pregnancy while I was still blaming my nausea and fatigue on the flu or the stress of walking away from the cheating Hawk.

"Ah, yeah. Well. Sitting around the campfire tonight I just had the oddest feeling that this whole thing with Tommy Joe Lyons? Not his part in it so much, but our decision to set the trap for him here. In this forest. It feels like it's all, I don't know, ordained or something. Set in motion by what happened six years ago. My encounter with the family of Bigfoots. The way the female marked my belly with her lifeblood, like a blessing on the unborn Dharma and Victoria."

He untwines his arm from mine, lifts my hand to his mouth, kisses the sensitive palm before laying it against his scratchy cheek.

"I failed you once before." His voice is barely there, a mere phantom of his thoughts. "Always thought I'd walk through fire, take on anything to protect you. And that night I let those creatures keep me in the truck cab while you were on the other side of the mountain. Hurt. And alone."

"I wasn't alone. The Bigfoot family was right there with me. The female carried me through the woods like a child. I wasn't even hardly wet when I came to the next morning and, honey, it had rained all night long. They, or she, protected me somehow from the elements. I don't believe they left me in that bed of ferns until moments before I woke up."

Dharma swings her arm in one of those roundhouse punches of hers. I trap her hand moments before it connects with her sister's nose, pull her warm body tighter against mine.

"Still." Bubba's voice like a penitent in the dark of a confessional. "I wasn't there when you needed me. Won't happen again, I don't care if I have to fight my way through an army of the hairy, big-assed creatures."

"Honey," I whisper, "it's Mother's boyfriend that's the enemy here. Not Bigfoot. Remember that."

"Ah-huh. Still and all. I'm explaining to you that I'm packing the Glock 17 and my grandpa's Colt .45. The M1 Garand my momma's daddy smuggled back from the Pacific in Dubya Dubya Two is right here.

Something, anything, gets in the way of me protecting you or the girls? I ain't gonna worry 'bout who or what gets hurt."

His cheek is like coarse sandpaper under my palm. A hunk of wood slips on the fire outside, dancing shadows flicker as flames reach momentarily for the sky. Banned from the tent, Rufus whines softly into the night, his footfalls moving from the warmth of the fire to just outside the tent flap.

"I have the third watch," I remind my husband. "Wake me at three."

IN MY DREAM I'm being carried through an ancient forest. A forest I almost recognize. The sweet smell of rot, of death and rebirth, heavy and rich, floods my senses. The breasts of the creature in whose arms I'm cradled jounce at each stride. We've almost reached our destination. Almost there.

A howl of terror and rage startles me upright. My sleep-drenched mind registers a large shadow on the nylon dome. Something big passes between the campfire and our tent. A second banshee song of fear and confusion banishes the dream and brings me smack dab into the middle of now.

No! No! Rufus.

Disoriented, still fighting my way up from the dream. Adrenaline and fear flood me with power.

Desperate to aim that weapon in the correct direction. Confused in the dark. My hands find my unzipped belly pack under the pillow, the .38 not one bit reassuring.

The sound of the zipper of the tent flap opening. Bubba's width blocks my view of the night.

"Move, goddamnit." Bubba struggles around Rufus, who's backed tight against the tent.

The dog's huge, shaggy head is thrown back. Wide open mouth aimed at the starless sky. A sound like the end of the world pleading into the night.

I see a slice of dying campfire through the sideways U-shape of the open tent. Nothing else. Blackness speckled with orange sparks, like blood splatter behind a suicide.

Hawk was on guard duty. Where the hell is he?

I'm on my feet. Rufus an immovable object at the tent's opening. Bubba nowhere to be seen. My right leg tangles in the nylon flap as I squeeze my way around the howling dog.

From the pitchy black on the other side of camp, Gloria's voice screams in panic.

"Mom? Mom!"

Hawk's tenor comes from the same spot in the night.

"Hush now. We'll find her."

My hand on Rufus's head, the dog roils down from his fever of pitched cries, whimpers pitifully at my side.

I can't see a damn thing. The remains of the fire we gathered around for warmth and comfort a few hours ago now draws my eye, robs me of my night vision.

"Samantha!" Mother's frightened voice off to my right somewhere. "Please! Help me!"

I take a step toward the voice. Squint into the night.

"Stay," I tell the dog whose cries escalate at each step I take away from the tent.

"Samantha? Darlin'?" Bubba. Somewhere to my left.

Something heavy hits soft unprotected parts of a body. Bubba's breath whooshes out into the night. Scuffling. Someone falls. The crack of bone colliding with rock.

Hawk's voice.

The screams of a woman.

I run toward the spot where I last heard Bubba.

A gunshot in the dark freezes everything. Stops my feet, my thoughts, my breath. There is a moment of utter clarity. No matter what else happens. This instant. Air tainted with gunpowder. Sparks dancing into the black night. The whimpers of a wounded animal. This moment is my life, condensed. A black hole into which everything else, before and after, will forever be drawn.

The instant passes.

There is movement in the dark behind me and to my left. Twigs snap. Nylon brushes against heavier fabric. A child screams. Boots move over the dead wood of the forest and thud hard against some fallen limb or exposed rock. A thin, mean voice that sends shivers up my spine cusses.

"You bite me again and I'll break your fucking little neck."

"Rufus! Mommy! Daddy!"

I stop my movement toward Bubba, race to the tent. Victoria leans over the dog. Something dark spreading across the front of her My Little Pony nightgown. Rufus at the entrance, on his side, struggles to lift his head, to reach me.

Dharma!

The inside of the tent is moving shadows and light from the fluttering fire. A man-sized hole cut in the back wall, nylon flapping obscenely.

Dharma? Dharma!

An inhuman roar comes from outside the circle of firelight directly behind the tent. There is the movement of something big. Something that pushes through, not around, inconsequential material barriers like brush and small trees. The overpowering smell of rot and animal musk fills me with hope. For a split second I'm back in my dream. Safe. Secure. On my way to a promised sanctuary.

A moment out of time between fear-driven heartbeats and then my screams meld with those of the creature. In one movement, I sweep Victoria to my hip. Her legs straddle my waist. My hands search her body for harm, find only what I pray is Rufus's sticky, still hot blood. I run, thinking of nothing but getting to Dharma.

Less than five feet into the woods, in the shadowy world where our fire loses its power and the forest reclaims the space for darkness, the female Bigfoot stands. Still. Quiet. She looks deliberately into my eyes. There is a moment of communion so deep, so primal it feels outside of time, eternal.

In that moment, knowledge of this female creature's calm determined rage settles over me like a warm blanket. We know each other, she and I. Something has been settled between us. Dharma will be returned to me, the world will return to its rightful order. The thought is still slowing my heart, settling my breath when she disappears, vanishes into the dark forest from which she came.

twenty-eight

WAVERING LIGHT FROM the Coleman lantern dangling in Hawk's hand throws the backseat of the Suburban into rippling yellow waves. The light washes over Gloria, who strokes the top of her jeaned thighs as though she's rubbing a talisman. Mother's face seems to melt and warp as she looks beyond me. She hasn't spoken a word since I explained to Hawk that he was to take her directly to Bobby Rossi. Accomplice to kidnapping are the words I threw over my shoulder as Bubba and I rushed to organize the search for Dharma.

The gash on the back of Bubba's head is still bleeding. He needs stitches, but that concern is a small thought far in the back of my mind. He won't bleed to death and he doesn't seem to have a concussion. We need to go…. GO. Each moment we hesitate takes Lyons farther away.

Carries Dharma deeper into evil.

We used precious minutes loading Rufus into the back of Hawk's Chevy and more time slipped irretrievably away while I wrestled with entrusting Victoria into Hawk's care and protection.

Then there was a fight with my remaining… no, no no, not remaining… a fight with the twin of my baby being carried through the forest or possibly already being loaded into a vehicle and driven away from me.

Victoria fought to ride in the back of the Suburban with Rufus who, from a quick hands-on feel of the giant dog while Bubba, Hawk, Gloria, and I lifted him from the ground to the vehicle, had been shot in the shoulder. Blood seeped slowly from both entrance and exit wounds. The bullet missed both bone and artery. I hope.

Now, Victoria strapped into the backseat, I take thirty seconds to turn to Hawk, lean so close my mouth touches his soft ear.

"You were on guard duty. I trusted you with the safety of my babies and, just like old times, you followed your dick, ran off into the woods for a quick feel instead of keeping your daughter safe from a predator. When this is settled, I'm going to kick the holy shit out of you. That's a given.

"Now, because I don't see any way around it, I'm entrusting you with Victoria. If anything happens to that child. Anything bad at all. I'm going to slice off your balls with a rusty knife. Slowly. Then I'm going to break every bone in your fucking body. Are we clear?"

His head nods, my mouth still pressed against his ear like that of a lover.

"Get Rufus to Doctor Thompson on Samoa Boulevard. Have Gloria look up his number on her phone. Take Mother directly to the sheriff's office. Have Gordon Clark or one of the other deputies we know call the DA direct. Bobby's the one knows what's going on with Mother and Lyons."

"Ready," Bubba calls from the other side of the fire.

I resist the urge to bite the lobe of Hawk's ear clean off, feel the need to draw blood and his is as good as any at the moment. Instead, I turn my back on him, kiss Victoria good-bye, do my best to fake confidence and reassure her that everything will be all right as I double-check her seatbelt, breathe deep her sweet, irreplaceable scent.

Hawk has the Suburban humming and I hear the click of its heavy doors locking before I turn and run to Bubba.

The barrel of the Garand .30-06 protrudes from behind Bubba's shoulder, points into the night sky. The ivory grips of his Colt reflect the firelight from their resting place in the holster on his hip. Knowledge that feels older than war itself tells me this arsenal will not help us one bit in the rescue of our child. But carrying the weapons is as natural to my husband as pulling on pants in the morning. I'll not waste time explaining my premonition.

Besides, it's possible I'm wrong and this firepower is exactly what we'll need when we find Dharma and Tommy Joe Lyons.

I have all I can do to fight the low, constant refrain of the panic beating in my gut.

My baby. My fault. Yes, all my fault. We're coming, Dharma. Daddy and I are coming for you.

I push this song of terror deep. If fear wins, Dharma is gone. Of that truth, I am certain.

"Got any ideas on how we're gonna track 'em?" Bubba's voice is shaky, cracks just along the edge of each word. "In the dark. With no dog?"

His fear, like an electrical switch, cuts off my own panic. His hand is wide, warm in mine, and the only bit of comfort I've got right now.

"No ideas," I whisper like a plea to a loving God. "We just begin."

The boom of a Bigfoot's deep-throated, primal roar slices the night, answers my prayer.

Beside me, I feel a shiver pass through Bubba even as he moves toward the bellow. I follow the call blindly. Plead for my faith to be justified. Pray I'm not confusing hope with shock and denial. My footfalls on the carpet of fallen needles and leaves beat a nightmare chant to whatever power is listening.

My fault. Keep her safe. My baby. Protect Dharma. My fault. My baby. My fault.

Our flashlights switched on, two small cones of light are pale tunnels in the pressing darkness. The beams are also fine targets for Tommy Joe Lyons if he's close enough to see them. All he has to do is aim at the source of the light and pull the trigger. Bubba and I spread out. A shot from Lyons may take one of us down, but the muzzle flash will also pinpoint his location for whichever one of us is still standing.

I trip over the exposed root of a fallen tree, break my fall with my hand against a moss-covered boulder, rise from an awkward half-squat, and keep stumbling toward the sound of snapping twigs and the occasional deep rumble. Bubba's light flashes between trees off to my left like some indecipherable Morse code.

My brain strobes out its own electrical prods. *We're coming, Dharma. Hold on, baby. We're coming for you.*

We're being led up the backside of Blue Mountain. Toward the cave. The knowledge that Dharma is safe and protected comes to me as a full-blown vision. Or delusion. A prayer leaps from my center to my lips, bypasses my brain completely.

"Let this vision be truth. Help me in my unbelief."

I keep putting one foot in front of the other, continue to follow a creature many call mythical. A wild creature who has made me no promises whatsoever and yet a being I am trusting with the life of my child.

This is insane! I truly am a lunatic. The word conjures Dharma's sweet face, the velvety feel of her skin, the way her mouth tilts slightly lopsided when she tells a joke, as though her joy can't quite be contained. The incredible miracle of holding her towel-wrapped body against mine after her nightly bath. The sweet spot at the back of her neck where I lift her heavy hair and press my lips.

My baby is gone. Stolen. My fault. My fault.

No.

A whisper.

She's safe.

A voice, a spiritual caress as sure and true as life itself.

Dharma's warm and unafraid. Waiting in safety for you and for Bubba.

Murmurs from a place in my center, a part of me I first began to recognize when I woke from that bed of ferns five years ago blessed with a big handprint on my belly. A mark put there by the female Bigfoot I now follow through this night forest, a sign pressed lightly on my body made from her life blood and, I suddenly realize, designating me and my babies as chosen.

Dharma's under our protection.

How could that be true?

Don't know. Don't care. I choose, right this moment, to believe.

I flash my light twice, turn it off. The ribbed switch under my thumb is rough, part of a reality I left for a moment or two but to which I now return. In the dark, Bubba's beam of light makes its way to me. I breathe in the resin of evergreens, the warm, wet dirt of early autumn, exhale panic and terror. Imagine the fear dissipating into the heavy air of the forest, absorbed and transformed by a power greater than any a mere human might possess.

"You okay?" His voice is scratchy with fear.

"Turn off your light."

"Darlin'? We're burning time here."

"She's safe." I want him to share this knowledge, ache to take from him the panic of losing our child, the terror of worry over what this predator is doing to her even as we stagger through the woods in pursuit.

In the dark Bubba's arms are love's embodiment. I am encircled, pressed hard against his broad chest.

"Dharma's at the cave," I say. "Safe. She's not afraid. Knows we're coming for her."

His shoulders tighten, he squeezes me harder against his length, cups the back of my head in a mighty hand, and touches his warm lips to my forehead.

"Sherriff's chopper will be here in the morning," he says.

"What?"

"I told Hawk to call Rossi the minute he had cell phone service. We need help here, darlin'. Search parties and dogs and eyes in the sky."

"Bubba. Honey. She's all right. I promise."

"I hear you. And I'm powerful glad you have that faith. For me? The rules changed the minute I saw the back of that tent cut open. This Lyons has my child. First, we get all the help we can to find Dharma. Once our girl's safe, I kill him."

I stand in two worlds, caught between a twirling mist of what most would call reality and the dead certain reckoning that promises all this, every word, every deed has been foreseen, and maybe even arranged, by a loving power.

In one world, Dharma has been stolen by a predator who may right this moment be roughly touching, wounding my baby, even as I continue to breathe in and out, taste the green of the woods on my tongue. In the world of faith, a promise has been extended to me, a pledge that my child is safe. A vow has been exchanged. I need only believe. Dharma is safe. She's at the cave.

I choose the second world, the world where I overcome the shaking, trembling terror that threatens to rip my heart and lungs from my body. The world where I go forward in, if not complete faith, than at least the firm hope, that this night will end well. That my stubborn insistence on dealing with Tommy Joe Lyons on my own hasn't irreparably harmed by child.

Bubba's body shakes against mine, an earthquake of grief splitting him open to the core. His terror seals my own fear deep in my gut. I stand protected by hard walls of rock-hard faith, my grief closed off as swiftly and as thoroughly as sliding a metal cap across the surface of a deep well. It is the oddest feeling.

My body, my mind, simply shut down, disallow the fear. The raging terror is still there, but it calms, lies dormant while my husband needs my comfort. A thought from some primitive part of my brain pushes its way to the light, flashes like neon on a stormy night.

One of you must stay focused at all times.

A low, soft call echoes from just above us on the mountainside, a voice deeper than any man's, as though the sound comes from the very earth beneath our boots. Bubba wipes his face with the rough sleeve of his jacket, our flashlights click on almost simultaneously and, hands linked for two extra seconds before we separate, follow the beckoning howl.

Within minutes, the manzanita brush thins and I stand on the forest service trail that connects Blue Mountain with Bluff Creek. From here the cave is less than a mile away. We'll make better time if we stay on the trail. We'll make better targets too. How sure am I that Dharma is at the cave? And, even if what I saw was a true vision and not my grief-stricken and shocked brain creating some comfort, how do I know Tommy Joe Lyons is with her? Could be Dharma's safe and Lyons still walks the woods, weapon in hand. Still, it seems incredibly unlikely that he'd be this close with Bigfoot right here and we'll make so much better time on the trail. Twenty minutes on a smooth path as opposed to hours of forcing our way through thick underbrush and heavy forest.

"We need to stay off the trail." Bubba's husky voice from the other side of the path.

"I'm not so sure."

"I ain't losing both of you." Bubba's voice is under control, but the fear is right there under the surface, threatens to slice its way through his calm. "You dead is as good a way as any to keep you from collecting any inheritance."

"Bubba. Honey. Tommy Joe isn't anywhere near here. Not with Bigfoot this close."

"Stay under cover in the woods, Samantha."

"Dammit! Listen to me. Dharma's at the cave. The sooner we get there, the sooner she'll be back in our arms." And, just like that, the thought of my arms closing around my baby unlocks the grief. The shaking begins in my gut and, within seconds, I'm kneeling in the black dirt and dead fir needles of the trail, howls of terror rising up from my soul, piercing the night with pain.

Brush cracks, boots break small limbs and push through dense ferns. Bubba kneels on the trail facing me. Tall silhouettes of ancient fir are living rafters to our left and our right. His flashlight already off, he finds my hand, pushes the switch that drops us into darkness.

The night is velvety black, thick and heavy with the forest's incense. I close my eyes. Breathe the musk of the rotting needles we've disturbed under our knees, cooling dirt already devoid of what little heat it absorbed from yesterday's dappled sunlight.

"Look here, darlin'. If you're right and Dharma's at the cave." He rubs my hands between his calloused palms. "Safe. Safe at the cave. Then a few more hours to find her won't make any difference."

I open my eyes. The forest is a comfort and familiar balm around me. My hands move automatically as though caressing beads between my thumb and the inside of my index finger. My lips move in a silent plea. Pray for us sinners now and at the hour of our death. The breeze shifts and, from the path ahead of us, the strong scent of musk lifts my head.

"The female, she wants us to stay on the trail." My voice cracks, betrays my uncertainty.

"Listen to me now, Samantha. You know I love you more than life. And I got nothing but respect for your intuition and for your... link... with this creature. But...." He lifts his hands, strokes my cheeks, thumbs away the tears. "I will not trust my baby—Dharma—to some vision or communion you got with this hairy critter. There's a spot just near that cave where we got ourselves cell phone service and the sheriff's helicopter can set itself down. So, I'm willing to follow your lead here, but if you're wrong and this Lyons is out here waiting, on the trail, he'll pick us off easy as snatching June bugs from a chinaberry tree."

The female Bigfoot calls again. Her soft whine comes from farther up the trail. We need to follow. Now. I put my hands on Bubba's wide shoulders, push myself to my feet.

"We gotta go Bubba. Right this minute. Dharma's waiting."

He stands now. Close enough that all I can see or feel is his big body. His presence dwarfs me. The right decision is to follow the female, stay on the trail.

His voice is strong and clear in the night. "I will not lose you too. We follow, but we use the woods for cover."

The female cries again, her plaintive voice farther and farther away.

I cannot do this without Bubba, lack the strength of belief to risk my baby and my husband on the same night. The woods close around me before I switch on my flashlight, Bubba's light already a meager beam off to my left.

twenty-nine

WE LOST THE female Bigfoot over an hour ago, not long after that we somehow veered too far right, or possibly left, and the trail simply disappeared.

Surrounded by thick, pants-ripping brush, Bubba and I thrash our way up the backside of Blue Mountain. Sheltered under the deep green canopy of virgin pine and fir, the forest undergrowth here never dries. We are soaking wet. I weave through the thick black of a night that feels more menacing with each struggling step. Always pushing toward my best guess as to the direction of Bluff Creek and the cave at the backside of this mountain.

The truth—that I have no clear idea of where we are on this mountain—hits periodically, ever increasingly, like a punch to the gut. My pulse pounds an erratic beat of fear in my ears. The ghostly slice of moon is a thin crescent of yellow light leering through a heavy scrim of slow-moving clouds. My watch claims the time is just after 4:00. Endless, heavy hours still separate night from dawn.

At the crest of a narrow ridge, I stand still.

Where the hell are we exactly?

The certainty that wrapped me in its protective arms a few hours ago—the sure knowledge that Dharma is safe and waits unafraid at the cave—has dissipated like fog exposed to the burning sun. Stumbling through darkness, every stumble, each collision with a low tree branch or clinging, tearing

Manzanita bush has scraped away at my faith until I stand now, emptied of all but the desperate need to feel Dharma safe in my arms.

I flash my light twice toward the weak cone of Bubba's flashlight, fight to catch my breath, which panic and the struggle up the mountain has stolen. In the viscous black of this endless night, a loop of guilt hisses numbing venom in my soul.

My fault. All my fault.

Stupid, irresponsible decision to use my babies as bait for this predator. After all the history that Hawk and I share, still I trusted that he understood the blood-red threat Tommy Joe Lyons was to our girls. I counted on that wounded, irresponsible man to take the first watch. Trusted him even when I knew he was hot on my twin's trail. What was I thinking?

And Mother. Why on earth did I trust the woman who abandoned me? Was I so damn desperate for her love that I ignored the danger she posed to my daughters? No one else could have told Tommy Joe Lyons where we were camping. *Where exactly will be we camping, Dear?*

It was her screams that brought me out of the tent where the girls slept like puppies, safe between Bubba and me.

Everything she said was a lie. None of it was true. Not even that one soft word spoken as her French-tipped nail brushed the back of my hand. Not even that. And all those gooey, idiotic, warm, mushy feelings that ached to ooze out of me? Every desire for her acceptance based on nothing but a big, fat, manipulative lie that I was dumb enough to fall for like some needy child.

Bubba's breath is slow and deep, rasps in the night as he joins me on the exposed ridge. The voices in my head snicker at the comfort it brings when his hand slips into mine, but the accusations back off some, quiet a little.

"You know where we are?"

After so many hours in the company of self-blame, hearing nothing but the snapping of the occasional dead limb and the soft brush of wet brush against my legs, his voice so close to my ear seems unreal, like magic in the night.

"No."

If the moon where a little more full, if the heavy cloud cover would lift for just a moment, if we had stayed on the trail and followed the Bigfoot....

"I think we need to crest this last ridge and then we'll drop down to Bluff Creek, but I've got no idea how far away we are from the cave. I think that last copse of Manzanita forced us too far east, but I could be dead wrong."

Don't say dead. Do not free that word out into the night air.

I'm no longer certain that Dharma will be there when we find the cave. From the moment I chose to ignore my instincts, to turn my back on the female Bigfoot I believed was leading us to my baby, sinuous blackness began to swallow belief. Faith in my vision of Dharma safe and warm, unafraid, seems now like nothing more than the denial of desperate mother. I push on toward the cave because I can't see another option, but all belief that Dharma will even be there when we arrive is gone, as hidden from my view as a featherless baby bird in the belly of a serpent.

All is lost. Nothing remains but to press on, plant one boot in front of the other in dull hopelessness and black desperation.

"Darlin'?" Bubba pulls me into his chest and my wet Carhartt presses tight to his soggy fatigue jacket. "I'm sorry I wouldn't follow the Bigfoot. Stay on the path. Could be that decision has cost us… might be I was horrible wrong. But, Baby, to me this critter ain't nothing but a big-ass ape, some kinda dumb animal." He tightens his arms as I tense along his front. "Please, Sam. You can't expect me to risk your life to a faith I don't share."

"If I'd insisted? Followed the female and my instincts and stayed on the trail? Would you have come too?"

Some small, ordinary animal scuffles in the underbrush. Warm, wet air blows up from the creek waters below us, breathes into our faces the smell of algae and mud, spawning salmon and hope.

His heart still pounds under my ear, steady beats muffled by layers of wet cotton. His voice rumbles his chest. "No good talkin' like this. You ready?"

"What if I'm wrong?" The fear, spoken aloud, picks up the wet air, gains substance. "What if Lyons has her? What if, right now while we're lost in the dark on the side of this damn mountain, he's… hurting her?"

"That. Is. Not. Happening. You got your beliefs, darlin'. I got my own faith. It don't do no good to give power to them kind of thoughts."

One more squeeze from his mighty arms and we put fifty feet or so between us, force our way through the underbrush, one step at a time, toward the ridgeline. A sudden tear in the ragged clouds reveals a thin fingernail moon hung alone in the endless night sky like the prayer of an atheist.

An hour later we stumble along the slippery edge of Bluff Creek. We've come way too far east. Over a mile out of our way. But I know where we are now. Less than an hour from the cave. Only a few more running, scrambling steps and Dharma will be in my arms.

Or…. *No!* Visions of an empty cave. Emptiness against my breasts. *No!* Dharma is at the cave. Period.

The trees along the ridgeline to our right are black silhouettes against the cobalt blue of false dawn. We slip our way through the coldest hour of the night. Each exhale is visible now, vaporous clouds I hurry through. A few yards ahead and on my right Bubba's dark shape is a stooped shadow. Watching him there, his wide back like a beacon, I am struck with an unwelcome insight. He does not share my wavering vision of Dharma safe at the cave. We travel the same path separately, both on our own private journey even as we track our child. The thought staggers me with its implication. Had I followed the Bigfoot, stayed on the trail, I'd have reached the cave hours ago. I, famous for my independent, stubborn nature, chose the comfort of my husband over faith in my vision. For better or worse, Bubba and I are joined.

Please, please don't let this be one more bad decision born of my own weakness. Please don't let Dharma have been harmed because of my weakness and need for my husband.

Across the lightening sky come high-pitched screams of terror. Primal. Lunatic. The cries of a man whose soul is being ripped from his body, his beating heart held high, exposed to an impossible, foreign reality.

I run. My boots slip on wet, smooth river rock. Right knee slams hard into a jagged chunk of bedrock. Get up! Keep running. As though the last few hours have been a dream and that scream the alarm that wakened me, dropped me once more into reality, the woods, the creek, the dawn suddenly alive.

Water murmurs rounding the granite rocks of the creek bed.

Wind is a morning promise in the tops of the tallest branches of the evergreens.

The primal smell of spawning salmon, rotting pine and fir needles that are the eternal cycle of the forest—the air is a wet, cold brace.

The crescendo of screams builds, rising, hitting heights of terror impossible to imagine.

I run harder.

Bubba stumbles as I reach his side. His eyes are wide, his breath vaporous fear around his face. The barrel of the Garand he's packed over all these miles through the tearing, cloying brush still protrudes above his wide shoulder. For a moment our hands touch, clasp, and then we run, side by side, until the mouth of the cave for which we've searched is a wide dawn-bloodied gash in the dark granite above Bluff Creek.

We smell her before we see her. Musk so heavy it coats the lungs at each gasping breath, seeps into the pores of our skin, tears our eyes and clears our brains.

Wide-legged in surprisingly shallow water stands the female Bigfoot. She's facing us with the sun rising behind our backs so that we stand, Bubba and I, stock still as dawn reveals the scene. She cradles the naked man almost gently in her arms. Like a toy broken by a careless child, his body splays lifelessly against her pendulant breasts. The sheer bulk of her mahogany-haired body dwarfs the man whose eyes stare wildly into mine.

In a moment that seems to stretch like saltwater taffy on one of those machines in ocean front candy stores, I look up and into the face of this creature who marked me, joined me to her so many years ago. Her massive body turns and for the first time, I see the male Bigfoot on the granite ledge above the creek bed, his size so unbelievable I almost miss seeing him altogether. My eyes somehow refuse to telegraph his existence to my brain until he shifts his position slightly. Less than ten feet from the mouth of the cave he stands, loose-limbed, his back against the stone face of the mountain, appears for all the world to be nonchalantly standing guard.

The *whoop-whoop* of a landing helicopter breaks the spell of the scene. The female, still pressing the naked man to her hairy breast, strides up the face of the mountain in a long, easy lope. The male opens his massive mouth and bellows once into the break of day. At the mouth of the cave appears a young Bigfoot who looks once back over his shoulder into the dark before he joins his parents and the three vanish into the richness of the Pacific Northwest forest.

thirty

BUBBA REACHES THE cave before me. I stand, cold creek water invading my boots, hollowed out, emptied of this world and its attachments. The encounter with the Bigfoot family has dissipated my fear for Dharma's safety, like fog vanquished in the sun's heat. This feeling of sublime lightness won't last. But just for now, I let myself feel the breath of the forest.

The thick musk of the Bigfoots coats my tongue, blankets me for just a moment longer in some secret, ancient magic. Then the sounds of heavy-footed men stomping a path through the forest comes from the direction of the meadow to my left. Bubba appears at the mouth of the cave, Dharma cradled in his arms in the same pose the female Bigfoot used to carry the monster that stole my little girl.

"Mommy!"

I run. Reach my baby as Bubba steps from the ledge down into a bed of dark green sword ferns. He kneels in the lush foliage and I drop to my knees across from him, Dharma safe between us. My hands run over her squirming body. Nothing broken. No blood. Still wearing the black sweatpants and sweatshirt I dressed her in before tucking her into the sleeping bag. Last night? Less than eight hours ago?

"I'm sorry you was scared Mommy. Daddy." Her clear blue eyes still hold innocence and trust.

My own eyes are leaking like a water spigot in a spring thaw. Trapped too long in desperate need for logic and action, the tears fall now in an unending drip of relief.

"Baby." My palms cup the soft, precious skin of her rounded face. "Honey, what happened?"

"We played, Mommy. In the cave. But first his mama took me from the bad man and then his daddy carried me."

"Were you scared, Baby Girl?" Bubba's arms are wrapped around both Dharma and me, the two of us happily trapped in a soggy-jacketed circle of protection.

"I don't 'member." She wrinkles her forehead for an instant, shakes her head. "I musta been scared when the bad man came through that hole in the tent. Victoria screamed, I 'member that."

"Did them big hairy critters scare you, baby?" Bubba's voice breaks.

The rescue party is almost upon us. The noise of a large group of bipedal creatures moving through the forest is as loud as an invasion of rampaging black bear, if bears wore Wolverines and combat boots. Very soon our reunion is going to be interrupted. Hard questions will need to be answered.

Dharma laughs, a sound that closes wounds and dried tears.

"Noooo Daddy," she sings. "I knowed them from afore. We talked like Victoria and I used to could do, from our insides. You know, before we learned our letters and the names for things that you and Mommy taught us." She bounces happily against my chest, smiles at Bubba's confused face. "I couldn't unnerstand their names exactly. They said it didn't matter, they'd be the same no matter what I called them. They called me Littlefoot."

I can't help myself, my own laughter wells up and joins with Dharma's clear crystal tones in the dawn forest.

"That's funny, huh Mommy? 'Cause that's what we call the little kid Bigfoots. Right Mommy?"

"Ah, yeah. I suppose it's only right they name us."

Boots splash through the creek, knees collide with hard, water-slimed rock, profanity mixes with the sound of breaking branches and squishing boots.

"Drop your weapons!"

I pull Dharma behind me and push myself to my feet. My hands behind me, I grip the forearms of my daughter who stands so close I can feel her warm breath on the back of my thighs through my wet jeans. I can't see the men, only the broad back of my husband who's slipped around to form a living wall.

"Drop your weapons!" This command comes with the adrenaline-charging sound of shotgun butts pressing against shoulders sheathed in heavy jackets, the sharp intake of breath of men with their hands on narrow slivers of metal, steady for fire.

"Y'all need to take it easy here. I'm the child's daddy. I'ma take this Garand offen my shoulder now. Lay it here in the ferns real gentle like."

"Stand down! This is the father of the little girl." The voice of Bobby Rossi slices through the tension.

Held breath is released into the cold air, the audible click of the safety mechanisms of shotguns sliding into place pushes my own breath from my lungs. I peek out from behind Bubba to see three men in a triangular pattern along the rocky bank of Bluff Creek. The men kick the toes of their boots against boulders, roll their shoulders, do their best to release unused energy. I don't care where they aim their special cop mix of adrenaline and testosterone, as long as they've stopped pointing it at my husband.

"Hey, Bobby. Thanks for coming," I say as though welcoming the District Attorney to dart night at VD's. "Dharma's here. She's okay."

The DA aims his stare directly at me. Dharma slips around from behind my back. From the corner of my eye I see her lift a dimpled hand in the air, wave at the men arrayed along the creek.

"I am truly delighted to see you young lady." The DA waggles the fingers of his right hand at my daughter, making her giggle. "We snoop around here some, we likely to discover a body?"

"I'm not sure what you'll find," I say.

"Ain't none of my weapons been fired today," Bubba says quietly. "And if ya find Lyons, I'd bet my back teeth you ain't gonna find no bullet holes in him."

"What the hell did you two do?"

"See, Bobby." I lift Dharma up so her legs straddle my hips, her silky hair just under my chin. For the first time I notice the scent of the creatures who rescued her rising off my baby in waves. "You're asking the wrong question. Moving in the wrong direction. What you oughta be asking is 'Where did the Bigfoots take the monster they captured?'."

"Jesus, Mary, and Joseph." Bobby's hands flow in an automatic blessing— forehead, heart, shoulder to shoulder. "What, in the name of all that's holy, have you two done?"

thirty-one

THREE SHERIFF'S DEPUTIES in wet camouflage gear huddle around the campfire in the back of the cave. The storm hit two hours ago, hindering the search for Lyons and grounding the helicopter in the meadow on the back side of Blue Mountain. Jerry McGarran, the pilot and my eighth grade biology lab partner, sits on his folded jacket, slices slivers of deer jerky from the hard stick in his hand.

The District Attorney, in soggy jeans and a brown fleece-lined denim jacket that steams in the heat of the fire, stands nearly inside the flames. Our backs to the cave wall, Bubba, Dharma, and I enjoy a small picnic of Swiss Miss hot chocolate with eensie-beensie marshmallows, the honey granola bar left in the pocket of my Carhartt from God alone knows when, and a shared stick of jerky.

We've all three told our stories to the DA, recited them again into the blank face of the lead sheriff's deputy. The two lower-ranking deputies returned a few minutes ago, dripping wet and shivering, to report they tracked whatever-in-the-hell-they-were-chasing over the mountain and then lost the trail somewhere between Onion Lake and the Wichipec leg of the reservation. It was Bubba that found Lyons's torn and soggy clothing below the entrance to the cave.

I have a dozen questions but don't want to ask any of them within

Dharma's hearing. The pleading, insane eyes of Lyons as he lay naked in the arms of the female Bigfoot are going to haunt me for a long time. It'd be good if I could label as sympathy the feeling I had when I looked into those terror-filled orbs.

But the truth is, in that moment, I rejoiced.

How do you like it, Mr. Lyons? A real monster trapped by a creature others call by that awful name.

"Mommy? What about Victoria? And Rufus and Daddy Hawk? Are they at camp with Gramma and Aunt Gloria?"

Cuddled between Bubba and me, caught up in the drama of the rescue, Dharma seems happy for our undivided attention, for once not required to share us with her sister and the running of the bar and the dozen other priorities that sneak into each ordinary day.

Bobby overhears the question, tells Dharma, "Your grandma's visiting with a good friend of mine in Eureka."

"I think you might be on fire," Dharma tells the DA.

"There's a fine line between steam and smoke when you're standing that close to an open fire." I grin.

Bobby beats at his coat front. The cave fills with the laughter of men enmeshed in a situation they don't understand, happy for a simple release of tension.

"Thanks for the heads up." Bobby grins at my daughter. "Rufus is going to be all right. Your mom was right. A clean shot. The bullet didn't hit bone or vital organ. Big as that dog is, it's a wonder the slobber factory even knew he'd been hit. I spoke with your Daddy Hawk a little bit ago. He said to tell you he loves you and that your sister is safe and sound. He and Victoria are staying at your house with Grandpas David and Victor until you get back."

Bobby looks at me, the right corner of his mouth curves up. "Hawk told me to tell you, Samantha, that he expects to be gone before you get back to the house. I had the impression he already had his escape route planned."

"When did you talk to Hawk?" Bubba shaves a long, thin length of deer jerky, balances the slice on the razor's edge of his knife, and offers it to the DA.

"Cell phone reception in a two-foot patch of meadow a few yards behind the helicopter. Got a call in just before the storm hit. Talked to a couple other folks as well." Bobby kneels to accept the jerky, cuts his eyes to the cave's entrance, works the dry meat slowly between his molars.

The silky hair at the crown of Dharma's head is so infused with the musky smell of the Bigfoots I reel back a little when I plant a kiss there.

"Be right back, baby. I'll be right over there, checking out the weather. You doing okay?"

God I do not want to leave this child, not even to walk twenty feet, stare out into the storm, and talk with the man who will decide how far to pursue the investigation of what he's begun to call the incident.

Dharma snuggles into Bubba. "I'm finer'n frog's hair, Mama." She smiles beatifically at me.

"That," I say to my grinning husband, "is your doing."

From the ledge just inside the cave's overhang, the full menace of the storm is revealed. The sky is thick and low, swirling with the greenish-black colors of tarnished silver. The underbelly of the clouds explodes periodically with light and elemental collisions. Primitive joy ignites in me even as I startle at each nearly simultaneous flash of lightning, growl of thunder.

Bobby stands so close I can feel the heat of his smoldering jacket all along my left side. He turns his head, places his mouth inches from the knit cap keeping my head warm, covering my ears.

"The Trinity County District Attorney is making noises about investigating this incident."

I pull the watch cap from my head, hold it loosely in front of me.

"We in Humboldt or Trinity County here?"

"My best guess is you camped in Humboldt County. This cave right here? I'd guess it's across the Trinity County line." He points with his chin to the shadowed forest in front of us. "Out there, where the trail ended? That's the rez."

"I'd say that's about right." I nod, slap the cap against my thigh.

"You've disguised the truth some over the years. Left out parts of stories if it suited your interests. But, in all the time I've known you, you've never, to my knowledge, outright lied."

"If this all goes to court, Bobby? Do me a favor and tweak that ringing endorsement some, will ya?"

"The new DA in Trinity County is a guy name of Tesler. Richard, not Dick, is the way he introduces himself. Richard Tesler. San Francisco born and bred. About five-four on his tippy toes. Rumor has it he has political ambitions. He's made over a hundred arrests so far this harvest season."

"Huh. With at least half the economy of Trinity based on the cultivation of marijuana, that seems a bold and not necessarily politically astute stand."

"Except he's not trying to impress the locals. He's looking to run for state senator."

"What does any of it have to do with me?"

A low rumble of thunder coincides with a flash which lights up the mountain. We stand at the brink of the storm's power. Bobby sidles closer, slips his arm around my shoulders, presses his warm mouth to my cold ear.

"Tesler's already heard about this case."

I jerk my head toward him, my face almost touching his.

"What happened to *incident*? Now it's a case?"

"Rein in that famous temper. I need you to concentrate on what I'm telling you."

The forest is illuminated by a low, three-pronged strike of electricity. I'm at two Mississippi when the rumble booms through the air, resonates in my chest. If Bubba and Dharma weren't here, if I had no one to worry about but myself, I'd step out into this storm. Dare the primitive power to do its best to erase me from the earth.

"Tell me," I say.

"Here's how it looks to Little Dick. You and Bubba endangered your children by bringing them into the woods with full knowledge that, and I'm quoting here, a misguided individual was stalking them."

Bobby tightens his grip on my shoulders.

I refrain from twisting away and decking him, stare out into the rain and do my best to absorb some of the storm's elemental power.

"Your claim that, not just one mythological beast, but an entire family of the creatures, somehow intervened, rescued your daughter, and stole away with the alleged stalker? That looks to Little Dick like insanity that runs in the family. Sam? He's not just talking about opening a criminal case here. A missing person's report naming you and Bubba as suspects. He's pushing DHS, Department of Human Services, to open a case of parental neglect. Armed with California's new law, AP Three Four Nine Five, that allows the removal of children from the custodial home when the DA's office has adequate suspicion of law breaking, he's pushing to take Dharma and Victoria from you, place them in foster care until this whole thing is settled."

thirty-two

THE DOOR OF VD's is propped open with a neon bowling pin, a new addition that showed up in my three-day absence. A rectangle of weak light around the door wavers on the dark plank floor, dust motes lazily exposed in the slice of sun. The front window broke in the storm. Bar towels and a ratty plaid blanket lie haphazardly along the baseboard, soggy with rain. At the table under the fur-bare elk head, Lefty cleans his nails with a tiny pocket knife, won't look up at me standing directly in front of him, hands curled into fists at my sides

"Wanna explain to me why there are a bunch of big-ass posts in the courtyard of my bar?"

Bubba and the girls are across the street having a breakfast of pancakes in the shape of feet. Dharma's idea. She's enjoying rubbing it in to Victoria that she's had an adventure her twin missed out on. Victoria, not to be outdone. Ever. Is having a difficult time eating while waving her shocking-pink glitter fingernails over the breakfast table like flickering glow worms. Dharma may have spent time with Bigfoot. Victoria hung out with her glamorous Aunt Gloria.

"What the hell did you do to my bar while I was gone? Three days, Lefty! Three goddamn days and there are eight-freaking-foot poles around my courtyard!"

"You're welcome." He digs the dirt from his thumbnail, props his sneakered feet on the chair across from the one on which his skinny butt is parked.

"I'm not in the best mood and the people I'd really like to kill aren't in this room. Explain to me what you've done. Quickly."

"What I've done." He folds the knife shut, nails no cleaner than when he started as far as I can see. "I've brung this ole bar of yours to the attention of the WWF. Got a promoter name a Jimbo Bowdeen gonna be here next week Thursday to scope out the situation, see 'bout bringing some greenbacks to this establishment a yours."

On an ordinary day, I'd kill him. Just reach across the table and wring his scrawny neck. But this is no ordinary day. This is the day our family sits down with lawyers and advocates and mediators and, God save us, social workers, and we do our best to persuade these educated strangers that Bubba and I are fit parents and should be allowed to keep our daughters in our home. This is the day the politically ambitious district attorney of neighboring Trinity County tries to lock my husband away and bring him to trial for murder. Today, turning the courtyard of my bar into a cage-fight ring for the World Wrestling Federation is of little importance to me.

The sun bathes the chair on the right side of the table where Lefty sits tapping his foot. I lower myself into the seat's temporary warmth.

"Look. Here's the deal. I know that somewhere under all that scheming crazy you've got buzzing over there is a fellow capable of running this bar for a few more days while Bubba and I sort out this mess with Lyons and the custody of the girls."

My voice cracks on the last few words, fear closes my throat, threatens to well up and spill.

"Lefty. If you can't do what I'm asking, say so. I'll shut the bar down until everything gets back to normal."

It will be back to normal. Any other possibility is too God-awful to contemplate. I swipe at my face, blow my nose on the paper towel I used to wipe up a puddle of stale beer from behind the bar. Never in my worst nightmare did I foresee the possibility of losing my girls and my husband to the state.

Lefty's feet make soft thuds as he lowers them to the floor.

"You don't gotta worry 'bout the bar. I give you my word on that. Take care a them twins. Caroline and me, we'll take good care a all this."

He sweeps his right hand around in a half-circle as though pointing out riches beyond compare. Cold air seeps up from between the hundred-year-old planks at my feet. The moth-eaten heads of deer, a bedraggled elk, and the poorly-stuffed bear we call Gladly—in honor of our personal rendition of the old hymn "Gladly the Cross-Eyed Bear"—watch from the walls. The open door frames a small cluster of muttering homeless accosting guileless tourists. This world is as dear to me as any mansion, but it's easy to see how a city-bred social worker is going to see the environment in which I'm raising my daughters.

The shaking starts as a twitch in my left eye, works its sneaky way down to my chest where it squeezes. Hard.

"Get rid of those poles. Call whoever the hell it is you've got coming here from the WWF and cancel. Now. Same pay we agreed on before you dug up my courtyard. Call Arcata Glass and get somebody out here to fix that front window before the health department shuts us down for good."

Leaving my old friend to gather up dripping bar towels, I stomp across the street. In less than an hour, a cadre of enemy will be descending on my home, doing their worst to take my babies and my husband from me. Little Dick has promised to indict Bubba for murder, or manslaughter, or whatever he thinks might stick if he throws hard enough.

A consonant-enunciating social worker from CPS or SHIT or whatever-the-fuck acronym employs her, will be making the judgment as to whether or not our home constitutes a safe place for the twins. Bubba and I would already have disappeared into the mountains if it weren't for the assurances of the Humboldt County DA, the Humboldt County sheriff's league, and both the attorney we hired to protect the girls and the shark representing Bubba—everyone tells us to hold on, this too shall pass.

My breathing is almost normal when I unlock the front door and step into my home. Where reality rises up and slaps me in the face.

I'm greeted by a scowling stranger. Who, I'd be willing to bet a free night in the Bigfoot cave, does not have in mind the best interests of me or my family. The woman rises from my couch, extends a nail-bitten hand. In her early thirties, dark hair pulled back into a twist and secured with a butterfly clip, sensible low-heeled navy blue shoes that match her androgynous suit.

"Who are you?" I deliberately tone the anger down, leech it from my voice. So it surprises me some when she actually flinches at my words, hesitates in her movement toward me as though afraid I'm going to follow through on my desire to kick the shit out of her pompous ass.

"Shelly Markson. Managing supervisor, CPS. You're just in time. I only arrived a few minutes ago."

I stare into her gray eyes before taking in the wounded and tranquilized-out-of-his-gourd Rufus, sprawled on his new orthopedic bed in the corner next to the floor vent of the furnace. The twins sit on the sofa flanking a smoldering Bubba in jeans and a forest green sweatshirt, his bare feet still in slippers.

Dharma's dressed herself in black tights and a black sweatshirt that was a gift from Lefty from his trip to Idaho last summer. The sweatshirt is too small for her now so that it stretches tight across her narrow chest, the fluorescent orange cursive letters on the front stand out like glittery blood. *YOU PRAY. I'LL SHOOT.* Victoria is wearing her silver tutu over purple leggings. She's still fluttering her fingers, admiring the glamorous effect of those enameled nails.

"CPS? Child Protective Services. We have an appointment." The intruder speaks.

I walk past her. My girls wiggle out of Bubba's arms to tackle my legs.

"The lady is early." Dharma lifts her arms and I scoop her up, hold her against me.

"We don't like her." Victoria's whisper is loud. She clings to my left leg like a monkey. I drag her with me to the sofa where I lower myself beside Bubba, and she scrambles to his lap.

"I am early," Ms. Markson says. "You'll have to forgive me, but unannounced visits often produce the best results in my line of work."

No way I have to forgive her. Not for anything. But I keep my mouth shut. Truthfully I'm not sure I could squeeze words out if I tried. Instincts honed over thirty-four years, sharpened by motherhood, now blade-ready for combat, must be sheathed. There can be no bloodletting. This conflict between what I so very much yearn to do and what I must do to keep my babies is a knife in my own gut.

Bubba sounds dead calm. "The District Attorney should be here in about an hour. At the time you scheduled this interview."

A hard knock at the front door startles me.

"That will be my assistant. I've asked her to join us so she can remove the children while we have a nice little chat."

Bubba stands, cell phone in hand, towers over Ms. Markson. He's already talking over her objection into the tiny phone in his big hands. He holds up his index finger to the social worker, ignores completely her squeaks and fluttery commands for him to hang up.

The pounding on the front door continues intermittently. Bubba speaks clearly into the cell. He's sounding the trumpet call for help from the authorities wearing our colors.

Ms. Markson, a small bird harassing an effortlessly soaring eagle, circles, reaches for the phone, chirps and squawks, all with no effect. Finally the social worker accepts temporary defeat and lowers herself stiffly into the threadbare chair across from the couch. From behind us the dog moans his protest. The girls cut their eyes to me and giggle.

"You shouldn't sit there," Victoria explains to our intruder.

"Oh? And why is that, sweetheart? Are there rules in your house governing who can sit where?" Markson leans forward, her voice saccharine sweet. Makes my teeth hurt. Though that might be partially due to my grinding them.

"That's. Rufus's. Place." Victoria speaks slowly, enunciates carefully.

"Oh? And who might this Rufus be? A friend of your mama or your daddy's? My goodness this Rufus must be here quite a lot if he has his very own chair."

Dharma slides from my lap, scrambles over the back of the sofa. She stretches herself on the giant pet mattress, wraps her arms around the dog's big head.

"This is Rufus," she says, as though explaining some obvious concept to a developmentally challenged child.

"We loves him a lot," says Victoria, "but he stinks."

"Ah, yeah," Dharma says. "That's why we don't never sit in his chair."

I slip my phone from the pocket of my hoodie where it's entangled in a beer-soggy paper towel. Jesus. I smell like stale beer from cleaning up that mess across the street. Nothing for it now. Dad answers on the third ring. Ms. Markson brushes at the butt of her navy blue suit. Ain't no way she's ever going to get rid of all that dog hair and stink.

"We're under attack."

The social worker jerks her head toward me, takes in the phone in my hand.

Rufus, doped up on pain meds, lets loose with a rumbling fart that seems to actually stir the air. Talk about breaking wind.

"Now?" Dad asks. "Already?"

"Ah, yeah. Hurry."

The knocking continues at the front door.

"We're three blocks away. Hawk's driving."

Victoria kneels in my lap, waves her pudgy fingers and painted nails in my face—a human fan. Her head twists sideways, from over her shoulder she explains to Ms. Markson, "We tole you. Ruffy is a good ole thang, but he do stink."

From the direction of the courthouse five blocks north, the sound of a siren grows louder, announces the progress of the cavalry Bubba's called.

The front door swings open. Dad, David, and Hawk escort a young woman in a gray suit into our home. Bubba scoops up Dharma from her reclining position next to Rufus and sits beside me on the couch. The open front door reveals three cop cars—one unmarked Crown Vic, a mud-brown Humboldt County Sherriff's Chevy Suburban, and a Eureka Police black-and-white with the flashing blue lights still strobing in the gray morning.

From the couch, with the door open, I have terrific view of a collection of homeless, evidently spearheaded by John and Oscar in a lopsided triangle across the street in front of the bar. John carries a cardboard sign that, in huge black letters, proclaims *FREE VD*. Perhaps not the best sentiment to impress a social worker, but his intentions are good. From the size of the sign, the creation of his support required the sacrifice of his refrigerator box summer home.

All of this is a tableau of movement around me, the surreal shifting of props between scenes in a play. A horrible play. I could press Victoria to my breasts. Bubba, Dharma secured in his arms, could rise with me. We could flee this nightmare production, escape quietly into the cleansing rain.

It's not fear that makes me shake. It's not! It's the beating down of the desire to coldcock the CPS worker and escape. Flight or fight and neither will work in this situation.

The Humboldt County DA, my old friend Bobby Rossi, takes charge. Little Dick, the Trinity County DA has not yet made his arrival, a blessing for which I thank Jesus, Mary, and Saint Martin, patron saint of drunks and losers the world over.

"Miz Markson," Rossi says to the social worker, "I am disappointed in you. DHS has, up to this moment, had a good relationship with the office of the district attorney. That you went behind my back on this, and chose to ambush these good people, who have already been victimized beyond the endurance of most, well, as I said, it's a disappointment."

"AP Three Four Nine Five gives me the right to be here. I did nothing to…." Ms. Markson stands, compulsively brushes her backside.

"Not now," Rossi shakes his head, holds up a hand that ends her justification.

He points a finger at Bubba, Hawk, and me, motions us to the kitchen. The DA nods to Dad and David, points to Victoria and Dharma, and then cuts his eyes up the stairs.

It's all I can manage to release Victoria, stand her at David's side, watch her small hand disappear into his age-spotted clasp while Bubba kisses Dharma's cheek and transfers her to Dad. I don't move until they disappear up the stairs.

I trust Dad and David, old hunter/warriors that they are, will soon be barricaded behind the thick door of the girls' second-floor bedroom. Besides, Gary Hollbrock, dart player extraordinaire and Eureka City cop, has already taken his position at the foot of the stairs.

Bubba, Hawk, and I follow the DA into the kitchen. Partially eaten pancakes in the shape of feet. Smeared butter like a slug's trail between the melted yellow stick and the plates of both twins. Golden brown syrup, sticky and sweet, drips from table to cold tile, its smell homey and falsely reassuring. We seat ourselves around the edges of this lovely mess, look to Bobby for guidance.

"Listen close, we don't have much time. Little Dick will be here any minute." To me, the DA says, "No questions. Listen."

I nod my head, too frightened to fight.

"Here's the way the home life of the twins looks to Miz Markson out there."

Bobby dabs at a puddle of syrup, sucks the finger clean.

"The legal father, Bubba, is a former pot farmer and the current owner of a veritable armory of weapons which may be legal in his home state of Georgia but are illegal here in California. The mother of the girls is the leader of a band of fanatics who believe in a giant, primitive creature—a faith most of the world finds bizarre. The children are being raised in and around a bar owned by the mother. An establishment which, at one time, was a brothel and which is now known by the charming name VD's.

"Said bar is in an area of our fair town which exposes the children, on an hourly basis, to a wide variety of homeless, lunatics, and addicts. The putative father is a known alcoholic."

He cocks his head and glares when Hawk squirms in his seat and attempts to interrupt.

"Recovering alcoholic, but known to fall off the wagon a couple times a year. However, by virtue of his position as a tenured professor of anthropology at Humboldt State University and the fact that he is Native American, Hawk has a strong tribal and legal claim to said children."

Hawk's eyes widen. I'm halfway out of my seat when Bubba's steady hand on my arm guides me back into the chair.

Bobby leans across the table, smears butter on the frayed cuff of his suit coat.

"If it comes to that, Sam, Hawk's a better temporary alternative for the twins than foster care." Never a fan of the charming and irresponsible Hawk, the DA stares across the table at the biological father of the twins. "Let's hope it doesn't come to that.

"Now." Bobby wipes at his greasy sleeve with a paper towel. "Bubba. All you need to know is to keep your mouth shut and do whatever your attorney tells you. Tessler can stir up a shitpot of trouble but he cannot charge you or anyone else with the disappearance of Lyons. Not without a body. And by the way, Sam, your mother was released two hours ago. I got the same problem as Little Dick. What am I going to charge her with? Screaming in the night forest?"

The sound of a knock, the front door opening, and then a voice like a weasel on steroids.

"What's going on here, Miz Markson?"

This is, no doubt, Richard Tessler, Trinity County DA and wannabe state senator from the great state of California. Little Dick.

Bobby grabs my hand as I push back my chair.

"Two more quick things," he says. "Miz Markson's maiden name is Larsen. Sound familiar?"

"As in Jerry Larsen? The kid whose front teeth I accidentally knocked out in third grade when he called Dad a Bigfoot Fucker?"

"The very one. And it's difficult to categorize the incident as an accident. You tackled him like a linebacker. I was standing by the swing set watching you clobber the little bastard. Our social worker is his little sister."

"Shit."

"It gets worse. Word around the courthouse is that Miz Markson is cohabitating with Little Dick."

thirty-three

I'M IN A tunnel. A black, rapidly shrinking tube with air that, breath-by-panting-breath, is vanishing. Every instinct screams for me to run, to dash upstairs, grab my babies, and rappel out the second-story window.

Movement. I need movement.

Cannot breathe.

Mouths move in the blackness of the tunnel. Nonsense words. Robbing the air of oxygen. I shake my head, force my mind to slow, to focus on the words emanating from the pursed mouth of Little Dick.

"There are tracking teams in the Bluff Creek area as we speak. Sooner or later we'll find the body. In the meantime, I will be charging the Johnsons, both Mister and Missus Johnson, with reckless endangerment. As you know, state law gives me the authority to recommend the removal of juveniles from the home when there is a strong suspicion of law-breaking on the part of the parents."

The mouth of the yappy weasel finally closes.

"Removal to the home of the putative father is your best option." A woman's voice that pumps up my desire to flail, hit something with my doubled-up fists.

"…temporary. If the county removes said children, the girls will be in the children's emergency shelter for at least a week until a judge can straighten this mess out."

"Darlin'." Bubba. His voice warm on my face. His arms holding me upright and preventing me from killing someone with my bare hands. "This is best for the girls. Nothing official. Just a nice visit with their Daddy Hawk. Keeps our chil'en out of the system."

Hawk is wide-eyed. His hands shake when he runs them through his hair.

"I'll have a TA take my classes at Humboldt State," he says. "Stay with Victoria and Dharma every minute. Never, I promise you, never let them out of my sight."

"Miz Johnson." The bitch's voice like a file scraped on jagged metal. "You may be a fairly big fish in the tiny, muddy puddle of Humboldt County. Buy your way to favor among the local good ole boys with your looks and free booze. May have written some ridiculous book about some make believe creature and earned your fifteen minutes of national fame. But you're nothing special to Child Protective Services. My job is to make sure the children of this state are free from harm and provided at least the legal minimum of care. To that end, one way or another, the twins will be removed from this environment of alcohol, neglect, and violence. Today."

The blackness narrows to a pinpoint, a mass so heavy it pulls me down into its depths. Requires movement. Demands bloody violence.

"I'll be honest with you, Mister and Missus Johnson."

If she doesn't shut up I'm going to give her the same treatment I used on her dumbass brother on the playground of Alice Birney Elementary.

"I'd be willing to work with you on this if you'd admit to lying about what happened in those woods. Children wander off occasionally. In this case, against all odds, the child was found safe and sound. But your insistence on the intervention of some imaginary creature, your ridiculous claim that this Bigfoot rescued your daughter and packed off a man you claim kidnapped her. Well, I'll be recommending a psychiatric evaluation before the girls are returned to your custody."

A whisper surprises me, catches me off guard with its calm and reason. The sensation of warm breath on my ear jerks me back into my body, returns me to my crowded living room.

"Ain't nothing important 'cept our girls. This solution'll work. Keep 'em safe. Give us a few days to sort through this here deal without Victoria or Dharma ever even knowing there's a problem. Be a vacation for them."

The pressing blackness lifts, dissipates in the breath-warmed air around me. My girls are not being removed. Fuck Ms. Markson and her sensible suit and matching shoes and her official vocabulary. Does she think that disguise hides the pointy black hat of bureaucracy balanced on her evil head? Dharma and Victoria will simply, reasonably, visit with Hawk for a few days while Bubba and I concentrate on sorting through this mess.

"Samantha?" Like the good witch of the west, Gloria glides toward me from the open front door. So beautiful I can easily imagine the air sparkling with glitter as she moves through it. My twin pushes her way into the circle of Bubba's arms, kisses my cheek.

"Hawk called. I'm going to stay at his place while the twins are there. Those girls are going to be sooooo spoiled when you get them back in a few days, it'll take you the next year to get them straightened out."

She presses her mouth directly against my ear, her words warm and tickly.

"I talked to Mom this morning," she says. "The woman is scared. It may not look like it at this moment, but you have the upper hand now. Use that power wisely."

I sneak a peek at my Wolverines, half expect the old boots to have transformed to sparkly ruby slippers.

The wave of terror and anger subsides, replaced by the calm of slack tide. It'd be soothing to believe the love and support in this room has beaten back the bad intentions of Little Dick and Ms. Markson. But the reality is my mind can only take so much emotion and then it simply shuts down, regroups, and rests until it can rise up and attack with accuracy.

"You." My anger at the CPS drone is flat and hard, my glare aims shards of obsidian at her black soul. "And you." I walk to the Trinity County DA. A good half-foot taller than this little man, my boots stomp to within an inch of his oxblood loafers. He holds his ground for a beat, thinks better of it and steps back. "Get out of my home. Both of you. You'll have to trust Humboldt County law enforcement to do the job you've forced on them."

IN NO TIME at all, my babies are gone. Victoria's pink suitcase packed. The black gym bag Dharma favors for overnights stuffed with black cotton outfits. Kisses and hugs exchanged, bright smiles plastered on aching faces. And they're gone. The house is instantly, starkly empty, as though I've wakened from a lovely dream to a cold, dark room.

The kitchen table is bare, wiped clean of smeared breakfast dishes, bits of pancake, and hardening maple syrup. The wadded dish cloth in my fist makes a widening wet ring on my jeans where my hand rests. Did I clean the table? It was Bubba who made the coffee. I watched him measure it carefully, pour the water in the open lid. As though ordinary life were moving forward.

I'm in a sort of wood between the worlds. A time out. Real life has paused while I stumble in the dark, hope I'm moving in the correct direction toward my girls. The table is crowded with the three men who are my solace and light.

"You want," Dad says, "David and I'll go on up to Bluff Creek, see can we track down this Tommy Joe Lyons."

The skin of his hand is smooth and dry under mine. His words bring no hope or comfort, but the very timbre of his voice soothes me.

"Anybody, you or the law, finds the bastard? Might make things worse." Bubba scoots his chair against mine. His arm around me, his thumb strokes my shoulder. "Plus, I got no confidence whatsoever he's among the living."

David sips at his black coffee.

"Nobody saw Lyons out there but you two. That right?"

"I don't know what Mother saw."

The word is bitter in my mouth. A sip of heavily creamed coffee does nothing to remove the taste.

"Huh," Dad says. "Be in her best interest not to have seen her lover boy. Wouldn't it?"

We all stare at him. My mind catches his pitch, a grin curves my mouth.

"It just might and we all know she can be counted on to pursue her best interests. Only trouble is," I say as the consequences of Dad's suggestion catch up to me, "if Bubba and I change our story, claim Dharma simply wandered off in the night, it means denying what we saw."

Bubba's hand cups my arm. Dad traces my lifeline. David studies me with those dark eyes so much like Hawk's it gives me the shudders. The last time I turned my back on what I knew was the correct course, Bubba and I stumbled around in the woods and arrived at the cave long, long hours after we could have if we'd only followed the female Bigfoot. Could I have saved Lyons from whatever happened to him if we had stayed on the trail? Would I have saved him? Certainly I felt very little empathy seeing him in those hairy arms. Though the memory of his eyes, crazed and pleading, does sear my soul.

"Let's see if we can come up with a plan that doesn't require denying what we saw," I say.

"Given the nature of the truth, that ain't gonna be easy, darlin'."

thirty-four

BUBBA'S GOT EVERY weapon he owns spread out on the kitchen table, stacked along the tiled counter, arranged neatly on the seats of wooden chairs. The Glock 19 is in pieces in front of him like some steampunk sculpture. I stand at the kitchen window, watch the rain drip from the eaves of the brick office building behind my home. The sixty-watt above the sink shimmers my husband's reflection on the rain-dimpled glass—his head bent to his work, the soft white towel in front of him displays a gunmetal-black barrel, one tiny spring, and a crosshatched grip.

Gun oil mixes with the smell of coffee sludge and a burnt bagel still smoldering in the toaster. Late afternoon overcast mottles the dirty brick less than twenty feet from my window. Maybe I am a bad mother. I bought this warehouse without a second thought about its location in Old Town other than to be grateful for its proximity to the bar. Eureka has quiet neighborhoods, streets where children ride their bikes on safe sidewalks and play in backyards with swing sets and tree houses. Never once did I consider raising the girls in one of those picturesque family settings.

Not for one damn second.

I'm pushing against a heavy current. Each word, every movement seems muted, requires an enormous effort. I turn from the window, lift myself to sit on the counter facing Bubba. The dark blue tiles are cold even through my jeans. This is where Dharma sits while I make dinner. Victoria with her dolls or beads or crayons spread right there, where Bubba now has the Glock arrayed, until the last minute before it's time for the girls to set the table.

"Bubba?" My voice a whisper. "You saw them this time, right? You saw all three of them?"

He leaves the gun broken down on the table, rises from his chair. I open my legs wide and he steps between my knees, lifts me to him, and rocks me against his chest.

"I seen 'em. At first, it was like the way you see a mouse from the corner of your eye just when he disappears into a hole. Or the way a ripple on the water'll catch your eye, let you know something—fish, sea lion, something—just ducked down under the water."

"But they were right there! You saw the female with Lyons!"

"I did. I did see her and Lyons, but that vision took a while comin' to me. At the time all I really saw was the mouth of that cave. I was thinkin' to get there, prayin' to find Dharma. Afterward, us talking about it… yeah, I saw her. Ain't something I'm likely to forget."

We stay like that, my head against his hard chest, his arms holding me until the kitchen is dark but for the focused light of the gooseneck lamp shining on the pieces of the Glock spread out on the table. I blow my nose on a paper napkin, kiss his salty mouth.

"You got any idea what the creatures'll do with him?" he asks.

"Been thinking about that. The female knew Lyons tried to hurt Dharma. Why else would she have intervened? Christ, Bubba, they must have packed her to the cave. She sure as hell didn't walk all that way. All her life she's heard talk of Bigfoot. Wasn't even scared when a family of them showed up."

He rubs his face in his hands. A shiver passes through him. It's like watching an earthquake shake a mountain.

"Ah, Lord. I don't like thinking about this here. If I hadn't been 'bout half out of my mind with worry for Dharma, seeing that female there in the creek? Lord I'da been near 'bout paralyzed. Was way beyond fear. Looking into those eyes near 'bout froze me in place."

"I knew you saw her."

"That ain't necessarily a good thing, darlin'."

"But you did see her with Lyons."

Rufus whines from his bed just outside the open kitchen door. The rain's let up. Be good to take him out now.

"Saw enough to know the man was stark raving mad with terror. Imagine. Naked. Completely vulnerable. "

I slip from the counter. "He was having a whole different experience with that female Bigfoot than I did five years ago. That's a fact. I'm gonna walk Rufus. Wanna come?"

At the sink he rolls up the sleeves of his chamois shirt, a homey strip tease that would normally send me into overdrive. I lay my head against his back for the briefest moment, leave him to his washing up. Rufus's collar and leash are on the sofa under Dharma's black hoodie. The cotton releases her strawberry-tinted scent when I press it to my face.

"Darlin'?" Bubba comes up behind me, pulls me against him. Gun oil and wet flannel, like ammonia nitrate, snaps me back to my body. "It 'bout kills me to see you cry like that. The girls are fine. They been gone longer than this on overnights to Hawk's plenty of times.

"Want I should take off my shirt? Let you blow your nose, wipe your face?" His voice warm and teasing.

"Ah, yeah. You did that once before." A smile breaks free. I push my face deeper into his shirt.

"Yep. You was pregnant with the twins. Didn't know which a way to turn. I promised you then it'd all turn out good, didn't I?"

I nod.

"This here situation ain't no different. You and me together? Ain't nothing we can't handle."

Rufus struggles to his feet. His right shoulder is hidden under a swatch of gauze and fraying tape. The dog staggers toward me. Unsteady on his feet, he sways like an enormous bobble head doll. I kneel to slip the pink collar around his neck and he lays his head on my shoulder, moans, and gives the side of my face one good lick.

"Let's get you outside." I bury my face in his neck. The medicinal smell of his wound mixes with that of a rumbling fart. Why those odors trigger another bout of tears I don't know. Bubba retrieves a roll of paper towels from the kitchen and I tear off a handful and wipe my face. The towels come away coated with a goodly portion of wet, salty dog hair.

Once out the door, Rufus lifts his head, sniffs at the cold air. Our motley band of supporters have taken their signs and vanished from the sidewalk across the street. Jonesy, in full camo, is hunkered down in the alley under a desert poncho stretched between the clinic and a Dumpster. He throws me a salute. Bubba kisses my forehead, strolls over for a visit with the Iraqi vet.

Ten feet from the door, on a sparse patch of grass at the base of a telephone pole, Rufus makes quick work of his duty, turns immediately and staggers for home. Across the street Bubba waves a plastic bag in the air above his head, nods his chin for me to go on inside with the dog. I actually smile. Talk about chivalry. Who the fuck cares about flowers or candy? A man who'll pick up the shit of a dog as big as elephant for you. Now that oughta be every little girl's dream.

My phone rings as I unsnap Rufus's lead from his flashy collar. I fish the cell out of the pocket of my jeans, follow the dog into the kitchen where he slops water over a three-foot area around his stainless steel bowl.

Hawk's number lights up the screen.

"Hello!"

"Hi, Mama. I gots black sparkly stuff on my fingers and toes!" My Dharma.

"Hi babies. Am I on speaker phone over there?"

A duet of giggles, and then a harmonious, "Yeeees."

"We watched a really old movie with a bad evil witch."

"And a lion and a, what was that one guy what wanted a heart?"

I talk over Gloria's voice, want my girls all to myself. It's not that I'm not grateful to my beautiful sister for taking my babies. God, without her help the twins might well be in some glorified prison shelter run by well-intended social workers. But I want to be the one watching *The Wizard of Oz* with Dharma and Victoria. I want to be the one cuddled up with them on the couch watching Toto and Dorothy escape the Wicked Witch. God, I am such an ungrateful bitch.

"That's a great movie. I'm glad you're watching it with your Aunt Gloria. Just today I was thinking how she reminds me of the good witch Glenda." Acting like a generous human being sometimes works.

"Mommy?" Dharma asks. "Is Rufus okay without us there?"

"He misses you both a lot, but he's fine, honey. You'll be home in a few days and by then the old swamp ape will be as good as new." I yank the paper towel from the pocket of my hoodie, wipe my face. My nose will have to wait. No point in worrying the girls with sounds of nose blowing.

"Guess what we're, like, having for dinner?" Victoria. God, she already sounds like Gloria. "Toads in the hole!" Her belly laugh triggers silent wails on my end of the phone.

"Mommy? Is it because a me and what happened with the Bigfoots that we had to go away?"

"What? No baby. No."

One full breath. In. Out. Rufus swings his head toward me, strings of watery drool hanging suspended from his jowls. The dog turns from his bowls, his tail thuds against the cabinets, the gluey cascade flowing from his mouth makes a slime trail on the tile of the kitchen floor.

"Dharma? Listen now. This is hard to explain because when grownups make mistakes the consequences sort of multiply like… like…."

"Like when The Grandpas got us Flopsy and Mopsey for Easter and then, at Christmas time we hadda pay all those people to give homes to so many bunnies?"

"Pretty much exactly like that. Listen. Both of you. This is a misunderstanding between grownups. That's all it is. Daddy and I thought, while we work everything out, it'd be fun for you guys to have a visit with Daddy Hawk and Aunt Gloria."

"We know," Victoria sings. "I'ma go and help aunt Gloria stick the toads in the holes." Giggles. "Bye Mama."

"Bye Baby. Have fun."

"Mommy?" Just Dharma now. "It's because some people don't see the Bigfoots like we do, right? So they think you and me and Daddy are lying 'bout what happened."

"That's a part of it, honey."

"Don't worry, Mommy. Everything will be awright. I promise."

"Well. You and Daddy have both given me that promise in the last fifteen minutes. I guess I'll take that as a sign that things will work themselves out just fine and dandy."

"I gots to go or else Victoria is going to do my toads. Bye Mommy."

"Bye Dharma. Enjoy your dinner. Suck those toads down good."

Into the giggles comes Gloria's soft voice. "Hey. I'm taking you off speaker phone. Listen, I know you miss 'em but the girls are, like, having so much fun."

"Ah, yeah. I could tell. Funny you had 'em watch *The Wizard of Oz*. I was just thinking of that story today. I had you cast as The Good Witch."

"Really? That's so cool. I was channel skipping and that show just popped out at me. Though I think I was thinking more of Mom as the Wicked Witch."

"And Miz Mark-fucking-son as one of the flying monkeys."

Another duet of twin laughter. This time grownup twins. The left leg of my jeans, from mid-thigh to mid-calf, is now thoroughly wet, dog slobber already stiffening the denim. Rufus's head droops nearly to the floor. I rest my left hand on his wide head, shuffle slowly to his bed, and point to the mattress. He seems grateful for the command to lie down.

"Well, with the threat to charge her with conspiracy to kidnap, I think you now have in your possession just the bucket of water you need to melt Mother's evil intentions, once and for all."

"I hope you're right. The lawyer, a Miz Hofstein, Marley Hofstein She's confident that, without a body, Little Dick'll have to drop all the charges. They may be able to string Bubba up on an illegal weapons charge. Some of those guns he's got came into California from Georgia, which has a whole different attitude toward firepower."

"Does this Hofstein think she can plea that out or something? Bubba's no threat to anybody. I mean, unless they come after you or the girls."

"Here's the ironic part of all this. With no body and no evidence except some soggy clothes, the state couldn't charge us with anything they thought might have happened in the woods. But just the suspicion of us having committed a felony gave them the right to take the girls. The cache of weapons? Which may end up being all they can charge Bubba with? The guns they didn't take. We still have them. Cleaned, oiled, and ready to lock and load."

"You think they'll find Tommy Joe?"

"Bubba asked me that same thing a little bit ago. I don't know. If they do, he's not going to have any gunshot wounds. That much I know for certain."

The front door opens. Rufus's tail thumbs twice on the thick mattress. The excitement of seeing Bubba releases another fart. I back away quickly, wave my free hand in front of my face. Holy cow, we either gotta keep the windows open or get something for this dog's stomach.

thirty-five

"HEY! SAM! BUBBA! Look at this." The remote in Dad's hand points at the television, my front door wide open from his and David's arrival. Wind from off the bay carries the smell of fish and salt and seaweed. The small screen comes to life, illuminates the living room.

Rufus's smelly chair throws a zillion dancing dust motes into the air when I collapse into it. Bubba leans a hip against the frayed upholstered arm, lays his hand over my shoulder. The camera must be set up on Fifth Street. The screen shows the steps of the courthouse, a wide view of what looks like everybody to whom I've ever served a beer, delivered left-over chili, or told a Bigfoot story.

Dad fumbles with the remote, finally finds the sound button. "…known Samantha Jean since she was a precocious little girl attending catechism at Saint Bernard's each and every Saturday."

Sister Mary Martha smiles sweetly into the camera.

"So you know Missus Johnson and her family well, Mother Superior?"

"Well, of course I do young man." The voice hard-edged as the click of rosary beads. "The Johnson family, Samantha and Robert, Bubba as I believe he's known, are a big part of our school community."

Generally speaking, a messy, unruly part, so it's nice of her to pick and choose her words so carefully.

"I understand, Sister, that the four-year-old twins, Victoria and Dharma, have been involved in a number of bullying incidents at the school. In one instance a child was actually taken to the emergency room due to injuries inflicted by one of the Johnson girls."

"Young. Man." Swish as the ruler descends toward an exposed palm. "That is precisely the type of irresponsible reporting and unsubstantiated supposition that we are here today to protest. Let us be clear. The Johnson twins have been the recipients of the bullying by other children."

"So you're saying the children are often victimized by bullying?"

"For a reporter you are a poor listener, young man. Those twins have never in their lives been victims. I believe the expression the kids use is, 'They don't start a fight, but they know how to finish one.'"

The camera pans back and the screen fills with another shot of the wide front steps of the courthouse blocked by a milling crowd. A dozen or so homeless and a number of off-duty cops eat what look very much like Marcelli's subs.

I squint at the screen. Pick dog hairs absently from the knee of my sweatpants.

David points at the TV screen. "There's the crew from Nooner's."

I can't help but be tickled at David's excitement over this show of local support, though whether or not this demonstration benefits our cause is a dicey call with that crowd.

John's *FREE VD* placard has been attached to the lone, scraggly redwood tree on the courthouse lawn. Letticia weaves through the crowd passing out what does look like meatball subs. I can almost smell the tomato and garlic. In the background a Channel 3 reporter interviews our attorney, Ms. Hofstein, a half-circle of homeless fanned out behind her—a backdrop of gap-toothed smiles, mismatched clothes, and the disturbing and vaguely obscene, tardive-afflicted face of John's cohort, Oscar.

A hesitant knock at the open front door raises Rufus's head. Weak as he is, the dog's growl is loud enough to send reverberations through my own chest.

"Yoo-hoo, anyone home?"

Well. Now my day is perfect.

Dad turns from the TV.

"Sit down, Rose. We'll be with you in a minute." His voice is firm but his hand trembles just a little when he points toward the couch.

Mother's skinny black jeans are topped with an oversize scoop neck sweater the exact same shade of blue as her heavily mascaraed eyes. Even on this gray, cloudy day, her hair seems to collect its own light. A golden halo shimmers around her head.

"For pity sake, this is the way you greet your mother?"

Fueled by a raging anger that ignites instantly at the sound of her voice, my butt clears the chair.

"Sit. Down. Shut. The *fuck*. Up."

Bubba's hand, like the double hammer of my Colt, keeps me from exploding into Mother's face.

Dad turns up the volume on the TV.

"Mister Tessler has said that he believes Mister and Missus Johnson lured this" —the reporter looks down at the wind-ruffled papers in his hand— "Tommy Joe Lyons into the woods where they shot and killed him, burying his body somewhere in the forest they claim is protected by a local legend known as Bigfoot. Does that mean your clients will be charged with first degree murder?"

"No. It most certainly does not mean Little D—the DA of any county plans to accuse the Johnsons of any crime whatsoever. We have a system of laws in this country. One must have actual proof before charges can be brought against an individual, not simply wild speculation. The question you should be asking is why Richard Tessler is harassing my clients, who as you see" —a sweep of an arm in a dramatic demonstration of the crowd behind her reminds me of Victoria's Vanna White impersonation— "are widely loved and admired in this community. What you should be asking is why this highly ambitious man, Dick… Richard Tessler, is using his elected position as District Attorney of Trinity County as a vehicle for his personal political aspirations."

The pointy toe of Mother's spike-heeled leather boot tap, tap, taps against the wood floor. Her jasmine scent insinuates itself into the swamp ape smell of the living room. I hate that fucking perfume! Hate the mushy feeling in my center it elicits. After her part in the kidnapping of Dharma, my feelings for her are clear, concise, without a shred of ambiguity. I hate her. And that damn perfume.

I force my focus back to the television. John, part-time resident of my front porch, has gone to some trouble to present a dapper appearance for the camera. His favorite purple t-shirt is tucked neatly into the waistband of fluorescent orange sweatpants. It's unfortunate that the image of South Park's Carmen mooning the world with his big fat cartoon butt is clearly visible on the front of the shirt, but still, it's touching that John went to the trouble to clean up for the interview.

"You might say all us fellows is unofficial godfathers." John rubs his thumb and forefinger above his upper lip, manages to remove most of what I assume is tomato sauce.

"So, you spend a good bit of time with these children, then? What are their names again?"

John adjusts the jaunty red scarf I gave him for Christmas last year. His eyes squint at the reporter.

"You know young man, just 'cause I'm homeless, that don't mean I'm stupid. Those twins are being raised up fine by their mama and daddy what loves 'em and would do anything in this world to protect em."

"Ah huh. So, if they, say, thought someone was stalking one of their little girls, it's your believe Mister and Missus Johnson could be counted upon to take the law into their own hands?"

"It is my belief that the government cannot be relied upon to protect the innocent or the downtrodden in this country." John stretches his neck, leans toward the camera. I have a clear shot of those unruly nose hairs of his. "The bastards are still lying to us about UFOs, ya know." He winces as though suddenly reminded of some danger, cuts his eyes heavenward. "Next thing them black choppers'll be landing right here on the front lawn of the courthouse."

Ah. So close.

The picture cuts to a shot of the reporter directly in front of the *FREE VD* poster, his suited back to the milling crowd. "The hearing to determine the placement of the children of Mister and Missus Johnson will be held here at the Humboldt County courthouse four days from now, Wednesday morning at nine. The results of that hearing will very likely hinge on the out-come over the mountain in Trinity County where District Attorney Richard Tessler is still determining exactly what charges will be brought against local Bigfoot author Samantha Foster and her husband, Robert Johnson."

Dad clicks off the TV and turns to face the couch and the woman en-sconced on a frayed cushion. Her long legs crossed, one booted foot swing-ing like a metronome, Mother looks ten years younger than me. Of course, pure evil is known to be a natural preservative.

"If you gentlemen don't mind, I'd like to speak with my daughter alone." She runs two fingers under the neck of her sweater, lingers a moment too long where her viselike bra has forced her boobs to meet in a deep valley of soft flesh.

Bubba's mouth is warm on mine, his kiss quick and firm.

"I don't mind at all," he tells her. "Be my pleasure. Leavin' you two alone with no witnesses being a kind of a dream of mine."

Mother stiffens, her fingers pause in their leisurely exploration of her cleavage. Bubba's smile is beatific. He wiggles his fingers at her, waves bye bye. Dad winks at me. David cocks his silver eyebrows at me before the three men troop out the front door, shutting it firmly behind them.

"You could offer me a drink. Cup of coffee. It's the expected social eti-quette when someone comes to your...." Her cat eyes sweep over my living room. She sighs before completing her sentence. "Your home."

I pick at the brown and white dog hairs that coat my gray sweatpants like bad mohair. "I don't believe I'll offer you anything. But I do have a couple questions for you."

My hands are steady, breathing slow and deep. But there's a vibration like a tuning fork in my gut.

"You know, Samantha Jean, you may have this righteous indignation routine down pat, but I'm the aggrieved party here. Not you."

"No kidding? This ought to be good. Do tell."

From behind me comes the sound of dog nails on hardwood, a deep moan and then Rufus appears. His head is heavy in my lap for a moment and then he positions himself between mother and me. His big head inches from her swinging foot, he lowers himself to the rug. Dog hair floats up around him, hangs suspended in the air before settling back down, more or less, from whence it came.

Mother's nose wrinkles in what I assume is disgust, though it could be allergies. I hope it's allergies. Swell her lying throat shut. Save me the trouble of strangling her.

"Despite your histrionics, that child of yours wasn't harmed in any way. I'm the one who spent the night in that disgusting jail cell like some common criminal. I'm the one whose boyfriend is missing."

The image of her in a piss-smelling jail cell is kind of delightful. I linger on the mental picture for a minute, Photoshop in a couple of crab-inflicted hookers, let a warm smile linger on my face. With this woman I figure I'd better take the warm fuzzy feelings where I can get them.

"I thought Lyons was an admirer? Now he's your boyfriend?" My stocking feet are warm on Rufus's broad back.

"You brought this on yourself. All you had to do was sign that paper. Accept my generous offer and get on with your pathetic bartending and Bigfoot hunting life. It's not like you even knew John Ambrose existed. What right do you have to any of his estate?"

That booted foot swings so hard now she may just save me the trouble and kick her own self in the head.

"I'm the one earned that money. Don't ever think I didn't! Those liver spotted hands of his. God it took me hours just to work him up so I could fold him inside me. I earned every goddamned penny of his money. And then we... he finally dies and I discover he's cut me out! Given half his money to Gloria and the rest to YOU. A child he's never even met! "

"Ah, yeah. I understand. The ole Anna Nicole Smith rationale. The only thing keeping you from being a cheap whore is the amount of money you receive for the blow job."

Mother's booted foot hits the floor an instant before a growl vibrates like the bass of a rap song through an open car window.

"That close to the dog," I say, "it'd be better if you calmed down some. Let's talk about your part in what happened out there in the woods."

She's halfway to a standing position when Rufus lifts his bulk from the floor. His deep bark rattles the windows, sends a shot of primitive fear through even me. Mother lowers herself back onto the coach cushion.

"He's a little grumpy from when your boyfriend shot him. Be better if you just stayed where you are."

"I thought, once we got this nonsense over with your father's estate, you and I might be friends." Her voice is soft, seductive. It might even be pensive, but I doubt it. "I actually envisioned you visiting me in the city. The two of us shopping. I thought I'd take you to James. The man is a genius. He could do wonders with that hair. Manicures. In something besides jeans and flannel you could be almost pretty. Look at your sister. She's never going to have my beauty, of course, but she's certainly knows how to play up her best features. Why, Gloria's quite attractive. You could be too, Samantha Jean."

"Always a goal of mine. Now. What the fuck did you do out there in the woods? I already know it was you that told Lyons where we'd be so the only real questions are—did you know he was going to kidnap Dharma, and did you help him do it?"

thirty-six

THE CEILING OF the first floor of my home is almost twenty feet high. The tall, narrow windows along the top of the west-facing wall were salvaged from the sunroom of an old Victorian Lefty helped tear down. These tall, narrow panes of uneven glass rise un-curtained along the entire length of the old warehouse. For a few minutes, on days when the sun is not obscured by clouds, my ordinary living room transubstantiates into a cathedral of light. Today, with Mother sitting on the couch across from me, on the cusp of asking the bitch all my burning questions, this afternoon of all days, the clouds part and the heavens pour this blessing upon me.

My legs tucked under my butt on Rufus's stinky chair, I study Mother, luxuriate in the warmth of the sun. She's straight-backed, stiff on the edge of a couch cushion katty-corner from me. This miracle of Humboldt County sunlight will last twelve minutes and thirty-two seconds. Dharma and Victoria and I watch for this phenomenon. The girls call it water light.

Our tradition is to sit cross-legged on the sofa, the girls like little Buddhas, and drink in the rare warmth. Bubba and I, on rare sunny days when the twins aren't home, have developed our own, less meditative, and more physical, way of celebrating this Eucharist. Today, I'm determined not to waste this short miracle on my hatred for the woman sitting across from me.

"Did you wonder about me as a child?" I ask.

Mother pushes back on the couch, swings her skinny-jeaned right leg over her left knee.

My finger traces a languid pattern on my thigh. Sunlight blends with the haunting scent of her perfume, transports me back to that upstairs bedroom across the street. For just a moment I am again that lonely child, running my finger over the only picture I had of my mother, a death grip on that damn jasmine-scented, hourglass-shaped bottle.

"The first words I ever sounded out, taught myself to read, were Jean Paul Gaultier and Classique."

For the grieving child I was, the essence of my mother somehow remained in the hard, cold glass in the shape of woman's body.

Mother leans forward on the sofa, shifts a few inches toward me.

"You know I left that perfume for that very reason." Her voice sounds pleased, though whether it's because she's telling the truth or because she thinks she's found a chink in my armor, I can't tell. "I hoped Victor would save it for you, imagined the lovely scent would remind you of me somehow."

Now she sounds like a little girl, hopeful, dreamy, so terribly disappointed in the horrible way life has treated her poor little innocent self.

"Big of you. Leaving me an empty bottle of perfume."

Something has shifted between us since we sat on either side of a leaping campfire. There's an emotional gap now. From within this newly constructed, thin wall of psychic protection, I ask her the question I've yearned to ask since I was old enough to realize that other little girls had mommies.

"Why did you leave me? How could you have left me?"

She flutters her hands in the air. The nails are gold tipped today, with tiny, sparkly, fake jewels stuck onto the surface.

"Don't be a child, Samantha Jean. Grownups make difficult decisions sometimes. One day you'll understand that."

"I stopped being a child a while back. Pretty sure it was the exact moment I realized you lured me away with your screams for help so your accomplice could kidnap my daughter."

The air is magic with dust motes and dog hair, ordinary life transformed by the sun into something holy. I wait for some final benediction.

Mother looks away from me. If this wavering late afternoon light has any effect on her, I can't see it. She flicks her hands through the air again, swats at dancing dust or maybe at hovering demons. She turns back to me and something changes in her face. She looks me directly in my eyes, begins to tell what looks like the truth.

"I was twenty when I met your father. John Ambrose wasn't as rich and successful back then as he is… was when he died, but for a girl from Whetstone, Arizona, he was a dream come true."

My father is not John Ambrose. My dad is Victor Foster, the man who raised me, loves me, and has been there for me every day of my life. But there's no point in breaking the flow of Mother's story to point out this obvious fact.

"It wasn't difficult to convince him to fall in love with me. I slipped onto his arm and into his bed easily enough. John had just turned forty-five. Never married. But I wasn't about to waste my beauty and my youth on anything less than a marriage contract." She lowers her eyes. Studies her hands folded in her lap.

The walls around us are lit now with a watery rose-tinged glow. My arms rise of their own accord. I stretch my hands high, throw my head back to expose my throat to the sun's warmth.

Mother glances over at me stretched toward the light. Her soft laughter sounds almost genuine.

"You're an odd one, Samantha Jean."

"Ah, yeah. So how'd you get John Ambrose to marry you?"

"Old trick. I got pregnant. But then his attorneys insisted I sign a prenuptial agreement."

"That's when you showed up here?"

I sweep my arms down in a wide circle, end with my hands palm up in my lap. The angle of the sun has already shifted, the walls more delicate pink now than the deeper rose they were a few breathes ago.

"My obstetrician in San Francisco discovered I was carrying twins. So I had a two-fold reason to run. I told John he could marry me with no prenup or he'd never see me or the baby again. The old fool was ecstatic about the pregnancy. I knew, if he believed my ultimatum, was confronted with my absence, he'd defy his attorneys and his meddling business partners in order to keep his child.

"But twins? There was no way I was going to spend eighteen years raising two babies. God. One child would be manageable with a nanny and all the help money could buy—boarding school as soon as feasible. But two?"

She shudders. Glances around and seems to see the light for the first time just as the sun slips down below the high windows on its path into the sea.

"Well. Two children were simply unacceptable. I had a friend drive me up here from the city. My original plan was to put one infant up for adoption and then return to John with the remaining child. But I got bored hanging around the Red Lion, waiting—waiting in this horrible gray, rainy place. Does the sun never shine?"

If I cared at all, I might feel sorry for this woman, or I might simply hate her. I keep my mouth shut, wait for her to finish the story.

She waves those flashy nails in the air again. "You know the rest. I figured since I was stuck in this Godforsaken place I might as well explore the nightlife."

She tilts her head back. Her laughter is brittle. When the hard sound stops, I expect to see tiny shards of evil like shrapnel falling through the air, embedding in her soft skin.

"When I walked into Victor's bar, he refused to serve me a drink. Gave me a lecture about alcohol and pregnancy. Which ordinarily would have pissed me off, but I was bored. And I'd already talked with an adoption attorney and it was damn obvious that nothing that goes through the court system is going to be hidden forever from somebody with as much money as Ambrose.

"Long story short, the idea came to me full blown. I'd leave one of the babies with Victor."

"Really Mother? Just like that. Here's this stranger who seems nice. I think I'll give him my baby?"

"Well, of course it wasn't just like that! Honestly Samantha, you do insist on painting me in the worse possible light."

The theme for *Spongebob Squarepants* interrupts our intimate mother/daughter talk about how my darling mother abandoned me as a baby like a scraggly pup dumped at the dog pound.

"Mommy?"

"Dharma?"

"I'm here too, Momma." Victoria.

The air around me lightens. I can't explain it any better than that. The molecules have more space between them somehow, each extra little millimeter filled with the love of my girls.

"Hey, babies."

"Did the water light come Mommy? Aunt Gloria was reading us from a new book. There's a boy named Mowgli and a bear and a black panther and a big snake. But the snake's not scary, just nice. Did it come, Mommy? The water light?"

"It did come. I sat in Rufus's chair and enjoyed every last drop of it."

"We was outside on Daddy Hawk's porch 'cause that's the only-est place where we could be in it."

"We was like little Buddhas, Mommy. Were you the big Buddha?"

"I was." I swipe tears. God I miss my babies.

"Aunt Gloria said we was joined with you in the light. We were, huh Mommy? We was all together 'cause we was doing the same exact thing and thinking about each others, right?"

"That's right. All of us together."

My throat closes around my words.

"We miss you Mommy! Daddy Hawk is gonna go and get us pizza for dinner."

I manage to say goodbye without scaring the girls with my crying.

"For goodness' sake Samantha, they've only been gone a few hours."

Mother. For just those few moments I forgot the woman was here. My legs have gone to sleep under me. Pins and needles prickle as I unfold them and plant my feet on the floor.

"I want coffee." I don't wait to see if Mother follows me into the kitchen.

Behind me Rufus growls low in his throat. The woman must be coming with me.

"Come on Big Guy," I say. "Let's find you a liver treat. And I think it's time for your next pain pill."

I take two cups from the cupboard, lift the glass pot from the coffee maker, tilt it at Mother.

"You don't have anything stronger than that? Bourbon? Even vodka'd work for me."

She's holding a full cup of black coffee before I open the refrigerator and dig around for supplies. I hide an antibiotic capsule in a mushed together ball of hamburger, bury a pain pill deep in a meatball. Both slide down Rufus's throat without so much as a tooth mark.

My coffee is doctored with thick cream and a heaping spoon of sugar when I pull out a wooden chair. There's just enough late afternoon light coming in through the east-facing windows to see each other across the table.

"Victor almost messed everything up, you know."

She speaks casually, as though discussing the near miss of a terrific deal on a pair of designer shoes.

"He insisted on marrying me. When I feigned the inability to drag my heavy body to the courthouse, some damn judge he knew came to that awful bar of his and married us right there."

I laugh delightedly.

"You were married in front of the picture of Patty?"

"Patty?"

"The picture of Bigfoot over the bar."

She sighs, flips her golden hair off her shoulders.

"Yes. I suppose I was. Honestly, Samantha Jean, you have the oddest sense of humor."

Then her own laughter mixes with mine in the coffee and the raw hamburger and the doggie smell of my kitchen.

"Why me, Mom? Why'd you keep Gloria and leave me?"

From the sidewalk outside the back door comes the everyday sound of the homeless trading news of the day, bragging about found bottles with a sediment-speckled half-inch of Dago Red left in the bottom, talking to themselves on their way to the mission on the corner where dinner will be served soon.

Mother is quiet for so long, I think maybe she's not going to answer, when she says, "You actually rejected me."

"I was a baby."

"True. But you were born knowing what you wanted. Gloria would lie quietly, suck on her bottle where I had it propped. She was the sweetest little monkey. You." She glares at me across the table. "You refused to drink a drop unless you were held. Flung your little fists around until you managed to knock over the bottle. Kicked and screamed like a demon until I picked you up. Sweetie, within two days of that nonsense I knew you and that over-protective Victor were meant for each other."

"Ah, yeah. I guess you're right."

There must be a hundred pictures of me cradled against Dad's chest, his big hand making tiny circles on my back. He says when he got tired, David took over. Those two old men still draw those circles on the small of my back every chance they get.

"Thanks, Mother."

"For what?"

"For having the good sense to leave me with my real parent."

The light is gone from the kitchen, our coffee cups empty before she speaks.

"I'll talk to the DA," she says and if I didn't know better I'd suspect her of tears. "I was desperate for the money. If John's will can't be broken, I'll lose everything. My beautiful home, my position—I'm on the board of directors for the Museum of Modern Art. The whole city looks forward to my fundraiser each May. I can't lose all that Samantha. I can't."

"What did you think would happen if you kidnapped one of my children? Did you really think I'd just sign over my inheritance and let you and Lyons walk away scot-free?"

The dog plants his heavy jowls in my lap, moans his concern. I stroke his head, my sweatpants already wet with drool. I should get up and turn on a light, but the glooming darkness seems right for this conversation.

"I may not have a lot of motherly instinct myself...."

Laughter, like a cork releasing bubbly gas from a bottle of champagne, explodes up out of me.

Mother talks through my laughter.

"But, I know the symptoms of parental attachment when I see it in others. So, yes, Tommy and I assumed if we threatened your precious babies, you'd be happy to hand over money you never even knew you had in order to protect them."

The blue glow of the streetlight outside throws just enough light into the kitchen that I can see the fluttering tips of Mother's gold-tipped fingers, like fireflies at dusk.

"Your boyfriend overplayed his hand when he gave Dharma that necklace."

"Yes, well. Brawn and brains. A difficult combination to find in a man."

Again, my laughter is released in a burst of hilarity that even as the sound floats around me I know is a better alternative than my anger. If released, my rage will happily kill the woman sitting at my kitchen table, but it'll take me with it.

"Out there in the woods, that scream for help that brought Bubba and me out of our tent? That was you setting the girls up to be kidnapped?"

"No! No. God what kind of a monster do you think I am? Tommy was supposed to cut the tent. Show you we could take the girls anytime we wanted. That's all. I swear. But then the idiot actually grabbed the one little girl and this… this… thing came out of the woods and everything flew away from me. All my plans destroyed by that stupid man and that… that… *creature*."

thirty-seven

BUBBA AND I are cresting the hill above Redwood Valley, halfway to Weaverville, when my cell phone rings and the screen lights up with Tessler's private number.

I put the Trinity County District Attorney on speaker phone, punch the little button of the recorder my old friend Bobby Rossi gave me. Bubba pulls the Ram diesel over at the next turn-out.

"You recording this?" The very first words Little Dick speaks directly to me.

"Ah, yeah."

Must have a good bit of technical equipment on his phone too, bug detection and such.

"That particular action doesn't demonstrate a great deal of trust on your part, Miz Johnson."

"Nope."

The windshield wipers, set on intermittent, sweep an arc of momentary clarity across the glass.

"You got something to say to us, Mister Tessler?" Bubba asks and I know the tinny speaker receiver is pouring the rattling boom of my husband's deep voice into the ear of the DA.

"I've recently had the opportunity to converse extensively with Rose Ambrose, the widow of my good friend, John."

Bubba and I stare at each other, our mouths open in full, wide *O*s of astonishment. This must be one of those "Ah-ha" moments I've heard so much about.

"Rose… Missus Ambrose," Tessler continues, *"having begun to heal from the shock of her horrendous experience out there in the woods of this great county, has recovered some additional memory of the events of that night."*

"So Mother is there? In your office. Listening to our conversation?"

I'll bet dollars to doughnuts the woman is running an index finger along the scoop neck of some sweater, one long leg crossed over the other, swinging a booted foot while leaning forward just enough to distract Little Dick without giving away the milk before the man buys the cow.

"The location of the widow Ambrose is not the issue at this point in time."

Eight years of college and the man can't talk without using redundancies.

"The reason for this courtesy phone call, Mister and Missus Johnson, is that after being afforded the opportunity to conduct an extensive interview with the grandmother of the children, who as you know is a key witness to the events of the night in question, and subsequently reviewing the evidence collected at both the campsite as well as at the cave known as C One Seven Eight—"

"Get to it," Bubba's voice echoes in the closed cab of the truck. "You ain't running for office, just talking to a couple of rednecks whose chil'en you stole."

"Yes. Well. I would hardly characterize the removal of minor children to the home of their natural father for a few days as stealing children, but nonetheless, as I am attempting to explain, I have instructed the court to drop all charges against you and your wife."

A logging truck loaded with second-growth redwoods no bigger around than my waist rumbles past on its way to one of the two remaining mills on the coast. Bubba waits for the truck to pass, opens his door on the traffic side of the truck carefully, comes around to stand on my side of the vehicle. He leans in the open passenger window, covers my tightly fisted hand with his.

"What exactly happened out there in the dark and confusion of that night will probably never be known, but, I'm convinced at this point in time that neither of you, Mister and Missus Johnson, are guilty of a provable offense."

"We told you what happened, Mister Tessler." I lift my free hand, cup

Bubba's rough cheek. "I told you. My husband told you. My daughter told you. Your own Trinity County Sherriff's department collected foot casts and hair samples. You simply refuse to consider the evidence."

"Yes. Well. It was, as you yourself reported, dark and the entire incident was confusing. Given your belief system and tendency toward drama, you can perhaps be forgiven for allowing your imagination to run a bit wild. Be that as it may, I'm calling to inform you that, having come to a more clear understanding of the situation, all charges against you and your husband have been dropped. I have spoken with Miz Hofstein at CPS in Humboldt County and she agrees that, at this time, it is safe for the children to be returned to your home."

"Mother? Are you there?" I open the truck door, step into a light rain and Bubba's warm arms.

"Happy now, Samantha Jean?" Mother's voice manages to be both syrupy sweet and meanly sarcastic. The woman overflows with natural talent for meanness. A gift from her overlord is my theory on the origin of this ability.

"Thank you, Mother." It's all I can manage to squeeze out. My throat closes with grief and fear I didn't know I had until this moment when it lifts from my shoulders.

"Perhaps, Samantha, I'm not the horrible mother you make me out to be. I'll be in Eureka this evening. Mister Tessler and I will stop by that... establishment *of yours to say good-bye before I return to the city."*

"It's a *bar,* Mother, and you bring that man anywhere near VD's and his new nickname is liable to be No Dick."

I flip the phone shut. The stench of fear washed away, the air new and green and expectant. Bubba's mouth welcomes me back to the land of the living. He comes around the front of the Ram, waits for a cabover camper towing a wide, shallow-drafted river boat to pull past, then climbs behind the wheel of the truck.

"Hawk and your sister got the girls up at Trees of Mystery. Be gone all day. Come back to us with pictures of the two of 'em standing beside that three-story-high statue of Paul Bunyan, posing like angels under the bowling-ball-sized testicles of Babe the Blue Ox."

I laugh so hard I pee my pants.

Bubba grins, winks wickedly. "You know what we ought could do?"

My eyes are dry but I really do need to find a bathroom. And a new pair of jeans would be swell.

He kisses me soundly. "This close, we might oughta drive on over to Weaverville, see if there might be anybody we know standin' around outside that courthouse."

We both know who's standing around outside the Trinity County Courthouse. Dad and David left the coast last night. Their plan was to drive over the mountain and spend the night swapping stories with Al Hodgson at his place in Willow Creek, then drive on over to the county seat just after dawn. The Tri-county Bigfooters are already in Weaverville. I talked with a few of them last night. Almost a hundred men and the usual small contingent of women are camped on the courthouse grounds, spilling in and out of local bars, having themselves a helluva good time by all accounts.

Bobby Rossi, Humboldt County's fearless defender of justice, has interviews scheduled on the steps of the Trinity County Courthouse with no less than five Northern California television reporters. Just about now my ole buddy Bobby should be waxing nostalgic for the good old days when the Tri-county area of Humboldt, Trinity, and Del Norte was left alone without the interference of big city money and influence.

At Lord Ellis Summit, like magic, the clouds part, fog lifts, and we're nearly blinded as we drive down the backside of the mountain directly into the rising sun. At Willow Creek Bubba pulls into the parking lot of the Bigfoot museum. I hurry inside to use the bathroom while he chats up a new docent working the front desk.

I come out of the bathroom like a cat stepping through sand. Maybe the General Store sells jeans. And a new pair of underwear. When I married a man that makes me laugh, I maybe didn't think the consequences through completely.

Bubba's still deep in conversation with the young woman in skintight pants, combat boots, and a long yellow sweatshirt that would cover her just fine if her jeans didn't end at a millimeter above her pubic bone.

"From what I hear the female Bigfoot, like, took him. The guy what was trying to kidnap the little girl, ya know?"

The new, young docent fiddles with the thick braid of dark hair that hangs to the crack of her exposed butt. She lowers her voice, leans toward my attentive husband.

"Nobody wants to say it," she whispers, "but it's pretty commonly held that the female? She took the guy for, like you know... sex."

"No kidding." Bubba winks at me over the head of this earnest child. "Does that happen?"

"Well, it happened up in British Columbia. Way long time ago. Nineteen thirty or something I think. Guy name of Ostwhile? Ostman? Something like that. This family of Bigfoots took him. For... you know, sex."

"Wow." Bubba steps away from the guide. "Thanks for the information. I guess we'll go on up to Weaverville and see what's going on."

Having used the bathroom, I figure I should buy something. The museum has a new postcard. I chose the classic Patty, frame 352 of Patterson's tape, and a new one with Bobo from Animal Planet's *Bigfoot Hunters* peeking from behind a giant fir tree, his shoulders hunched, arms hanging low, doing his best impersonation of Bigfoot.

"Stop on the way back if you hear anything, 'kay?" the young woman says as she rings up my big purchase. "I'm thinking, like, sooner or later this Lyons guy will wander out of the woods with a story to tell."

I slide the postcards into my jacket pocket, wave over my shoulder as Bubba holds the door for me.

thirty-eight

COMING INTO THE old mining town of Weaverville, now the county seat, we hit traffic. Lots of traffic. Mostly the brown and white SUVs of the Trinity County Sheriff's department with a few California Highway Patrol black-and-whites and what looks like every stripped down Crown Vic in the Tri-county area. All with their light bars strobing blue into a light rain.

"Something going on here besides a few Bigfooters gathering at the courthouse." I point to the yellow-vested sheriff standing in front of his Chevy Suburban directing traffic. The SUV is parked sideways, blocking 299, the highway that curves through this little mountain town.

Bubba pulls into the parking lot of the Joss House, a museum documenting the contribution of the Chinese to the area. They're gone now, of course, the hardworking Chinese, chased to San Francisco or an early grave by the area's white population. I'd like to think my ancestors were part of the tiny percentage of the population that spoke out against this atrocity, but I've got no basis whatsoever for this hope. It's far more likely my kin were part of the pigtail cutting, gold stealing mob that ran the Chinese out of town once the railroad was completed. My family, my real family, has been in this area for eight generations. Every single event in my life is layered with a shimmering, variegated veil of past mistakes and hopes and triumphs.

Bubba locks the truck, we pull up the hoods of our sweatshirts and, hand in hand, run east into the sun, toward the courthouse on the far side of town. A nondescript, one-story brick building set back in the dark green of the forest, the courthouse is surrounded by a crowd so dense even Bubba can't push his way through.

"Hey! Sam! Over here." The crowd reluctantly parts for Bill Riley, Yurok Tribal Council Elder. It's not so much that this mob knows enough to respect the old man working his way toward us as it is the determination on the faces of Bill's three grown grandsons who form a V and clear a path for their grandfather.

When he reaches us, the old man throws an arm over my shoulder, his leathery face inches from mine.

"We got him." His voice, soft and sandpapery in my ear, produces an image like brushing against a sleeping shark. "Tribal police found him wandering the dirt road into Peckwan 'bout four o'clock this mornin'."

"Lyons?" My hand tightens in Bubba's.

Riley bestows upon me a near toothless grin. He turns, leads us toward the doors of the courthouse. Inside, the tribal elder talks us past security. Truth be told, cops love drama as much as the most bored housewife. A chance to observe an encounter between me, local Bigfoot looney tick, and the man who stole my daughter and was then kidnapped himself by Bigfoot? Well, that's a chance they're not likely to pass up.

Inside the security door, Bobby Rossi greets me with a wide grin.

"They have Lyons in an interrogation room." Bobby leads us down a maze-like corridor to a door marked Authorized Personnel Only.

The room is dimly lit, crowded with law enforcement of every stripe. I blink, keep my hand firmly in Bubba's. On the other side of the one-way mirror, Lyons sits in a grey metal chair. A faded, navy-blue sweatshirt is tight across his wide back as he hugs himself, hunches over the scarred table in front of him.

"He was naked when they found him," Riley says.

A bald man in the brown uniform of a sheriff's deputy leans in between Bubba and me. The name tag pinned to his chest identifies him as Pete Willis. "That Lyons?"

"That's him all right," I say. "Except… his hair was dark."

The man on the other side of the glass sits, arms crossed, rocking himself slowly back and forth. His hair is wild and snow-white, his eyes are those of a lunatic. This is Mother's boyfriend, but it's not the same man who went into the woods at Bluff Creek intent on stealing my daughter and blackmailing me into signing away my inheritance.

"Can I talk to him?" I ask Willis.

"Nobody can get anything out of him. He just sits there rocking."

My hands in my jacket pockets, I grin up at the deputy.

"What would it hurt to just let me talk to him? You'll hear everything I say, right?"

The deputy leans into me again, the expression on his face, the confessional quality of his voice, tip me off to what he's going to say before he's spoken two words.

"You know, I saw him once. Bigfoot. Fishing trip back in two thousand two. Near Hobo Gulch."

I nod. Meet his eyes. That's all he wants. Recognition that he's not crazy.

"Sheriff's hung up with the news teams out front," Willis says. "Be quick."

"You sure 'bout this?" Bubba's hand on my arm is rock solid assurance.

Already moving toward the door to the interrogation room, I turn, grin, and wink at my husband before going inside to confront Dharma's kidnapper.

Lyons doesn't appear to know I'm in the room. His eyes remain vacant, the rocking doesn't change when I pull out a chair across the narrow table from him and lower myself into his line of vision.

"You remember me, Tommy Joe?"

Nothing.

"It was my daughter you stole."

Probably be good for my soul if I could feel pity for this hollow man. Instead I hear a voice hissing into a phone. Lot of baaad people out there. Be a real shame anything happened to one of them little girls.

"I suppose you've spent pretty much your whole life intimidating folks, taking what you wanted, not worrying much about the consequences."

Same rhythmic rocking. No indication he hears me. Whatever

happened out there in the woods around Bluff Creek, Tommy Joe Lyons is going to be spending a good long time recovering from it. Lot of people would claim the Christian thing to do would be to wish him well on his healing journey.

The little bag from the museum in Willow Creek crinkles when I take it out of my pocket. I pull out the postcard I want, run my finger over the face of Patty looking back over her shoulder, heavy breasts swinging with her movement.

The flat of my hand hitting the tabletop sounds like a gunshot in the room, echoes off the walls.

The front of Lyons's sweatshirt is a twisted knot in my fist as I pull him into me. I lean across the table, our faces almost touching. The crazy disappears from his eyes for the one second it takes to lift the postcard of the Bigfoot to his eye level.

Lyons screams, tears from my grasp, and staggers out of his chair, scurries on hands and knees to the far corner of the room. The door behind me opens. I'm running out of time.

"That's enough," says a voice that's probably Willis.

I'm up and moving toward Lyons, who's cowering in the corner, his screams high-pitched and frantic. Kneeling in front of him, I lay the postcard in his lap.

"Don't worry if you lose it," I say flatly. "No matter where you are, for the rest of your miserable life, I'll make sure you receive a copy every month. A small reminder of what happens when you mess with my babies."

His legs pump, feet slip frantically on the dull green linoleum as he tries to push himself away from me and the picture I insist on giving him.

"I ever see or hear from you again? I'll make sure she keeps you forever next time. You understand me?"

thirty-nine

BAY RUM, WET flannel, and the yeasty smell of beer are swept clean each time the door of VD's swings open and another well-wisher brings a cold wash of low-tide and wet, oily asphalt into the bar. We're having us a celebration.

Victoria's tutu is a flash of brilliant pink in a background of blue denim and plaid. Bobby Rossi's tie has been commandeered as blindfold for her eyes. Her legs and arms are bulky in the purple sweats I insisted she wear under the ballerina outfit. Lefty turns her in a slow circle, aims her at the painting of Bigfoot he's posted on the back wall.

My scrawny and consistently inappropriate friend arrived with a tiny cardboard cutout of a reclining, naked man so the girls could play pin the kidnapper in Bigfoot's arms. Lefty's depiction of Tommy Joe did have one knee bent artistically to cover his midsection. Still, I overhauled the game. The girls helped with the construction of a glittery paper crown to pin on the head of Bigfoot. Sparkly fairy dust now floats in the air like fish scales falling through a cloudy ocean. Pink sparkles reflect the light from every plaid shirt in the crowd.

Dharma sits on the bar. The soft heels of her black tennis shoes kick lightly against the wooden front. One kick for each bite of cake she forks delicately into her mouth. It's all I can do not to hug both girls black and blue. My hands ache with the need to touch their soft skin. The slightest whiff of the little girl smell of them is enough to set me off, solicit a flood of tears. The only reason I'm not still across the street with both little bodies snuggled tight against my own is that my need was beginning to frighten the girls. So, I'm faking it, pretending to be perfectly capable of allowing my babies farther away than arm's reach.

Dharma twists at the waist the way only the very young can do, points at the picture of Patty.

"I think that one is the grandma."

She waits, watches my face for a reaction.

I nod.

"Could be."

"Except nice."

I squeeze her to me. "Not all grandmas are like yours. I understand some are as wonderful as your grandpas."

"We have a secret," she whispers, "Uncle Lefty says you're gonna be really, really happy 'bout it." Her breath warm on my ear, she giggles, then in the next instant, turns serious. "You wanna know why I wasn't scared when I mets the Bigfoots?"

"I do. I want to know that very much."

"'Cause I knowed the grandma one." She points one dimpled finger at the picture of Patty above the bar. "I knowed her before."

"Before what?"

"Before here!" She giggles when she sees my face. "You're funny, Mama." She squirms in my arms.

I'm trying to digest this latest piece of information when another gust of fishy air ushers Mother into VD's. Calf-high purple leather boots with spike heels carry her across the plank floor. At the bar, she slips out of her leather coat, skips a finger absently through the fur of whatever unfortunate animal gave its life for the collar. Her pencil skirt hits just below the knee. The side split exposes her to the hip when she claims a stool.

"You don't have a coat rack?"

I ignore the stupid question.

"So, you're on your way back to The City?"

Bye bye and don't let the door hit you in the ass on your way out.

She turns away from me, watches the action in the bar. Bubba's in the corner, Victoria on his lap, her ballerina skirt a flouncy pink net across his green flannel shirt front. Dharma, Bobby's tie knotted firmly over her eyes, glitter-strewing crown clutched tightly in front of her, carefully slides one foot at a time toward the poster of Bigfoot. Dad and David sit near the back wall with a clutch of old hunters. A group of younger Squatchers gather at the table by the front door going over topography maps, planning their next Bigfoot hunt. Lefty, busy with the pin-the-crown-on-Bigfoot game, keeps glancing toward the door. I fear this is an ominous sign, but am too busy right now to check on the skinny troublemaker.

Mother swivels her stool, faces me. "You know, Samantha, you don't do yourself any favors, surrounding yourself with this— this *riffraff.* And don't think I didn't hear about your horrendous behavior at the sheriff's department with Tommy Joe. Honesty, I don't know what goes on in that head of yours sometimes."

I wave to Dharma who's succeeded, with much help from Lefty, in thumbtacking the crown on Bigfoot's left arm.

"Honestly, Mother? You have no idea what goes on in my head. Ever."

She crosses her legs, shows off more thigh. In the mirror behind the bar she scans the room, searching, no doubt, for what effect this latest exposure has on the males in the room. One old hunter at Dad's table glances her way, runs his eyes over that long, silky leg, shakes his head, and deliberately looks away. Mother glares at the side of his head in the mirror.

"Where's Hawk this evening?" she asks. "Surely the girls' real father is invited to these hillbilly shindigs of yours."

"Victoria and Dharma," I say. "Your granddaughters' names are Victoria and Dharma. And their real father is here. Hawk, on the other hand, has decided to avoid me for a while."

"I suppose your sister told you what your selfishness has cost me."

The cutthroat attorney recommended to me by Bobby Rossi met two days ago with Mother's weasel of a lawyer, along with Gloria's leashed killer, and the three of them presented their lies to a judge in San Francisco. Never actually legally married to John Ambrose, Mother, nonetheless, got the house. Gloria and I are to split everything else.

"I'm sure you'll be just fine, Mother. There are lots of rich old geezers out there looking for an attractive, middle-aged woman to grace their arm at social functions, warm their cold beds at night."

"Your cruelty is extremely unattractive."

Her glare puts a wide smile on my face.

"Ah, yeah. The truth can be a bitch."

"I suppose you'll end up turning your sister against me too. Already she's thrown over that gorgeous Hawk simply because he was once in some ridiculous relationship with you."

Gloria and I have plans next week to take Dharma and Victoria on the Skunk Train from Willits to Fort Bragg. We'll spend the night and ride the train back through the mountains the next day. My twin will manage the company we've inherited from Ambrose. I've already transferred my share of the unexpected windfall into a managed account for the girls. There's no reason to mention any of this to the woman sitting in front of me, fingering the front of her silk blouse.

It's the way Lefty's whole face lights up that tips me off, draws my eyes to the commotion at the front door. My scrawny friend scurries in a circle around a man as big as a small mountain. Lefty's grin is so wide I fear he may hurt himself. When the newcomer pulls the sweatshirt hood from around his face, my heart seems to jump from my chest, catch in my throat.

Mother is nothing if not quick to see an opportunity. She slides off the bar stool, unbuttons another button of her blouse, and sashays her way toward our guest.

Victoria and Dharma beat her to the giant.

"Hello, Mister Hogan." One tiny hand disappears into each of his giant paws. "Welcome to Victor and David's, the newest World Wresling Fedation ven... ven-ew." The girls grin up at Hulk Hogan, cut their eyes sideways to Lefty. "Is that right Uncle Lefty?"

Over the heads of the crowd, I catch Bubba's eye. He grins, shakes his head, shrugs. Oh Lord, his gestures say, there ain't no tellin' where this here is gonna lead. My smile is so wide my cheeks hurt. Tonight, after the celebration is done, the bar swept and wiped clean. After the girls are tucked in and Bubba and I have had our own private party, I'm going to head upstairs to my office. Finally, after all these years, I know how to tell the story of being raised by a famous Bigfoot hunter over a bar known as VD's.

PAMELA FOSTER is among the sixth generation of Fosters to be born and raised on the westernmost tip of the continental United States. *Bigfoot Mamas* is the second of her Bigfoot trilogy. After over two decades of travel, mostly in Latin America and Asia, Foster has returned to her hometown of Eureka, California, where she wakes each morning to fog draped redwoods, the ebb and flow of Humboldt Bay, and the comfort of finally being home.